Exhilarated

LISA AUSTIN

LISA AUSTIN PUBLICATIONS

CHAPTER 1

Aphrodite "Ditey" Greer

S limmy, Queen to my Slimmy
If it means I won't be here, from dyin' for your love,
Will you forgive me?

I nodded my head to the lyrics of Torey Lanez' *Queen and Slim* as it blasted through the speaker of my MacBook that rested on my lap. If I could dance, I would be swaying my hips all over my living room. Since I couldn't, I remained seated on my sofa, legs elevated on the matching teal ottoman, sipping from my wine glass. God knows I shouldn't be drinking, especially since alcohol was starting to give me a fucking headache. But I was caught up on all of my orders on this good Friday night, and that caused for celebration.

I didn't have shit to do over the weekend but vibe in my home and block all the troubles of the world out. Instead of letting the tart taste of my favorite wine, *Giulia,* get me tipsy, I needed to be looking at these houses my realtor had sent over since I was ready to finally purchase. I'm dreading putting my eyes on any of the homes she sent over simply because, what I really want, I can't afford just yet. A two hundred and fifty thousand dollar home just wasn't doing it for me. I yearned for some ridiculous ass shit. Like two point five million dollars, knowing damn well with just me, there was no need for all that house. But hey, I want what the fuck I want, and that's why I'd been renting the last five years.

I'm currently occupying a three hundred thousand dollar two-story, four-bedroom home. and The eighteen hundred dollar rent was getting too damn ridiculous. I make good money with my online boutique. Great money, actually, but I'm fed up with overpaying all this damn money renting. My least isn't up for another few months, and if I don't find anything by then, I'll do month-to-month instead of extending the lease another twelve months. At almost thirty years old, it was time for me to plant some seeds. I don't own shit outside of my home-based business and my five year old Lexus. I was ready to add homeowner to my list of small wins.

"Lord, please let me like at least one of these damn houses in this email." Emptying the remainder of the burgundy contents from my glass, I placed it down on the grey 8x10 shaggy rug that my two couches and ottoman rested on and opened Safari so that I could look at the prospective homes.

"Here goes nothing."

Ding Dong.

Picking my rose gold MacBook Air up, I pulled my oversized white shirt over my grey leggings to open the door for my unwanted guest. With my eyes scanning the computer screen, I unlocked the front door and walked back over to my awaiting warm spot on the couch.

His cologne greeted me before he did. The clanking of his chains talked before he could. A fine ass man coming to your house on a Friday night meant Netflix and Chill, but this most definitely wasn't that.

"Fuck I tell you 'bout unlocking the door and shit? No telling who behind it, Aphrodite."

The first house had me ready to slam my damn laptop close. Instead, I pressed pause on the music, sat it beside me, and gave this man my undivided attention.

"You look nice, Baguette."

He mugged me and grabbed the remote from my fireplace to power on the sixty-five-inch tv he bought me for Christmas. He was kind enough to even have it mounted, and although the gesture was nice, I wasn't a tv type of woman. So I had a feeling it was more for him, especially since he also purchased a surround sound.

I watched as he used one hand to scroll through the channels while he had the other tucked inside the front of his pants.

"I'm dead ass serious, Aphrodite. It could have been anybody at the door. I keep telling you this shit. I might not be as heavy in the streets as I used to be, but I'm still in 'em."

"And I keep telling you I'm good. If someone comes in here, they're getting blown off. Simple."

"That ain't the point-" he started with his eyes still on the screen. He'd settled on the Lakers game like I knew he would.

"I bought a pizza. Go help yourself." Bringing up food from our favorite pizza spot was one sure way to get this man off my damn back. Baguette could go on and on as to why I should bring a whole fucking AK to the door and make muthafuckas say a secret code in order for me to open it. I rarely got company outside of my package deliveries. I'm good. Don't nobody want my ass.

I glanced at my nails and reminded myself to go see my nail tech tomorrow. The light peach shellac had moved from my nail bed. I was a week overdue since I'd been swarmed with orders. I'm so proud of my business, but there were times that I'm so busy I tended to neglect myself.

"Damn, you ain't gone fix a nigga plate?"

I looked up at Baguette with a mug on. He had a sinister grin etched on his handsome face, but that didn't change the way I was looking at his ass.

"Baguette, two things. I'm not your bitch *anymore*, and you're not my child. Our daughter is dead, mmkay. Go fix yourself some pizza or don't eat. Either way, I don't give a damn. I'm full and was 'bout ready to take my ass to bed anyway." I yawned.

Today had been a long one, and I had fresh sheets, a heating pad, and two fans waiting on me.

"Cap. You was not about to go to bed this early on a Friday."

Baguette was what you call any bitch's fantasy. With skin the same shade as a worn penny, a low fade that was always crisp, and thuggish but clean look, he was more than easy on the eyes. The thing about him that made women bend to his will wasn't his over six feet stance but the deep dimple embedded in his right cheek. Not only was his ass paid, but he wore his wealth every damn day because he stayed in the latest.

"You're right. I was about to make this kitty purr and *then* go to bed."

My Rose is fully charged and so is my iPad. I already knew the Porn hub search for tonight. *Ebony lesbians eating pussy*. I'd never fucked a bitch in my life nor did I want to. However, it was something about watching lesbian porn that had me nutting in three seconds. Soon as I got my nut, I immediately prayed and repented. I felt disgusted with myself, but watching them carpet munchers shol' did feel good.

He shook his head and walked to the kitchen.

"And don't eat my cheesecake! It's peanut butter and has walnut crumbles!"

Baguette got on my last nerves, but he was my homie. Being best friends with a nigga whose face you used to ride every night is taboo, but that's us. At the beginning of our breakup, folks thought we were still fucking since we were so close, but that was the furthest thing from the truth. Baguette and I had been together from fourteen to twenty four and had practically grown up together.

He's a street nigga. A paid ass street nigga.

And the streets took a toll on our relationship.

We were young and having money, so the bitches flocked. Baguette was and still is fine as fuck, and with all his street status, he was slanging his big dick all over town. I got tired of fighting him and bitches over his ass, so I decided to walk away.

Shit was cool until a few weeks later, I found out I was pregnant. We chose to stay broken up but work towards a friendship that still included fucking and sucking. Shit was perfect until I pushed out a dead little girl. That shit hurt us to our core and changed us both for the better. I took our dying baby as a sign that our relationship was dead too. No more fucking. No more arguing with bitches. No more Baguette and Aphrodite. The shit was toxic and draining, and I didn't have the fight in me to hold us together any longer.

Although we were no longer together, we found ourselves talking and texting every damn day still. Baguette is fine. Any woman with eyes could see that. He isn't just regular fine, he's 'walk his tall brown ass in a room and command attention from everyone in that bitch' fine. But I'm not sexually attracted to him at all. We were best friends before anything, and that's how we are ending.

Our relationship caused turmoil in his dating life for the first two years, but eventually, the women he chose to give his time too saw that I wasn't going anywhere so, that drama shit ceased because they walked away or he cut them off. I didn't too much care for any of them hoes any way. When he brought a girl to me that I actually vibed with, I was so happy when he finally settled down with her. I hoped that would mean I would see less of his ass. Sadly, that wasn't the case at all.

The doorbell rang while I picked at my nails. Since Baguette was raiding my kitchen, I unlocked it again without looking and took my seat back on the couch. The wine had me feeling good, and I knew these two were sure about to give me some entertainment.

"Where that nigga at? I see his car in the driveway and I smell his cologne."

I shook my head at Baguette's girlfriend of three and a half years as she barged in the door dressed as if she'd just stepped off a runway. Tuscany Payne stayed on point and in the latest. Her long black bone straight weave was parted in the middle and flowing down her back. On her feet were a pair of red, pointed-toe ankle Prada boots. The black jean jumper she wore fit all of her slim thick curves, and to protect her from the winter weather, she had a red Fendi print crop bomber jacket on. I admired her red Chanel bag and shook my head because I see Baguette gave in. Her ass had been crying over that bag for the last few months. He talked all that shit but had her ass spoiled rotten.

"Hello to you too, Tusc. You look pretty," I snickered.

"Cut the shit, bitch. You and this nigga saw me calling both y'all funky-ass phones. Baguette!"

She screamed to the top of her lungs.

"Mane, stop all that fucking hollering. And Aphrodite, why the fuck you get peanut butter and walnut cheesecake when you know I'm allergic to both? I got a sweet tooth like a muhfucka'." Baguette came out of the kitchen, jeans slightly hanging at his waist and showing his briefs with a plate full of pizza while scrolling through his phone. Completely unbothered by his girlfriend's theatrics.

"My phone is right here and has not rung. Nor has my computer since they're both linked. If you called the business phone, it's powered off for the weekend. You know that." I shrugged and picked up my laptop again to finish looking at the bullshit houses.

"Baguette, you really left me? I thought we were going to the game?" She pouted and stomped her foot like the brat she was.

"Tusc, I told you if you weren't ready, I was leaving. You had all damn day to get dressed," he nonchalantly replied. He finally put his phone away and eyed her with lust.

"I really wanted to get out the house. I was almost ready."

"Well, we out the house now. Want some pizza? The game right here."

She eyed his ass before turning to me.

"This outfit ain't going to waste. Can you go get the ring light and take my pics, friend? Pleaseeee?"

I rolled my eyes. "Go get it yourself, Tuscany. I'll take your pics."

"'Cuz I sho' in the fuck ain't taking 'em. Ohh and one, baby! Let's fucking go!" Baguette yelled at the screen after he addressed Tuscany. He took another bite of *my* pizza, eyes still focused on the game.

Tuscany groaned and switched into my bedroom to grab the ring light so that I could snap her photos. Folk probably think I'm crazy as shit having my ex and his girlfriend all up and through my house like this, but truth be told, they are both my best friends. Outside of them, I had my mother and a few family members, but for the most part, these two are my partners in crime. Shit wasn't always peaches and cream with the three of us, but we were in a good space now.

Tuscany and I almost came to blows several times because she didn't understand Baguette and I's relationship. Once she saw everything was strictly platonic, her ass became clingier than he did.

All my life, anyone that met me clung to me. It's the same with my mother. Hell, when I'm not answering the door for Baguette and Tuscany, they're on my mommy's couch. When my mama is not up for their bored asses, they're at my aunt's. I don't know what it is about me that makes folk drawn in because I'm boring as hell if you ask me. All I do is work, build my brand, and sit my ass in the house. The only time I leave is to make post office runs, get pampered, and grocery shop. Everything else is ordered online. I go get a drink with Tuscany every now and again and maybe once a year she drags me to a lounge. I wasn't always a homebody though. I used to be fun and outgoing, but the death of my daughter changed me. It made me slow down and realize life is too short. I started looking at shit from a different spectrum.

Before the 180, all I did was spend Baguette's money, track his every move, stalk bitches he was fucking with, and be ready to whoop any bitch in regard to my nigga. Hell, I used to be ready to go toe to toe with him too. In the club, popping bottles, fighting hoes, and stunting on bitches. That's what I did. That was my life. I lived in the malls. Everybody in the city knew I was Baguette's bitch, and I basked in that shit. Nothing else mattered but my fucking title.

I was so caught up in that shit that I didn't notice the spark between us had died, and it had nothing to do with the cheating. All we did was fight. He would never put his hands on me, but that didn't stop me from trying to knock his head off his fucking shoulders. The shit was draining and toxic. I had no direction in my life outside of being a dope man's wife. All that money at my fingertips and I didn't once try to encourage my man to go legit. I just wanted to stunt on bitches. I didn't give a fuck that my man was taking penitentiary chances. Or that my reckless behavior on and off social media was attracting the robbers. All I knew was I was that bitch, and my man was that nigga.

That's why I like Tuscany so much. She's spoiled by her man, as she should be, but she came in and showed him a different route. Tusc was the one that put a bug in my ear to start a business, and that's how *Goddess Wears* was born. I studied all the big boutiques, took my paychecks from the call center I was working at, and now I made six figures doing this shit. It wasn't easy, but I did that shit. Anytime I got overwhelmed with orders, Baguette, Tuscany, my baby cousin Litty, and my mommy stepped in and was up all night with me packaging orders and printing labels.

Regardless of how a motherfucker felt on the outside, I rocked with them both heavy. I was happy for Baguette. He'd found his soulmate, and in turn, I got a new best friend. Tuscany was extra as shit at times, but she is my best bitch. I told him if he ever let her go, I'd kill his ass. Or better yet, I'd cut his ass off because that would kill him too. Baguette was like the brother I never had. Minus the fact we'd sucked and fucked every part of each other and had been in a long term relationship. I seriously didn't even look at him in that manner. We had our thing; it didn't work. We produced a beautiful child, and she didn't make it. It was okay. We were okay. I was just happy that he was happy and legit for the most part.

"Okay. Let me see 'em." I handed Tuscany her phone and took my spot back on the couch, letting her ass know I was done snapping photos. One of those better had worked or she was assed out because her man damn sho' made it clear he wasn't taking her any. I loved a good pic too, but Tuscany was the type to have you snapping photos for an hour. Nah, not tonight, playa. Especially since I didn't need her to return the love.

Not only was Tuscany smart, my girl was bad as fuck. Her slim thick build, light tan skin, slender face, pointy chin, bright eyes, and ass to hip ratio that was out of this world, kept men always turning heads. Hell, anytime we went out, we had to almost fight niggas off for them to leave us the fuck be.

"Ohhhh, these is bomb! Thanks, bestie." She slid out of her boots, left them by the door since that was where we took her photos and sat on the couch next to Baguette, placing her legs across his thigh. He grabbed her feet while still focused on the game and began to massage them.

"You been a lil' off since a nigga got here. What's up? Talk to me. What's going on with you?"

Since Baguette and I had been in each other's lives for over a decade, he was able to pick up the slightest things with me. Most of the times he knew shit was about to go wrong with me before it did. I couldn't stand that shit.

"Yea, what's up, boo? Work again? You need help with orders? Or you need me to roast one of them hoes on social media again mad they can't exchange some shit they wore? I still owe that Daphne bitch. Hoe know her nigga got all that money, but nahhhh, bitch gone make a post lying like a motherfucker scammed her. Ohhh, I'ma snack that hoe! I ain't forgot!" Tuscany tossed her weave behind her back while still on her phone, more than likely choosing a pic to post. I'm sure her photo would hit over two thousand likes on FB and ten thousand or better on IG since that's what she averaged. The fit was fly, and I was glad she was wearing an unreleased new arrival. That was one thing less I had to model next week.

One of the most draining processes with my boutique was being my own damn model and camera girl. My boutique took off like a rocket because of the way I presented my pieces. I didn't just put on an outfit and snap a pic in the mirror. Nah, my drops are a full-on production. If I received twenty new arrivals, I had to literally pair each fit up with heels and accessories, pose in front of the camera, go through all the photos and choose the best ones, edit them, and add them to my site. Not to mention I had to be sure to get my makeup and hair profession-ally done. I tried to switch up my styles according to the drops.

For instance, if I received tropical shit that would be fitting for vaca-tion, I was sure to get long wet and wavy hair or braids. Anytime Tuscany rocked my pieces, which was often, that was one less piece I had to model. Her ass had everything I sold and made sure she paid the full price. That's another reason why I love her. She supports me to the fullest.

I sighed and tucked my feet under my butt, "No, the boutique is good, and girl, she did all that on the book for her package to be at the house waiting on her. Had she tracked her order, she would have saw that. Fuck her. I blocked her from shopping from my site, but I think the bitch orders under a fake page or sum 'cuz she keeps my shit on."

Daphne is an irrelevant bitch that like to fuck after any and every-body. Long as she see's a nigga with money, the hoe gone go. The bitch played with me too hard back then and had the nerve to act like shit was all good now and shop with me. True, other boutiques sold what I sold, but what were the odds that Daphne wore all my new arrivals? Her ass was shopping under an alias. She placed a three hundred dollar order a while back and called herself blasting me on Facebook saying I was a scam and had took her money. I roasted that bitch so hard! When I told her I was on my way to her job, she was singing a different tune. The bitch is a secret admirer and a hater. You can't be both though, she has to pick a struggle. Long as she didn't pull that bullshit again, I would continue to take her money.

"See, I'm getting mad all over again. She always saying slick shit but still shopping. Girl, I'll comment and shut that hoe down. I even told Baguette that hoe is not allowed at our new house. Bad enough she came to the old one. I don't want that ran-through bitch in my space, period." Tuscany did the cut throat gesture like the City Girls, and I wanted so bad to call her ass Yung Miami. They had so many similarities, but Tuscany hated that shit. She didn't like to be compared to no one, so I kept my thoughts to myself. I swear they could be sisters, though.

"Mane, y'all stop gossiping about that damn girl. She ain't gossiping about y'all," Baguette inserted himself in our conversation.

"Nigga, I know you ain't taking up for this bitch?! The same bitch that busted yo' baby mama out on Facebook because she still bitter 'bout some back in the day shit. Better be glad I found out late you fucked that hoe because she would have never been in my space. Ion know what Goal see in the bitch anyway! You just let yo' friend know I'm on that hoe's ass anywhere. I don't give a fuck if we in the house of the Lord, I'ma stomp the Holy Ghost out that big nose bitch."

"Mane, you ain't gone do shit, and I fucked that girl so long ago it don't even count. That was before you. Yo' crazy ass friend already beat her ass once, so chill. Y'all handled it; she got her package, and that's the end of that. She still shopping, so evidently ain't no beef on her end."

Baguette bumped his shoulder and focused back on the game. I was so used to bitches not liking me still over Baguette. It didn't faze me not one bit. If the nigga I was fucking on bitch beat my ass once upon a time, I would be mad too. Crazy thing is, damn near all them hoes still shopped with me.

"Aphrodite beat her ass years ago; I didn't. Give me my feet back, nigga." Tuscany snatched her feet from out Baguette's lap, and I had to hold my laugh in.

"You done pissed me off. Why you had to fuck all them bitches anyway? Then this hoe just hop from hustla to hustla. Now she done bagged Goal and think her shit don't stank. Sour bitch. I'ma whoop that hoe, mark my word. She get by, not away."

"Okay, bae. Gimme then corns back. I know they barking. You should be glad we ain't go to the game, knowing damn well you can't really walk in heels like that."

Baguette hit her with his million dollar smile; showing off his one right deep dimple.

"Nigga, you tried it. They don't be corns when they be in yo' mouth. Don't show out," Tuscany spat.

"Y'all crazy. But I'm good. The boutique is great. I'm just stressing about this house shit."

I turned my nose up as I looked back at all the outdated ass houses plastered on the screen. They were either too close together, too old, too small, or the neighborhood wasn't ideal for me. I was now living in Conquoy, which was a semi-middle class neighborhood. I had been living here for the last few years. I loved it because it had so much to offer. It was still the suburbs, but I wanted a change of scenery. After renting out here so long, I didn't want to buy. It was out of the question. I regret I didn't buy a home the moment I left Baguette because the market was much better back then. Now that everyone has found out about Jagoda Bay and how our city is not only thriving but swarming with successful black folk, the world wants to move here, making the housing market skyrocket.

"So you ready to buy again? That's what's up. What's it to stress about? I know it ain't about no bread?" Baguette was talking to me but replying to something on his phone.

"Yes and no. The houses in my price range are too damn raggedy looking. The problem is I think I'm 'posed to live like I'm married to the fucking mayor or some shit."

"That's because you are, friend. You want what you want. But let me see the houses. I bet they not even that bad. They on there?" Tuscany asked as she snatched my laptop from my lap.

"The problem is you gots to get out and actually go to the properties. You be in this house like a damn prisoner. See, they be looking totally different in person. Like this one here... well... yea...or this one...umm... bitch, these all ugly."

"Aye, y'all like these Nike sets? Yea, y'all like 'em. Let me tell this nigga I want the mediums and larges. But about the house situation, just get what you want. We ain't worried about no price." Baguette continued to text on his phone.

"Yea, 'cuz this shit here a mess. Baby, what you buying us? Let me see." Tuscany sat the computer on the ottoman and leaned in to look at Baguette's screen.

"See, yea... no. That's not gonna work. I love y'all both, but I'm tired of being y'all damn third wheel."

They both looked up at me with shocked expressions.

I sat up on the couch so that I could explain to them better. I could see this going left fast, and that wasn't my intention. Every time I said something about being a third wheel, it put Tuscany and Baguette deep in their feelings.

"So what, you don't like us hanging with you?" Baguette asked, offended.

"No, it's nothing like that. Y'all are all I got outside of mama 'nem. I love y'all. But let's be real, Baguette. I'm not your woman. You shouldn't be buying me and Tuscany shit at the same time like this is a three way relationship. Nor should you be ready to go half with me on a crib. It just ain't normal. My man should be doing those things, not my best friend. I appreciate you both, but some things are just out of line, and that's one of them. Please don't take it the wrong way."

Baguette placed his phone in his pocket and slid to the edge of his seat.

"Watch out." He tapped Tuscany's feet so that she could move them.

I groaned internally because I already knew Baguette was about to speak his peace and leave. Anytime he was in his fucking feelings, he didn't want to be touched, bothered, or around anyone.

"Look, Aphrodite. What I do for you ain't for no motherfucker to judge but us. Ain't no weird shit going on. You my day one. The mother of my child. I vowed to my daughter's corpse that no matter what, I would always make sure you straight, and I'ma do that 'til my dying breath. Can't nobody or no one change that shit, and you know that shit."

He stood up and grabbed his jacket, making me feel like shit.

"Come on, babe. Don't leave. We're having fun. All Aphrodite is saying is that she don't feel comfortable with a lot of things you do. I don't mind at all. She's my best bitch, but she feel like certain things are for her own man." Tuscany tried to reason like she always did. She was forever trying to play peacemaker like I did with them.

"Well, she need to get a nigga then. Get her ass out the house and go mingle. Like normal single women. I'm out though. Come lock up, baby." Baguette bent down and kissed Tuscany on the lips while pulling her up so she could lock the door. With a look of defeat on her face, she followed him to the door, gave him another kiss, and locked it.

"You know how he is, Aphrodite. It's nothing you can say to make him feel less obligated to do for you, so just let him. Hell, it don't bother me at all. You're family. Y'all got history. He just want to see that you're straight."

Gripping the back of my neck to relieve the tension, I rolled it until I heard a few joints pop.

"I know, Tuscany. I know. But Baguette gotta back off a little. It's overwhelming sometimes. Him always stepping in. I love him like a brother but damn. He can't be taking care of me like he takes care of you. It's unethical as fuck. I appreciate all he does,, but buying houses and cars and shit is where I will always draw the line. I don't know why he don't get that."

Tuscany reached in her bag, pulled out a blunt, and fired it up. Once she took a few pulls from it, she passed it to me, and I happily obliged.

"I'ma tell you some shit that better not ever leave this room."

I waited for the tea as she blew smoke from her nose. Folk would say Tuscany and I were too pretty to be smoking but hell, only ugly mutha-fuckas posed to get high? I didn't smoke all day, but a few blunts a month kept my head above water. Tuscany hit the blunt again before passing it to me, and I greedily took it.

"Baguette still cries for Athena."

I damn near choked on the smoke hearing he cried over our daughter. It had been almost five years. He seemed like it was all cool. We visit her grave together every holiday, and I've never seen him shed a tear, not even when I pushed her stillborn body out. I'd never seen Baguette cry, ever. This was all new to me.

As for me, my daughter is something I'd learned to deal with. I would love for my baby to be here. She deserved to be here, but I couldn't live in that dark space. Life isn't fair, but it is what the fuck it is.

"In his sleep. He calls her name. He talks to her. All the time. With a face full of tears. It's been going on the entire damn near four years we've been together."

I'm truly at a loss of fucking words. Baguette is one of the hardest, toughest men I know. I'd been with him a huge portion of my life and hadn't seen him shed a tear. Crying seems like it just isn't in his character. However, he did lose his first and only child, as did I.

I passed Tuscany back the blunt as she sat with a far-off look on her perfectly made-up face. I was happy her damn lipstick was matte red because she was known to gloss up the blunt.

"The reason I say let him be there for you is not to just keep the peace, but it's because he really does feel bad about everything. He knows the reason you lost her was because of him. The late nights, the fights, and the cheating. He feels like his actions are what led you to delivering a stillborn. Yea, we're all cool. You and him are the best of friends but forreal. Deep down, you hold some type of resentment. Or maybe not even resentment. Depression."

I tried to push my back into the couch as far as it would go. I hadn't been diagnosed with depression, but I knew I was. If it wasn't for Baguette having a cleaner come through here once a week, my place would probably be a mess. There were days where I didn't want to leave the house or get out of bed, but I really can't say why. This started about a year or so before I even got pregnant with my daughter. But, since I'm not harming myself, I just simply learned to deal with it.

"Friend, the last man you've had sex with was my man. I'm not tripping. I know it's nothing between y'all, but it's time for you to put yourself out there. You're bad as shit. The minute you post a new arrival, that shit sells in seconds. Your body is lethal, your face is a twenty, and your energy is unmatched. You're the total package. Baguette knows he fucked you over, friend. He knows he damaged you, and tries to make up for it by being a shoulder for you to lean on and that financial security. You're the closest thing to his daughter.

He feels her through you. I understand the house may be too much, and I'll talk to him about that, but promise me you'll try to live for you instead of living through us. If you do get a man, Brock's ass won't feel so obligated to be there for you. It's the guilt, Aphrodite. It don't make it right, but it's the truth. He loves the fuck out of you."

My chest swelled with air as I wiped a fallen tear from my eye. I missed my daughter—every damn day. I wonder what she would look like, who she would act like. I missed the fuck out of Athena Dianne Cherman. Born and died on April sixteenth. My daughter would have been my little mean and outgoing Aries. She was my everything, and although I didn't get to see her alive, I felt her grow and move for nine months. Pregnancy was the highlight of my life, and if I never get to experience it again, I'm content with knowing I did it gracefully with Athena.

"I just don't want to cross any boundaries. Some things should be reserved just for you." I sniffed.

"Oh, a lot is being reserved for me. Like the dick and his pussy eating skills. If he was giving you that, then you'd be a dead bitch." Tuscany did a dance in her seat, causing me to chuckle. That was one thing her ass didn't have to worry about. I couldn't even remember too much how Baguette was in bed, and I wasn't trying to. It was just weird.

"Okay. Okay, TMI. But please talk to him. I never have and never will blame him for our daughter. It was God's plan. I love her, but it wasn't meant. I'm okay with that. I've made peace with it. As bad as I hate to say it, I needed for that to happen. Look at where that placed he and I in life. He met you; I met me. I found myself and my purpose. For too damn many years of my life, Baguette has been there to clean up the broken pieces of me. I don't feel comfortable with him saving the day, and he doesn't get that. But I understand what you're saying. I'll cut him slack, only if you help me find a house I can afford ON MY OWN."

Tuscany smiled, showing off her pearly white teeth. Anytime she smiled, her pointy chin stuck out even more, making her look like she was up to no good. My favorite thing about her, outside of her flawless skin, slim thick shape, and gorgeous facial features, was her tawny brown tones. I was only a half shade lighter than her, but it was something about the uniqueness of her color that I loved. She's feisty. Kinda like the old me before I got old and boring, and she challenged Baguette. She was perfect for him. She changed him from a boy to a man. I hadn't heard her complain of infidelity not once, and that's saying a lot from the boy that used to lay dick all around the city. I loved them both. I was happy for them, but I didn't need him or her throwing me a pity party.

I'm single because I choose to be. I spent all of my youth and early twenties chasing around Baguette. These last five years, I've learned so much about myself and grew from a girl to a woman. I pulled myself from that dark place, and I was damn proud of it. Just because I didn't have a man didn't mean I needed Baguette to step up and do things that a man should be doing. I needed him to be my friend and not my provider.

Although him filling that male role in my life wasn't cheating, because he and I were a thing of the past, I feared that the sense of him having two women on his side wasn't healthy for his growth. Maybe I was looking too deep into it, but I just didn't feel right having him take care of me when I was completely capable of providing for myself.

I decided to let the topic go and vibe with my girl the rest of the night. I loved Baguette, but I lived for moments when it was just Tuscany and I. We gossiped, planned for the future, discussed business, and had good ole girl talk. When I was in a relationship, I didn't hang with no bitches because I was too busy thinking bitches wanted to fuck on my man. Hoes was grimy. The city was already envious of me, so I rocked with my family or my nigga. Now, ironically I'm besties with my ex-nigga's woman.

Hanging with Tuscany showed me how much I was missing out on. We didn't get out much, outside of maybe catching a happy hour or brunch here and there, because just as much as she was my only friend, I was hers. Her family lived in Memphis, so if she wasn't with me or Brock, she was bored as hell. I was either at their house or they were at mine. The time we spent though was priceless, and I secretly wished I'd had more of this years ago. That sisterly bond. I have a sister on my father's side, but we'd never met. Bonding with Tuscany had me really wanting to reach out, especially if we could hit it off like this. Maybe it was time for Baguette to back off just a little and let me spread my wings. I didn't need him handling me like I was some fragile piece of glass. I'm a grown ass woman, and I don't need a man to rescue me.

CHAPTER 2

Goal Navarro

"Come on, man. I got a family. My mama sick with pneumonia! If I don't cater to her, that shit gone take her out, Goal. Don't do this shit! A nigga don't wanna die! On God, ion wanna diiiiieeeee!"

Cries from this bitch ass nigga echoed around the warehouse. All that begging and pleading fell on deaf ears as I watched this disloyal muthafucka dangle upside down from the ceiling. Every time he wiggled, the chain wrapped at his ankles clanked. Blood spewed from his mouth with each word he belted, revealing about eight missing teeth. His eyes were closed shut and were already swelling and discoloring. I'd beat the shit out of him, which was rare on my part. At thirty two years old, I no longer did any dirty work. I hired men for that shit. But this right here was personal for me. Not only was this nigga a liar, he stuck his hand in the cookie jar. That right there was a fucking no no.

My goons stood around us in a circle as I walked around this nigga, spinning him ever so often.

"Goal! Goal! Please!"

"Nigga, shut the fuck up. You know damn well you ain't getting out of this alive. As far as yo' mama, I got mad love for Ms. Natalie, so she will be well taken care of. You may as well stop all that fucking pleading because that shit ain't gone grant you another hour of life."

He began wiggling like his ass was a fucking worm. The nigga's arms wasn't even tied, so he could have easily swung up, grabbed the chain, and climbed his ass to the ceiling or some shit. Had I been in his predicament, I would have turned into Spiderman and fought my way out this bitch. This nigga had about a hundred pounds on me though, so his fat ass barely had the stamina to walk, let along make like Tarzan and swing up out of this bitch.

"All this for what? Over a bit-"

"Nigga, it's never over a bitch. Remember that. I get mo' pussy than a Sorority orgy party. Yo' mind so throwed off 'bout these hoes that you failed to realize your bag came up shawt again. I gave your ass a pass because at the time, yo' mama was just diagnosed with cancer, but this time, her pneumonia case can't save you. Leo! Hit the switch!"

My men and I involuntarily started moving backwards as the floor beneath us shifted. Steel was no longer underneath Wex. It was now fresh water infested with three twelve foot alligators.

I tuned this nigga's begging and pleading out and signaled for Leo, the controls worker, to lower the rope. Wex's body hit the water with a splash, and the clear waters turned crimson red in three point five seconds. I knew it wouldn't be shit left of him when they finished, not even bones. While Money, Power, and Respect were devouring Wex, I checked the planner on my phone to see what was on my agenda for the day. I had a meeting with my nigga B. After that I was clear to take my ass to the house.

Killing a nigga didn't make my dick hard like some motherfuckers. The shit actually drained my energy because I hated being the fucking bad guy. It had been so long since I had to lay my hands on a fuck nigga. Now that I had, the shit had me ready to shower, roll up, and eat in silence. But, I'd committed to this sit-down, and prided myself on being a man of my word. Just like I told Wex, if he came up short again, he was gone be Gator bait.

I stood on my word. If a man didn't have his word, he didn't have shit. I was gone make sure his moms and daughters were straight though. I took their sole provider away, so it was only right I stepped in. That's just the type of nigga I am.

Once I dismissed all my goons, I headed to the office reserved as mine in the warehouse, and Baguette had already made himself comfortable.

"Nigga, you still got them wild animals and shit, I see." He stood, and we embraced in a brotherly hug.

"What can I say? My nigga Wilde keeps me with some exotics, and they gotta eat." I poured a glass of Remy Martin Cognac Louis Xiii Legacy since that's what B was already sipping on. Shit was twenty five thou a pop but smooth as shit. Definitely worth every fucking penny.

My office was on the top floor, and instead of walls, it was encompassed in one way mirrors. Couldn't see in but could definitely see out. Wex was a big nigga at about three hundred pounds, so the gators were still down there doing a number on him.

"I see you, baby." I gestured towards his bust down and Cuban that was shining like new money. B always had a love for jewelry and that granted him the street name Baguette. He was flashy but not loud. There was a difference. He didn't catch the attention of the police but still let niggas know he was getting it, and his reputation let a motherfucker know trying to rob him was a death sentence.

"I just came here to bring you the rest of your bread personally. A nigga going all the way legit with this shit. I done made enough money and my businesses flourishing enough to afford me to live like a king for the rest of my days. I just wanted to tell you that shit myself, nigga, and pay you what's owed."

Baguette sat a Fendi duffel bag on the chair next to him. I leaned back in my brown leather chair and nodded. I'd been telling B to go legit for years now. I knew when a nigga's heart wasn't in shit no more, but the streets was all he knew. He didn't work for me. Never had. When I first took head in the Navarro Cartel, most the drug lords and kingpins that were copping from the old leader wouldn't do business with my ass. They followed who they were loyal too, and while I thought the shit was stupid as fuck, I respected them.

B is one out of three niggas that stayed on and copped from me. He didn't know shit about my ass, but the fact I had the Navarro blood running through me, he took a chance and had been eating better than he ever had ever since. The nigga was never late, never asked for a handout, and was never short. Over the last few years, we'd developed more than a business relationship. I considered him an acquaintance. I don't do friends or right hands or no shit like that, but B is solid as they come.

"What brought on the change?"

"Life, nigga. I find myself having dreams of my daughter more than ever now, and I don't know if that's a sign or what. I'm good, the home front's good, and I'm blessed to make it through this shit. Most niggas don't beat the streets, but we did. I gotta get out while I'm ahead," he stated more so to himself as he took another sip of the cognac.

I'm happy for my nigga. He has shit to live for. Family. A beautiful, loyal ass woman. Hopes. Dreams. All of that good shit. He needed to get out. Truth be told, the moment his daughter died, he should have gotten out. But I respected his hustle. The last three years, he and I had gotten extremely close, and that's when I noticed he wasn't in it like he used to be. Before I'd taken over the cartel, I sat back and watched every dope man copping from the Navarro's. There were a few niggas I was impressed with. B was fasho at the top of the list. I needed to know what the fuck I was dealing with, but I fasho didn't expect for most the men to jump ship on my ass. When they realized their loyalty didn't mean shit to a snake, they all came back, but the price was doubled.

I was happy Baguette was getting the fuck out though. I'd made my peace a long time ago that I would die in these streets. I had too many motherfuckers depending on me. Unlike my bitch ass sperm donor, I didn't have a son that could jump in my place. My lil' brother was too fucking spoiled and had NFL dreams, so him coming in was a no go. Walking away wasn't an option or even a thought. I mean, I got a family that I come from and take damn good care of, but I wasn't out here creating one of my own. These bitches out here for everybody and outside of B's and a few of the niggas women in my camp, I was starting to think it ain't no worthy bitches out here. B is blessed, and if I had some that looked like Tusc and with a rep as clean as hers, I would be thinking of a way to scale back from this shit too. Since I don't, I'm going all in 'til the fucking casket drops.

"That's what's up, bruh. I'm glad you finally came to terms with this shit. Now it's time to make an honest woman out of Tuscany. She a real one," I spoke from the heart.

Tuscany is for sure one of the few goodies. She don't have a past full of ballers and dope boys. She didn't hang with a lot of bitches, and her ass was down for whatever. They were a funny ass couple. I enjoyed seeing them love on one another. I knew he was in a relationship with his high school sweetheart for years, but I had never really met her. All I knew was Tuscany was a gem, and he did right to move on from whoever she was.

"Yea, that's the plan. When I do, leave D at the house because Tuscany is on her ass when she sees her."

I shook my head and rubbed my hand over my low cut, thick wavy hair.

"Tell her I'd pay her ass to do her dirty, on God. Go ahead and say I told you so." B told me not to fuck with Daphne, but that shit fell on deaf ears. I let a fat ass, good pussy, and a pretty face blindside me but never again. I knew he had fucked, hell half the ballers in the city fucked. But I tried to give her the benefit of the doubt. I'm a born hustler, so I respected hers. She hustled hustlers. When her stupid ass hooked the big fish, she was supposed to change. But there's no turning a hoe into a housewife, and I see that shit now.

"I hate that for you, my dog. I knew yo' ass was just blinded by the pussy. It was a matter of time though. Playas fuck up. You'll meet the one soon enough. I'ma get up out here though. Tuscany blowing my ass up." He shook his head, and I stood and dapped him up.

He was right. I wasn't happy to run home at the end of the day to lay under Daphne. I didn't get all mushy and shit at the thought of her. I couldn't even really sleep in the same bed with her Grizzly bear snoring ass. All she'd ever been was a wet pussy, deep throat opportunist. But her time was coming. Soon enough. I'd given this sour bitch way too much, and she was 'round here fucking the help.

Wex was so damn low in rank that it was embarrassing. He was one of the first niggas I stupidly put on and hadn't upgraded his life at all. The nigga seemed to go down in rank as the years progressed. He was a damn do boy, and she put the pussy on that nigga. My pussy on that nigga.

Fuck I look like sharing pussy with a nigga I was feeding? I knew Daphne had a past, but whatever happened before me was null in void when I stuck dick in her and gave her the fucking title she'd been dreaming of. She'd fucked up big time. I wasn't gone kill her though. I was gone break her ass down like a fraction. Her ass needed to be reminded that she was nothing more than a scutterfield cum rag. I was just the nigga to give her the memo. I was gone strip her ass down to nothing and then send her back to her mammy house.

"Aye. Before you go, you know somebody that's in the market for buying a home?"

B, who had his back turned, faced me with a stroke of his chin.

"Yea and no, nigga. If you talking about the house you had built, hell no. My babymama looking for a home, but she got a budget and shit. Before you say some, she won't take a nigga's help at all. She wants to make it happen on her own, and as much as ion like it, I gotta respect it."

I nodded. "I tell you what. Send her the address and have her and her realtor meet me there same time next week. I'll meet her budget."

B nodded and smiled.

"Damn, nigga. You really are done with that broad. My BM gone lose her shit when she see that house. Good looking. Holla at me."

I walked B out and grabbed my shit so I could head to my condo. I didn't want to be around that bitch tonight. I had a trick for her ass though. It would be the last time she fucked over a goon. Not only a Goon but a multi millionaire Cartel leader at that. Who the fuck? How the fuck? Bitch gots to be smoking dick or popping them pills down at her job to fumble a nigga like me. Stupid ass.

CHAPTER 3

Aphrodite "Ditey" Greer

"**H**urry your ass up! Damn! You worse than me! No wonder why Baguette be so damn annoyed with me when I'm getting dressed. You done scarred my man for a lifetime."

I ignored Tuscany as I switched my shoes out. I'd changed outfits four times already. The fourth one was the winner, but the shoes were a no go. I'd planned on wearing Uggs boots and a chill set since we still had a week left in February, but Tuscany came in this bitch like we were headed to Nobu in Malibu, so I had to change it up. I hadn't dressed up in so damn long that I didn't know what to wear. True enough, I put together killer looks weekly with my new arrivals, but that's only for the camera to sell my pieces. Once I get my pics, I take that shit right off. When I do leave the house, it's always in leggings or a Nike set. Since we were going for a girls' day out and Tuscany gave me no other choice, I had to get sharp. Plus, I was determined to change her perspective of me. I didn't want the pity looks, especially since she'd labeled my ass as depressed.

I gave myself a once over in the mirror and almost cringed at how over the top I was. Instead of dwelling on it, I grabbed my metallic Gsuwoo chain bag and my crop bubble jacket since it was cold outside and all my damn stomach was out.

My boots echoed through my bathroom as I switched to my bedroom, where Tuscany was laying in my bed on her stomach waiting.

"Yeap, he used to leave my ass too. He'll be aite. You ready?" I asked while pinching my mid-waist jeans up in the back since my ass always pulled them down. These jeans always looked good on me as a teen since I naturally had a long torso that curved in the back. You couldn't tell me I wasn't the thick black Britney Spears back then. I was so happy these jeans came back in style. I tossed my long ash blonde bone straight tresses behind my back. My hair was styled in a half up half down style and was 30 inches with dark brown roots. I wasn't feeling it at first, but by the time I got my lashes done, the frontal unit grew on me. It was something different for me since I was usually a black-haired girl.

"Hold the fuck up, bitch. GOD DAMN! Shit!" Tuscany jumped up, damn near taking my curtains with her. I rolled my eyes, sat my bag on my dresser, and slid my bubble crop jacket on.

"Bitch, you so fucking bad! Oh my God! My hoe don't play that shit! Oh my fucking God, friend! Like you too damn bad, mane!"

I pulled my hair out of my jacket and picked my purse back up, placing it on my shoulder.

"You so dramatic. You see me dressed up all the time in my boutique pieces."

"Keyword. Boutique pieces and most of your pieces don't show skin. This Instagram model shit right here you got going on is top fucking tier. It's the hair for me. No, it's the makeup for me. No fuck that-"

She bent over and grabbed her phone off my mid-sized cherry wood poster bed." I keep it so G, ain't no lies from meeee. Damn, that bitch bad! It's the eyes for me. Why she standing like that? It's the thighs for meeee!" Tuscany rapped to Rylo and Gotti *For Me* while recording me. I gave her a little show and bent over to touch my toes. Her gay ass patted my pussy print from the back all in the camera.

"Let me find out! Talking about you can't dance! I can't even touch my toes without bending my knees!"

"Come on, I ain't got time to play with you!"

I had to admit the outfit was the shit. I was in *So real* from head to toe, rocking a baby blue cropped collared shirt that featured baby blue stones all over with the matching bubble crop jacket. The denim blue jeans were mid-waist and fit me like a glove, and the stacked baby blue, thigh high suede boots set the outfit off. I was the shit and was feeling like a new bitch.

Wearing this outfit had me seeing my weight loss. I'd only lost about twelve pounds, but it wasn't intentional at all. I'd always been on the medium side, and no matter what I ate, my tummy remained flat. But seeing now how tiny my waist is, had me looking like I'd had a rib taken out. The ass-to-hip-to-waist ratio is fucking stupid right now. Being 5'7, I had Tuscany by two inches, but with the hair I appeared slightly taller. My raw Sienna-hued skin is a shade lighter than it normally is since winter is upon us, but I planned to be outside this summer, so I was looking forward to my tan. My face is still round and pie shaped though. Weight loss hadn't affected that at all.

"Send me that video too."

"And you better post it too, bitch. Come on, I'm driving."

I turned the light out in my bedroom but left the fan on. Winter and all, I had to keep a cold bedroom with a heating pad in my bed. The rest of my house was warm, but better believe where I slept, there was a fan on. My phone vibrated in my bag, letting me know Tuscany sent my video.

Our heels echoed through the house as we walked to the front door. Tuscany was killing it too in a hot pink and yellow sweater material bodysuit that was cut a little low in the front. On her feet are a pair of pointy toe yellow ankle booties. Her hair was styled in a frontal ponytail that came down past her ass and was long and black. On her neck sat an iced-out Cuban and of course on her wrist, a bust Down Rollie. I had my plain face Rollie on. I hadn't made it to the bust down leagues yet, but if these clothes keep selling like packs of dope, I'll have one. Hopefully by my birthday in August.

It feels good to be looking good. Everything is on point down to our makeup, and we smelled and looked like money. We bad as fuck, no lie. Dressed too damn over the top to just be going out for brunch and shopping, but oh well. Jagoda Bay gone get these looks.

Once I set the alarm and locked up, I double checked my bag for my pistol and followed Tuscany to her light pink S550. I loved when she drove this car. It was her 30th birthday present from Baguette. The insides matched the outside, making it the ultimate Barbie mobile. It still had that new car smell being that she just turned 30 in October. I snapped me a few selfies being sure to capture her name that's engraved in the seats. This bitch is bad.

"I love this damn car, man! He did this!"

Tuscany smiled while putting on her seatbelt. "Yea, baby did good." *In love ass.*

She pulled out the driveway and began blasting the same song she was just singing while recording me.

I found myself rapping to it and starting it over three more times before I realized we weren't going anywhere near downtown for brunch.

I turned the music down and cut my eyes at Tuscany.

"Where the hell we going, Tusc?"

She kept her eyes on the road, trying to avoid looking at me.

"Look, Baguette asked me to bring you by this house. Before you bitch, he isn't buying it. It's in your budget, and somebody he know put it up for sale. The seller is just ready to get it off his hands. Before he put it on the market, Baguette wanted you to see it."

I folded my arm underneath my breasts.

"Y'all always doing some shit. I swear."

I looked upside Tuscany's head as her skin turned a shade of red.

"Have you at least seen it yet?"

She shook her head no. "But the nigga that has it up for sale don't play that shit, so I know it gotta be worth looking at."

Sighing, I turned the music back up but not too loud to where we had to talk over the tunes in order to hear each other. I swear I'ma cut these motherfuckers off if they don't stay out my damn business. I know they meant well, but damn. They always had some shit going.

"Well, let me at least text my realtor."

"She's already on the way there. According to the GPS, we got another twenty seven minutes."

"Well damn. Y'all just had this shit all planned out, hunh? I swear I'ma beat you and your mans ass, bruh. I hope I don't even like the house! And where this shit at? Sparkling City?"

Sparkling City is in the next city over but super close to Jagoda Bay. It's a vibe out there too, and slowly turning up on the black excellence. They have more bodies of water than us that sparkle underneath the sun. That's where the name comes from. But, it was too far from my mom to move too—three hours to be exact. I thought about it because the houses were huge, new and cheap but, no. I might just need too in order to get away from Bonnie and Clyde.

"Bitch, what? Never! That's too damn far for me. The house is in Jagoda Bay Crystal Cove to be exact. Now sit back. You claim you sick of Conquoy soooooo."

"Yea, aite." I applied more nude lip gloss and held my tongue. It was so much I wanted to say, but I ain't wanna ruin the mood. We were looking pretty and feeling good. Plus, Crystal Cove is the shit. It's a bougie ass neighborhood that most of the politicians and judges lived in. Their mall was to die for, and one of my favorite Steakhouses had a location over there. I can't imagine anything over there in my budget, but we shall see.

"Look. I think I wanna reach out to my sister," I blurted. It had been on my mind for a while. My mama never really talked about her. All I knew was that we were around the same age. I think my mama was kinda bitter because my daddy chose that family over ours, but his ass was dead and gone. My mama and daddy were rocky before he even stepped out because she didn't even let him sign the birth certificate. I had my mama's family last name.

My ma didn't speak foul over my daddy though; she just never brought his other family up. Hell, the family he comes from all live out west, so I don't too much know them to ask them. My daddy left us when I was six for his mistress. Although he made sure to always show up and show out for me, he never brought me to his new house and family. My mama wasn't going for that, no way. He died when I was nine and although that was a long time ago, I had been thinking about my sister.

I knew firsthand that life was way too short. All the times I spent around Tuscany had me really yearning for that sister bond. What if she needed me? What if she was struggling? Or sick? I'm not rich, but I'm more than capable of helping her if that was the case. I just feel like it's worth the shot to at least try to look for her.

"Ion know how I feel about that. I mean, we good with just us. What if she messy or fake or hang with the wrong crowd? You know ion do bitches like that."

"And I don't either, friend. But it's just been heavy on my mind." I sat back in my seat and watched the cars on the freeway.

"Well, I say go for it. I ain't too sure about this shit, but I support you. Where will you even find her? How will you find her? Ms. Robin don't say much about her and might slap the shit out of you if you ask."

Tuscany was right. My mama flew off her rocker anytime I brought up my sister. It was gonna be hard as shit finding her, but I had hope.

"All I know is that her last name is the same as my dad's McDowell. That's not a common last name. Social media is the easiest way to probably find her."

"Yea, but nobody uses their real name on social media and you know it. But I'll help you, friend. We gone find your lil' ugly ass sister, and if you push me aside for her, I swear I'm beating both y'all asses. We here."

I looked around at all of the homes that were miles apart from one another and was taken aback. There was no way in hell I could afford anyone of these on my own. These had to be at least a million dollars or better. Wasn't no way in hell.

"It's this one here. Damn, this shit bad as fuck. It's killing my house. Okay, frieeeend! I'm really never going home now! Come on!" Tuscany hopped out the car while I didn't know whether to be pissed or amazed. In the circular driveway were a white Rolls Royce truck and a white Range Rover probably belonging to the owners. My realtor drove a red Maybach truck, so I knew she hadn't pulled up yet.

Tuscany was already switching up the driveway, so I had no choice but to follow her. I had to admit although I wasn't on the inside, I loved this home. The gorgeous estate was breathtaking. It was definitely everything I'd dreamed of in a home and more, and I hadn't even made it inside.

The cast iron grand double doors on the Mediterranean-styled home were open already, so Tuscany and I walked in, and our heels echoed against the marble floors.

"Girrrrl, this shit here is beautiful! Oh my God! You gotta get it!" Tuscany squealed while doing a 360 spin. The grand entry featured a winding staircase with a bronze chandelier hanging. From the front entry you could see straight through the backyard, which had a pool, and from the looks of it a guest house. Even though I couldn't afford it, I couldn't wait to see it.

Tuscany and I just stood in the entryway taking it all in, and of course her ass was recording for Snap. She lived on damn social media, I swear.

We could hear another pair of heels in the distance, so we turned our heads toward the hallway where the sounds were coming from.

"Oh look, babe, the interior designers are here."

My mood suddenly went from sugar to shit. *This bitch.*

There were very few people on earth that I considered myself hating. Very few. This blonde hair, one too many ass shots, blowup doll looking bitch is one of the few.

Before I could say something slick in response, my words were caught in my throat at the specimen that walked up behind her. Everything in this brand new ass house seemed to take on a clean brightness with his presence. It was like a fucking glow stemming from his long frame. We both locked eyes, and I be damned if this nigga wasn't the finest I'd ever seen. And trust me, I'd seen some fine ass men. This damn man was so very good looking, and the way my body reacted strongly to him had me alarmed.

I don't know if it was the grey eyes for me or his toast-hued smooth skin, the goatee that matched the hair on top of his head, which was in a crisp box cut. Or the thin barely there mustache that sat on top of his pussy pink lips. With his skin tone, there was no way his eyes should be grey. It gave him an exotic look, although he was all African American. Or maybe I sense a bit of Hispanic or Dominican in the mix. His eyes bore through mine as he placed a gold bottle of Ace of Spades to his wet lips and chugged it back.

God damnnnnnn, this nigga fine as fuck. And his swag is on fucking point. On his legs were a pair of Dior jeans with the signature logo all

30

over them. The shoes may have been Dior too but they didn't have the logo. Either way, he was hard. He complimented his look with a over-sized white T-shirt with DIOR written across it in light blue, and underneath the shirt, he sported a white long sleeved turtle neck. Speaking of neck, it was dazzled in diamonds, and so was the wrist feeding him the bottle.

With his left hand, he placed his Dior bucket hat on top of his head. Not once did we stop fucking each other with our eyes. He wasn't too big, but he wasn't small either. Not too tall, but he was far from short. 6"1, maybe? Give or take. Whatever he was, he's thuggish looking, rich looking, and fine as a motherfucker. His cologne was so strong that it suffocated me.

Those grey eyes that were piercing through mine, showed me our whole damn future. I was ready to propose to this nigga, give him my debit card, pop sixty grey-eyed babies out for him and suck his dick in front of my entire family if he asked. Yea, this nigga was toxic, and I needed to get far the fuck away from him. Pronto!

"Wassup, Goal? Baguette told us to meet you here," Tuscany spoke up.

He nodded his head at Tuscany, never breaking our contact.

"Sup, Tuscany. Tell that nigga hit me up later too."

Whew, he even sounds sexy. A little southern, deep, demanding ass tone too. His voice seemed to vibrate the whole damn house.

"Babe, how about we show them what we need done? Ladies, you can follow me." I almost forgot Daphne was in the room. Her ass was doing the most too. Had her arms wrapped around this nigga's torso while he was eye fucking me. She was cute, but she wasn't no us. Her high yella skin packed with makeup, and her blonde weave was pulled back in a low ponytail. Daphne is a bad bitch, but the see thru outfit with the pasties on her titties was a little too much for the daytime, if you ask me. Daphne always been the type to do the most when she really didn't have to do much at all. Her ass looked like she was headed to the club at 11 a.m. She had laid down on the table three too many times, so her ass-to-legs ratio was fucked up. She thought that shit was cute though.

"Daphne, you know damn well we ain't no interior designers.

Cut the bullshit. I hate to do you dirty in front of your nigga, but keep on and I'ma dog walk your ass up in here," Tuscany stated without an ounce of sarcasm in her tone. She was dead ass serious, and if Daphne didn't cut her shit she was going to get the worst ass whooping she'd ever had. I beat the shit out of her the first time, but I was going to murder that ass the second time. I'd been itching to beat the life out that bitch again. Yes, me and Baguette were a thing of the past, but the fact that this hoe played with my company online is what secured her on my forever shit list.

"Oh, I almost didn't recognize y'all. It's the sister wives. Baby, you know that's Baguette's first bitch, Aphrodite. She sell lil' clothes online now," Daphne snickered like she wasn't the same bitch buying my lil' online clothes anytime a new arrival dropped before I blocked that ass.

"Baby, ion see how y'all besties and ride the same dick. Couldn't be me. The weirdest shit ever, but I know Baguette enjoying that. He always knew how to juggle two bitches."

"Bi-"

"AHT AHT, I got this, Tuscany." Taking a few steps forward, I noticed this clown bitch was wearing grey contacts. Typical lame ass Daphne. She was the type of bitch that tried to morph into whatever nigga she was stalking at the time.

"You mean the same dick you sucked and fucked every chance you got? The same dick you got your ass beat the fuck out of in front of the entire hood for? Daphne, stop fucking playing with me up in here like you don't know how I get down. Don't confuse my growth for weakness, bitch. I'm still that same bitch from da bricks that will smack slob from a hoe in a millisecond.

Ain't no fucking sister wives going on. Fuck outta here. It's called being grown and carrying such a vibe that makes my ex *and* his bitch rock with me. Real niggas and real bitches gravitate to me. Some shit yo' rotten ran thru pussy ass don't no nun 'bout."

This red ass hoe smirked and sucked her teeth while her nigga continued to stare me down and drink from his bottle.

"Yea whatever, bitch. You ain't all that."

"Says the bitch who begged me to eat my Pussy AFTER I beat her ass. Stop playing with me up in here, Miss mamas."

"Bitch-"

"AHT, AHT, AHT. No need for profanity, sweetie. Sorry I'm late, Aphrodite. Traffic was bananas."

We all turned our heads to the entrance as my realtor stepped in. Quasie Lantis was dressed to kill. She was rocking different variants of cream. On her feet were a pair of sling-back red bottoms, hugging her frame sat leather pants with a snake print belt holding them in place. A sweetheart neckline bodysuit tucked inside her bottoms, while her shoulders housed a cream trench coat, and in the crook of her arms Christian Dior bag. Her hair styled in her signature middle part bob, and as always her makeup was flawless. Quasie had one of the best shapes to me. She's on the taller side, standing an inch taller than I did. Her hips and ass wasn't too much but damn sure couldn't be missed. I chose her to be my realtor because not only is she a customer of mine, but she's a bad ass successful realtor, and her style is impeccable. She'd also sold Tuscany and Baguette their latest home.

"Wassup, boo. You looking pretty." Tuscany hugged our bossed up ass realtor as Quasie tossed out an air kiss and strutted to the side of me, never taking her mug off of Daphne. She's a professional, but her ass could get with the shit quick, and I loved that about her.

"Who the fuck is you? Why all y'all in my house for? Baby, make 'em leave. Your dick down my throat wasn't enough. I need to sit on that dick." This nasty hoe licked her lips, letting us know she was just swallowing semen prior to our arrival.

"Well, I'm IS the realtor, boo, and we're here to hopefully make a deal with Mr. Navarro on *your* house. Let's tour the property, Aphrodite, shall we?"

The look on Daphne's face was priceless. Her light skin flashed a shade of bright red, and I could visibly see the sweat beads form at her lace. I guess she didn't get the memo that her nigga was putting her house on the market.

"Wh-wh-what? Baby, what the fuck is she talking about? My house isn't for sale! It was just built! I'm set to move in in two weeks. Baby!" Her nigga was still drinking and checking me out. He pulled her arms around from his waist. When she wouldn't let go, he gave her a slight shove making her hit the floor with a thud. This silly bitch got on her knees and started begging. I could fucking never.

"Please, baby! Tell me this a joke!"

"Was fucking the help a joke? Yea, it was a joke, but this damn sho ain't. Ladies, make yourself at home. Tour the property. Mrs. Navarro, let me know what you think of it," he flirted while looking directly at me.

Looking backwards and then turning my head back in his direction, I was trying to find out who the fuck he was talking to. Damn sure couldn't have been me.

"That's not my name."

This fine ass nigga looked me dead in the eyes. "Not yet."

"Well, I heard that. Tuscany, *Mrs. Navarro*, follow me. Let's tour this immaculate property. I love the grand entryway and custom marble floors."

We all turned on our heels, leaving Dumb ass on the floor. Before we could bend the corner, we heard a slashing sound, and I gasped seeing this nigga pouring the champagne on top of this bitch head. Whew. That was some disrespectful ass shit.

"I can't stand that whore," Quasie spat and shook her head. Tuscany was laughing her ass off. As bad as I wanted to gloat, I couldn't. I was disgusted. If it was one thing I couldn't stand, it was a foul ass, disrespectful nigga. That shit made me lose all respect for him. He was now labeled as a fuck nigga in my eyes. I don't like the Daphne hoe, but at the end of the day, a man degrading a woman has never been acceptable to me. You selling the damn girl house, put her out, and keep it fucking moving.

Touring the home had grey fading to the back of my mind as I fell more in love with the property. The six bedroom five bath, exercise room, sauna, office, library, and guest house did it for me. The home is equipped with everything besides furniture. It's literally move-in ready. It was all a shame that I couldn't afford it, although my realtor assured me I could. I just couldn't see that being possible. This is well over a million dollar home in a highly desired and sought out neighborhood. I had to hit the fucking lottery for this shit. Hell, I didn't even have the half to give Baguette If I allowed him to help me get the damn house. I was about to have to take my ass home and sulk because I wanted this place knowing damn well it was out of the question.

We were all standing in the kitchen discussing the fabulous home and how we could see it decorated. The vibes were so damn good that I forgot we still had company.

We could all sense him before we saw him because all conversations halted as this Goal character made an appearance.

"So, what do you think about the home?"

I said nothing, just stared at him blankly while chewing the inside of my mouth. Why the fuck do I keep tensing up around this man like I'm not used to good looking guys? Shit's embarrassing.

Tuscany cleared her throat, breaking my eye contact, and I wanted to smack that smug off her face. Quasie was on her laptop, possibly securing more closings. Her ass worked harder than me. Still, I could see the low smile she was trying to hide. *These muthafuckas.*

Mustering the courage to speak up so this man won't think I'm fucking slow, I licked my bottom lip.

"I love it. It's not in my price range, but if it was, I would definitely take it off your hands," I spoke honestly. This house is a Dream come true. It was the cream of the crop. Top tier. It was just wayyyy above my price range. Plus, what the hell was I going to do with all of this house?

"Do you want the house or not?" This nigga had the nerve to ask me.

"I ain't ask about no bread. It's simple. Yes, Papi, I'll take it. Or no, I'll move in with you instead." A sly grin spread across his handsome face.

"Mrs. Lantis, start drawing up the paperwork. No need for lenders and all that shit. The quicker you can get it done, the better for you. I'm letting my wife get it for the low, but I'll make sure you still get the commission as if we were selling this shit for the listing price. Let me holla at Mrs. Navarro real quick."

Quasie closed her laptop and grabbed Tuscany by the hand.

"Yes, sir. I'll get right on it. Take your time; we'll be outside inspecting the gutters."

These heffas left me in the kitchen with this damn stranger like it was cool.

"I don't know why you told her that. I can't afford this home. Especially with a cash payment. I don't know what Baguette promised you but kill it. He's not buying shit for me. He's Tuscany's man. Not mine. I'm buying my own shit." I was over these games and this back and forward.

"Baguette not buying you shit. I know that ain't yo' nigga, because I am. As far as you being able to afford this house, my bitch can have the world. Ain't shit off limits."

"But I'm not a bitch, nor am I your bitch. She's a few rooms over doused in champagne." The disdain I had for his act was shown in my expression, and he knew it because he smiled at the shit. There was some distance between us, but it felt like he was in my fucking skin.

"Yo' ain't no bitch but you most definitely my bitch. Come on now, you know what the fuck going on."

Cocking my head aside, I crossed my arms.

"Naw. I really don't."

"Yeah, you really do. I get what the fuck I want and I want you."

That statement shouldn't have had my slit flushing with warm liquid, but it did. The type of fucking man that knew he was fine was the worse type. He's the worse type. I had to get the fuck on.

"Cut the shit. How much for the house?"

"Your number."

"Nah, forreal. How much?"

"Your number. Dead ass. Give me a number, possibly let a nigga pull down on ya, and it's all yours. You can have the keys and title and all that." He shrugged.

"I'ma get ya number anyway, so you may as well give it to me now. Make this shit easy. But I fuck with a challenge." He licked his lips and stuffed his hands in the front of his pants.

"I refuse to share dicks with Daphne ever again. So my number is out of the question. Plus, disrespectful niggas like you aren't my type. You're too damn old to be pulling up on someone. Ask a bitch on a date. I like my steak medium rare with grilled shrimp on the side, and loaded mashed potatoes, and to wash it down with a lemon drop or a nice bottle of Giulia. That's neither here nor there though."

"Is dat right?" The southern drawl of his voice had my eye twitching, but I had to stay focused or else he was going to have me bent over this big ass island.

"How about this. I give you what I was going to spend on my home, which is three hundred and seventy five thousand. We draw up papers and have it listed at that amount so it can be approved by the lenders. What is the house worth? One point three mill? Give or take. You had it built for a bitch that ain't worth gum underneath a park bench, so something short of four hundred thousand should suffice. I've done the whole street nigga thing. I'm beyond that. So, do we have a deal?"

Those grey eyes pierced through me again. My breathing heightened as he slowly walked into my space, causing me to peddle backwards until his ass had me cornered against the counter. My throbbing breasts pressed against his hardened chest. He was so close, I'm sure he could smell the mint on my breath and feel the poke of my nipples.

"You wouldn't be sharing dicks with no bitch because it would be all yours. I'm only disrespectful to a motherfucker that needs to be disrespected. I ain't take you for a woman that be worried about the next hoe. And if I said all I wanted was your number, then that's what the fuck I said. Ion need the bank's money. I am the fucking bank. Don't play me on no broke shit, mama. You had a street nigga. A damn good one, but I'm THE street nigga. You ain't never had nan like me."

"I can smell that hoe saliva on your dick. Move, sir." My hands moved from gripping the cold countertop to his broad chest as I tried to shoo him from my space.

"You got a smart ass mouth. I'ma fuck that shit right on up outta you too. Yeaaa, let me see if you can talk all that shit with this dick in yo' guts."

I turned my lip up and scoffed, "I wouldn't fuck you if you paid me. Fuck out my face, nigga."

He chuckled. "We both know that shit's a lie. Keep talking shit. I'll bend yo' ass over right here, with the next bitch stankin' ass saliva on my dick." His voice boomed through the kitchen as I swallowed hard.

"Now let me tell you how this shit gone go. You gonna take this fucking house and you gonna be ready Saturday at eight and not a minute after. I'ma give you time to move the fuck in. You want a nigga to court you and shit? Cool. Wear a dress. Leave the panties at the house. When the realtor come back in here, let her know we got a deal."

"Nigga-"

Goal grabbed my neck with his massive hand and slid his right hand straight down my pants. His hand was so big and warm as it brushed up against the baldness of my opening, it caused me to shake underneath him. Once he cupped my pussy, I squealed and bit down hard on my bottom lip. I was so wet it took nothing for him to slide a finger in. That shit felt so good my eyes rolled to the back of my head. It had been so long since I'd been touched by a man that I was biting back a moan. I was already about to cum, and he wasn't even stimulating the clit. His big ass middle finger was just sliding in and out of me.

"That's right. Cum for Papi. It's been a minute since somebody played in this pussy, hunh? Is that why you on ten? You need to be humbled. You need to be fucked?"

"N...n...yesss!" I hissed.

"I know it. Now what you gonna tell the realtor?"

I squeezed my eyes shut, and he applied pressure to my neck.

"AHT, AHT. Open up. Look at Papi while he in that pussy."

I could feel my climax coming, and it had my legs stiffening. Butterflies swarmed in my belly just as it began to cave.

"I'ma...I'm...I'maa... ummmmmmm."

"Speak up."

"I'ma...I'ma tell her we got a deallll! Ohhh, fuck! I'm cumminggggg, shiiiit!"

"Ummm, you look so fucking sexy when you cum. Be ready for that date, since you like yo' steak medium well. Just know when I get you to myself, it's ova. You gone be sucking the skin off my dick right here in this kitchen, but that'll come in due time."

My entire body vibrated as the butterflies turned into cramps. I felt a strong urge to pee, and I held that shit back because I knew it meant I was going to squirt. I didn't have time to walk out of here looking like I'd pissed on myself. Having a man I didn't know telling me I was going to be sucking this skin of his dick would have me ready to curse his ass out, but this cloudy-eyed demon right here had me so fucking sloppy wet behind those words it was pitiful.

"Let Papi taste you." He slid his hand out of my pussy and placed his now milky finger in his mouth.

"Like sweet Fiji."

"Are we interrupting?"

My eyes ballooned, and I pushed his big ass off me while gathering myself. The high I was just on seconds ago had brought me back to earth as I adjusted my coat while Tuscany had her hand over her mouth and Quasie was grinning. I couldn't stand their asses. This shit is so fucking embarrassing. I don't even know where this nigga's hand had been. Nor did I know if Daphne was still on the property, and here we were in the kitchen doing nasty ass shit.

"Nah, not at all."

This nigga still had his finger in his mouth, making my kitty thud.

"You need time to decide? It's cool if you do. I have more listings to show you." Quasie raised a brow while looking directly at me. The looks we exchanged told her my answer before I could voice it.

This nigga cleared his throat, making me groan.

"No. We have a deal. You can get started on the paperwork, Quasie. Thank you. Tuscany, I'm ready to go."

I switched past everyone, shocked that this was happening. This house was too big and too much for me. I hadn't had a man to touch me in five years, and here comes one that I'd never even been in the same space with, making a bitch cum harder than my rose ever did off fingering alone. Not only that, it's Daphne's ex, who's friends with my ex. This entire situation is messy as fuck, but I'd be a fool not to take this home off his hands.

I made it to Tuscany's car before she did and caught Daphne burning rubber in a Range Rover.

My head hit the cold leather as I got lost in my thoughts. Taking this house meant now the crazy bitch knew where I stayed. I wasn't so much worried about Daphne as I was this psychotic ass nigga. If he could make my body do that with his fucking finger, I'm scared of his actual dick. *Fuck.* I'd just sold my damn soul to the Grey eyed demon for my dream home. This shit about to be a hot ass mess.

CHAPTER 4

Brock "Baguette" Cherman

My phone rang, but I pressed ignore before sliding it back in my pocket. I didn't it like any interruptions when I visited my daughter. She deserved my undivided attention, and I always made sure I gave it to her.

"Daddy brought you some little mermaid shit. It's what all the lil girls around your age liking right now. Ion know if you would, but if you're girly like ya mama, then you'd love it. We got a black little mermaid coming, and when they stock the shelves, I'ma get it all for you."

I looked down at all of the Arielle dolls and shit I'd purchased at Walmart and knew Aphrodite was gonna curse my ass out for going overboard again. My little girl had to have the best, even in death. Nothing was too much.

"I've been dreaming about you a whole lot. Daddy miss you, lil girl. I done did a lot of fucked up shit but one of the only things I did right was making you. You supposed to be here. You, Tuscany, and your mama are my world. Your mama mad at me because she feels I overstep my boundaries when it comes to her, but she gave me the greatest gift, and that was you. I'll forever make sure she's straight. Until I join you in the afterlife."

I placed a hand on her tombstone and placed the Louis frames before sitting in front of Athena's grave.

"Athena Dianne Cherman. Pretty ass name for a pretty girl. Did I ever tell you where ya name comes from?"

I paused as an elderly black couple walked by. I'd seen them here a few times before and on some nosey shit, walked by the grave they visited and figured it must've been their child too. The death date was from 1999, and according to the birthday, the child was nine years old at the time of death. Seeing them out here torn up over a child they lost over almost three decades ago let me know I would never get over losing my baby. Once they were out of sight, I stretched my arms out with my elbows resting on my knees and let my hands hang.

"Well, your grandma Deborah was fascinated with Greek mythology. She even got your mama on the shit hard. Let me stop cussin'. Yo' stepmama Tuscany told me that shi- that stuff not cool for me to be using bad words when I'm talking to you. But, like I was saying, yo' grandma likes Greek mythology. She named your mama Aphrodite, and Aphrodite is the Goddess of love and beauty." Swiping my thumb across my nose, I chuckled.

"She's for sure all of that. You have the prettiest mama in all the land. You come from good genes, kid. Yo' mama is so damn beautiful, she's the type of gorgeous that if you had a baby brother, he would have been ready to fight any man that looked at her. As far as love, your mother is the most loving person I know. She loves hard...so hard. She loves the fuck out of you, baby. She loves so good that it was too much for daddy, so she had to take the love she gave me and put it back into herself. Her love for you though, its unwavering. It's never too much." I closed my eyes and imagined my baby's face. Round and pie, just like her mama's. I knew she would have been so damn pretty.

"Your name doesn't mean beauty or love, but you have enough of that in you already. Athena is the Goddess of Wisdom, Practical Reason, and War. I know for sure you're the smartest little girl up there. I just hope you not in heaven leading wars. I'll have to come up there and clear all the angels out about ya... I know you leaving us had to be for a reason, but baby, that shit just ain't practical to daddy," I choked out.

My daughter is my greatest creation. Ain't no way in hell she's supposed to be dead. No way. It's muthafuckas out here I know for sure deserved death, but my fucking seed wasn't one of them. I know Aphrodite acts like she moved on, but losing Athena changed her. She don't have that sparkle in her eye no more. She stays in the house, buries herself in work, and won't give any nigga the time of day even if he paid her ass. She misses our daughter no matter how fucking nonchalant she appears to be. Aphrodite nor I will never be the same unless our baby girl came back from the dead. Real shit.

My phone rang again. It wasn't nobody but Tuscany, so I ignored it again and spent a little more time with my baby girl. Anytime I was feeling down or overwhelmed, this is where you could find me—kicking shit with my daughter. Most street niggas longed for a son but not me. The moment I planted that see din Aphrodite, I knew it was a princess. I did Aphrodite dirty for years. I mean, yea, I spoiled her, but that was it. Our relationship lacked honesty, excitement, commitment, and growth. All that shit was on me. She liked to blame herself, but that was all me.

I was a stupid ass young nigga that was getting way too much money too early, and got the fucking big head. I shitted on the bitch that was down for me when I was that dusty ass nigga on the block. A nigga stressed that girl so bad, I made her lose our daughter. All the bitches and riches in the world wasn't worth my child's life. This shit will never be okay. I will never be okay with my actions.

There wasn't no coming to terms with my baby being dead. It's so hard to explain the shit, but it didn't *feel* like she was dead. Like she was maybe out there somewhere waiting for me. Waiting for us. Call me crazy, but that's just how a nigga felt.

I know Aphrodite hated how much I did for her, but she was the one that was with me from the beginning. I could never shine with a bitch that came after her and leave her in the dirt. True enough, I'm not attracted to her in a sexual way. No matter how bad she is, she's my homie. My best friend outside of my parents. I loved her like a sister, and no matter what, that shit was gone never change.

Once I was sure my daughter was sick of my ass, I got up and headed to my McLaren. I usually only drove my baby on special occasions, but my daughter is a fucking special occasion.

Turning out of the cemetery, my phone rang again right on cue.

"Bay, I'm headed to you now." I watched my rearview mirror as I spoke to my baby. If I didn't answer the phone, her ass would blow me the fuck up.

"What was Athena doing? I would have come with you," she offered. We liked to talk about my daughter like she was still living, although we knew she wasn't.

"Listening to me vent like always. Tired of her old man probably." I chuckled while stroking my chin. A few hairs had surfaced, letting me know it was time to visit the barber. I tried growing my shit out, and it didn't work for me. Shit was patchy as hell.

"She will never be tired of you, baby. You're the best dad. I gotta make my way out there soon."

Although Tuscany didn't get the pleasure to meet my baby girl, she bonded with her spirit, and I admired that shit. Tuscany would be a great stepmother to Athena fasho. It was no doubt in my mind.

When Aphrodite left a nigga, I wasn't in the market to wife up no bitch. I was already fucking on women when I was with her, but the crazy thing is, when she left, a nigga felt so empty and sick. On top of grieving our daughter, I just fell the fuck back. I still got my dick wet, but instead of fucking several women, I would just deal with one. Every one that came along was threatened by Aphrodite and I's relationship. When she left my ass, we were on the phone the same damn night, and a few weeks later, I found myself sleeping on her damn couch. We were still like a couple, but we didn't do no intimate shit during most of the pregnancy. Hell, up until Tuscany, I was still spending the nights at Aphrodite's to the point she'd set up a guest room for me.

Running into fine ass Tuscany wasn't supposed to turn into a full blown ass relationship. I was just looking to find a constant woman to drain my dick, but when she came along and showed me some different shit from what I was used to, I fell like a muthafucka.

"Who do you think she would have looked more like? You or Aphrodite?"

I watched my rearview as I merged on the expressway.

"Aphrodite, for sho. I imagine that she's her mama's twin with my skin tone and big ass eyes. Bossy like Aphrodite too. Long curly ass hair like her big headed ass mama and smart and witty like me. She's perfect."

"And that she is. Aphrodite would have been the best mom. She would have been lucky to have y'all."

"Lucky to have us. All of us."

Athena's death changed nothing. Aphrodite and I still would have split. We weren't meant to be. I loved her when I was with her, but with Tuscany, it was different. That girl fed my soul. She is that one. My one. While Aphrodite is my person, Tuscany is my soulmate.

"I know, baby. I just hurt for y'all sometimes. Life is so unfair and unpredictable. Did you put any thought into the grief counselor I found? She comes highly recommended."

Tuscany had been trying to get me to sit down with this grief counselor for a minute. I shut her ass down every time. I didn't need no fucking shrink. My lil' girl was gone and was never coming back. A bitch with a pencil and notepad couldn't make me feel no better about the shit. I was good. Plus, I wasn't too keen on pouring my heart out to a complete stranger. That's why I passed on that shit every single time.

"It is indeed. You cooking or you want me to grab sum?"

"Grab some'. I'm tired, baby. I've been at the bars all day. I had some wings earlier, but that was hours ago."

I nodded like she could see me. Tuscany and I owned a chain of bars, and that shit kept us busy as fuck. It just now got to the point where they ran themselves, but we still liked to show face and make sure everything was a go. *The Bottom Sports Bar and Lounge* is my baby and afforded me to walk away from the streets. We have four locations in the city and nine more spread throughout the south. Getting thirteen locations up and running in two and a half years wasn't easy, but we did that shit. Life is straight and business is better. I just needed my baby girl here with me.

"Whatchu got a taste for?" I checked my rearview mirror again before going towards where I knew she would want. Although I'd paid Goal for my last few bricks and bowed out gracefully, a nigga still had to watch my back. I'm out the streets, but I'm having paper and a whole lot of it. Niggas will off you just because you got what they don't.

I looked at the screen to make sure Tuscany was still there since she hadn't told me what she wanted to eat. I don't even know why I asked. If her ass could eat Houston's fried shrimp every single day, she would. Even when she told me she wanted something else to eat, I know it was only to appease me. I didn't care one way or another. I was still that nigga who could eat a fried pork chop sandwich from the corner store. All the money in the world wouldn't change that. Long as a nigga ate.

I disconnected the call with Tuscany and parked. I already knew what she wanted so there was no need to keep her ass on the line. I loved my baby, but her ass just loved to hear a nigga breathe sometimes. My mind was way too clouded to listen to her ramble on about the employees from The Bottom and girly shit with her and Aphrodite. I was tryna be in and out of the restaurant, and being on the phone would her wouldn't help me accomplish that.

I love Houston's Restaurant just as much as Tuscany. It's small, yet the dim lights, candles on the tabletops, and choice of music gave it an intimate but laidback type of vibe. You could come here for a romantic dinner or you could sit back and kick shit with the homies. All of the political crooks stayed in this bitch at the bar. I hit a few head nods at some muthafuckas I recognized from being at *The Bottom* while I waited on our favorite waitress to give me our order. I'd already texted it to the manager, and Ms. Giselle spotted me walking in and scurried to go get it. Ms. Giselle had been working here for many years, and Tuscany had taken a liking to her. Hell, as a matter of fact, this is where I first saw Tuscany, but I didn't get her digits at the time. She was talking to Ms. Giselle the day I saw her pretty ass.

I tried offering Ms. Giselle a position at one of The Bottom's locations, paying her double what she really made, but she declined every time. Tuscany was begging her too. They think it was because she got a mother vibe from her, just like she took a liking to Aphrodite's mother. Her own mother wasn't bad, but she wasn't much to look up to. That was her story to tell.

I took a spot at the bar and signaled Donnie's square ass to make me a Manhattan. I was still in a fucked up space behind my daughter and needed to regroup. After downing the shit and the liquid going down with a burn, I signaled my hand to request another. I was feeling the effects after the second drink, and before I could request a third, I felt something hit my leg. Looking down, all I saw was ponytails. I bent down to pull the lil' mama up because I know her fall hurt like a motherfucker. I'm a solid nigga, and so were these floors. Before I could completely pull her up, she sprang straight up into action like her little ass just didn't take a great fall.

As she pushed her hair out of her face, I looked around for her damn parents. The restaurant wasn't big nor was this the type of establishment a child should be running around freely and shit. I couldn't spot her peoples, so I focused my attention back on the little girl, who I could now see a clear view of since her curly ass hair was out of her face.

"I'm sorry for running into you. Did I hurt you?" The child looked up at me with her innocent face, and I couldn't even formulate words to respond. My chest heaved in and out as my heart rate kicked it up a notch. An icy chill curled up my spine as I froze, eyes wide, struggling to comprehend. *What the fuck?* I'd seen this child so many times. Every time I blinked. Every time I slept. She was there. Staring up at me with big brown, concerned eyes. She rubbed my knee, where she'd just ran into, but there was no need. I'm two hundred and twelve pounds and 6' 2. I was more than okay.

"I'm really sorry. I shouldn't have been running. Now you're going to have a boo boo."

Her hands were intertwined behind her back as she twisted side to side. I tore my eyes away from the child, picked up my empty glass, and looked back down at her. *Nah, nigga, you tripping.* I'd just gotten a bad fucking case of deja vu. I swear I'd seen this child before.

"Ramira! Get your butt back over here. I done told yo' behind about running off! I turn my back once just so your brother can use the bathroom, and you turn loose!" An elderly stubby lady wobbled, scolding the little girl who'd run into a nigga.

"I'm sorry, Ms. Haddie! I was trying to catch my ball! I didn't mean to," she replied with pouty lips while continuing to do her innocent sway, making her pink and white striped sweater dress shift.

"Sir, forgive this child. She knows better than to run off. Ain't that right?"

She nodded her head up and down, "Yes, ma'am."

"Now come on, my grandson should be here any minute. We gotta get you and your brother back home before your father makes it." The elderly lady, that the child called Ms. Haddie, held her hand out for the little girl to take.

The kid leaned in, kissed my knee, and rubbed it again, "All better now. Bye!"

Ms. Haddie shook her head and gently grabbed the child's hand. A waitress walked up holding a tray. "Would either of you like complimentary peanut butter and almond bars? They're delightful."

"I'm straight. Allergic to both." I dismissed the bubbly waitress.

Ms. Haddie snapped her head up at me and gave me a strange look.

"What about you, ma'am?" Ms. Haddie immediately turned on her heels and scurried off to their table I'm guessing. I sighed and tried to ease the tightness in my chest by chugging back the last of what was left of my drink.

"I'm sorry about the long wait! Here is your order."

I pulled out two one hundred dollar bills and handed them to Ms. Giselle, prompting her to keep the change. I needed to get the fuck outta this damn restaurant because I was losing my damn mind.

I tipped Donnie again and made my way out of the restaurant so I could get home to my hungry woman.

"Wassup, family?"

"Damn wassup, nigga! I heard yo' ass was out. Fuck you been doing up in that bitch, body building?" I joked as I gave Kilo a dap and brotherly hug.

"Mane wasn't shit else to do up in that bitch. I figured the least I could do was get fit." He smiled.

"Yea, well, nigga you got fit fit. Swoll ass," I clowned. Kilo and I went way back. From when we were young niggas hustling the same block. Around the time my daughter passed, he got caught up on a body and ended up getting ten years. Me and Goal came together and hooked him up with the best attorney and got him to serve five years with no parole. We was hoping he didn't get that much time, but the

47

system is so fucked up they just had to see a black man behind bars. The fucked up shit was, Kilo didn't even commit the murder. A nigga in his camp did, but his prints were on the pistol. Shit was crazy as hell how it all went down, and better know that lil' nigga wasn't breathing no more due to his careless ass actions. We still trying to figure out how Kilo's prints were on the gun 'til this day. The law was so crooked, no telling.

"With how a nigga been eating, I'll be back flabby in no damn time. But what's good? I appreciate the fuck out of you and Goal too. Y'all ain't have to do what y'all did. If it wasn't for y'all, my grannie, and cousins, a nigga wouldn't have had no one behind those bars. Every bitch flaked on a nigga, except one, and that was the one I shitted on. I appreciate you though, forreal."

I rubbed my chin and nodded my head. I was no stranger to shitting on the one you should be praising. I'm a street nigga, so I knew how that shit went. I did time myself. None too crazy, but I was grateful for the one I had at the time. Them hoes scattered like roaches the minute them cuffs hit ya wrist. The ones that would stay only stayed around so that when a nigga got out, they could put 'em in position. The shit wasn't genuine at all. Kilo was worse than me and Goal put together back then when it came to hoes. He ran through 'em like water. I wasn't shocked that none of their asses stayed down. Typical Jagoda Bay bitches.

"It's all good. You a solid nigga, so it was only right we stood down for ya. I'm proud of you too, nigga. How is business?" Kilo managed to start flipping houses behind bars with the help of his grannie and cousin. He was still moving bricks; that shit hadn't stopped and probably never would. Hence the reason he gained the nickname Kilo in the first place. Nigga was moving so much of that white girl at a young age.

"Business is great, nigga. I know you still soaking up all this freedom and shit but hit me up when you get a chance. You can come by the crib and we can kick shit like we used to."

"I'll do that. Oh, and I'm sorry about y'all daughter. You talked to Aphrodite lately? How she been? I know you with fine ass Tuscany now."

Any other nigga would have asked about Aphrodite, I would have known he was tryna get down, but not Kilo. He'd seen Aphrodite and I here and there when we were in the streets heavy.

"Yea, Tuscany is my baby. Actually, me and Aphrodite pretty tight. Tuscany too."

He raised a brow like everyone did when they found out my ex, current, and I were tight.

"Nah, not no shit like that. Aphrodite a nigga best friend. We didn't work out but she still the homie. Tuscany fond of her too, so we all kick shit."

He nodded and rubbed his bald head. "That's what's up. I wish me and my crazy ass baby mamas could all be cool. I'm home now. It's 'bout time I take my son and daughter from their ignorant ass."

"Nigga, nobody told you to have a baby by a damn niece and auntie! Shit was a recipe for disaster," I clowned. Kilo was wild as fuck back then. It wasn't a shock at all to the hood when he got Kaisha and Ree pregnant. They stayed on that bullshit. I used to pull down on them and set their pockets straight, but I just couldn't deal with all that ratchet shit. I just sent whatever I wanted to give through Goal.

"On some dumb young nigga shit. But I'm proud of y'all though. It takes a lot of fucking maturity to get to that level. You loved the shit out of Aphrodite, so I knew you wasn't gone let her stray too far. I'ma hit you up though. My Grannie already gone roast my ass for being late." He leaned in and gave me another hug.

"Love, bruh."

I hugged him back. "Love, bruh."

It was good seeing my nigga back in his element. I knew with the life we lived jail sentences came with it, but we were just products of our fucking environment. So many of us black boys took to the streets because that's all we knew. We used our fucking limited ass resources to make a way. We wanted the money, the cars, the clothes, and the jewelry. So, we got that shit the only way we knew how. Either to take some' or make some shake. And maybe one person out the hood went pro and another went to college. That was it. The system set us up to be failures. Dumping us in the ghettos. We was destined to either be felons, baby mamas, or crackheads. But as for me and my people, we beat the fucking system.

49

Seeing Kilo was only a temporary distraction. By the time I pulled off the parking lot, I had that fucked up feeling again. I lifted the armrest and pulled out the only thing that was in there, which was a cool grey-colored business card with yellow writing. *Ella Dorsewood: Grief counselor.* Maybe it was time for me to face the fact that I needed to talk to someone. Today put a lot of shit into perspective, because I swear to God. I saw my daughter back there at Houston's.

CHAPTER 5

Aphrodite "Ditey" Greer

"**A**ye! Ayeeee! Aye, Ayeeee, get it! Get it! Aye, Ayeeee!"

Tuscany and Quasie slapped my ass as I twerked to Yo Gotti's *Watch Her Make It Work*. That was my shit back in the day, and no matter where I heard it, I showed my whole ass. I pulled my silver sequin dress down over my oval as I continued to show out. I could feel cool air on my pussy, indicating my pink thong was on display, but I didn't give a fuck. I'm drunk as fuck and enjoying the shit out of my night. I can't believe I let them talk me into getting out, but there was so much to celebrate. One reason being I'd closed on my house. I ignored all that bullshit Goal was talking about and had Quasie get him to sell it to me for three hundred and seventy five thousand dollars. The closing literally was smooth and quick. Since I'd already gotten a pre-approval, three days after seeing the home, I was signing my name on the dotted line and given the keys. I hadn't planned my official move-in day, but I'd bought boxes and moving supplies.

Bending over and grabbing my ankles, I looked back at my ass as I made my left cheek jump and then my right. That was one of the dance moves I'd mastered. Other than that, I'm a two-stepping bitch.

"Ohhh, get it, biiitch! Get it, biiitch!"

I'm still in a state of shock, and it really hadn't kicked in yet, but this was really real. I'm moving into my dream home and had gotten it for a fraction of the listing price. I was just sitting on my damn couch debating purchasing a home due to the weak ass houses on the market a few days ago. Now I'm a whole fucking homeowner in a prestigious ass community. It was truly unbelievable. When I asked my mama if accepting the house was a mistake, she told me to take my blessing and to not question the good Lord. Her ass was at the closing, standing in front of the house with a grin. She'd already picked out her room for when she never spent the night. That lady like being in her own damn space.

"Alright, Alright, ladies, we got another one for y'all! I need all the pretty and paid women on the dance floor!" The DJ spoke on the mic.

Quasie got her ass up and started twerking beside me as Money Bagg rapped. She was throwing her ass, and I was shocked because although she's cool, she's boujee. Like now, we are in the club, and her ass is drinking wine instead of Hennessy. I was surprised that she even took Tuscany up on the offer to come out and celebrate. Although we were at a club/lounge, I didn't take her for a woman that did this type of crowd. Her ass could dance too.

"Ooohhh damn! Y'all fine. Them asses sitting right too!" Some nigga commented. We'd declined a few offers from strangers to buy us drinks, but no one had blatantly stepped to us trying to cop a damn dance. I didn't even look up at the nigga because, for one, his bent up ass Air Force Ones were weak as hell. I'd just closed on a million dollar home. Even though I got it for a steal, I still had to be able to pay the mortgage, the insurance, the property taxes, and keep the maintenance up on it. There is no way in hell a broke ass nigga is about to get my time. I'm not looking, but if I was, he had to come with something.

Once the song was over, Quasie and I slapped hands and giggled while taking a seat back at our booth. We didn't want to all sweaty look-ing. Two songs were good enough for me. Once I cooled down, I may dance to another if I fucked with the song. I picked up my drink, and she took a sip of her damn wine.

"Uggh! I wish I could dance. Y'all get on my damn nerves." Tuscany rolled her eyes and downed the last shot that was sitting on the table. We'd ordered so much shit from our waitress and had only took a few bites out of the wings just to coat our stomachs.

"Awww, boo. It's okay. I'm the same way when I'm on my cycle. You did good to even get out the house." Quasie took another sip from her glass while using a napkin to wipe in between her breasts. We'd both worked up a light sweat but not enough to have us all smelly and sticky.

"Girl, only because I don't cramp like that. If I did, I'd be under the covers with my heating pad." Tuscany pulled her phone out and did a Snap video of herself. She was looking cute. Her hair was still in her ponytail, and since she'd gotten it touched up earlier, it was fresh. Instead of wearing dresses like Quasie and I, she rocked black leather leggings, black leather booties, and a sequence bodysuit that crossed over her breasts and had her back out. The theme of the night is sequins. I had a new shipment in and my vendor added sixty sequins pieces by mistake. Granted, the turquoise backless deep cut mini dress was the fucking bomb. I was mad as fuck because I never ordered that type of fabric after January. Since it would cost me more to ship the shit back to China, I decided to keep it. With the way I took my pics before the club, I was sure to sell out. I also did a few videos in my story. Hell, soon as Quasie saw me, she made me invoice her for her order.

Quasie was rocking a black sequin dress that was short and had belle sleeves with her signature bob with the middle part. We were all looking, feeling, and smelling damn good tonight.

"But about this house though! Congratulations, mama! I can NOT believe we locked in that deal. You're blessed forreal. I've been in real estate for five years and have yet to see something like that happen. Home had already been inspected and we literally closed in less than five days. Three, to be exact! That's unheard of. Thank you for choosing me to be apart of that. I just want y'all to know I'm the new third wheel. Ain't no getting rid of me." Quasie giggled and took another sip of her wine.

"Girl, welcome to the squad. We don't fuck with bitches like that, but you're a different breed. We love you, girl. I'ma warm you, Baguette's lonely ass be all up in our mix, but if you cool with that, then it's a go." We all laughed at that truth. I wanted to say I couldn't believe he wasn't here, but I'm sure he was somewhere lurking in the shadows.

"Thank you, Quasie. Welcome to the team."

"It's about time I freshen up y'all." Tuscany poked her lip out.

We all knew what that meant, so we grabbed our bags and headed toward the restroom in one single file line, with me leading the pack and Quasie on the tail end. This lounge is a whole damn vibe and packed as fuck. The ambiance of it is what really drew me in with its blue theme and large Aquarium tanks on every other wall making it an under the sea experience. Whomever the owner is, put a lot of thought and money into it. There's even a dance floor made of glass with fish swimming underneath. I love it here, and even though it's my first time visiting, it damn sure won't be my last.

Once we finally made it past the thirsty ass niggas and drunk ass bitches we walked into the bathroom, locking it behind us. It was something Tuscany and I always did. Once I told her about a time bitches jumped me in a bathroom, we always took that precaution. I wasn't fucking with nobody nigga, but bitches still held on to old ass beef because they were big mad a bitch was still intact. If a bitch had to pee while we was in the bathroom, they may as well hold the shit, use the men's, or piss on their fucking selves.

"Men are pathetic. I know they see this ring on my finger, but they still try to talk to me. It's disgusting." Quasie applied lipstick in the mirror while I played with my hair. I was ready to switch it up again, but I didn't know to what. I wanted to try something short like Quasie but maybe curly.

"Girl, niggas don't give a fuck. Especially Jagoda Bay niggas. They be ready to be a side nigga."

"That's crazy, but it's true," I mumbled.

So many niggas tried to talk to me when I was in a relationship and half of them knew who I was with. Pussy is pussy to men, rather it was spoken for or not.

I glanced over at Quasie's rock and almost went blind. The few times we'd been around each other, she never mentioned her husband, so I never pried. She didn't even have him on her social media. Her ass did everything alone or with her other realtor friends. For the most part, she was always working. I just thought Quasie's expensive ass rocked the ring because she could afford to, and it matched her fly. I never guessed that her ass is married. I'm the type that, if you didn't mention it, I didn't ask.

"Girl, where is this mystery husband anyway? Hell, I'm starting to think you married to Casper." Tuscany came busting through the stalls to wash her hands. I shook my head as she sat her Versace clutch on the sink and stuck her hand under the soap dispenser. I may not be nosey, but Tuscany sure in the hell is. She gives no fucks. If it's something she wanted to know, her ass is going to ask or figure out a way to find out.

"Girl, his ass *is* Casper. We're separated." Quasie put her Ruby Woo lipstick back in her Gucci clutch.

"Yet you're still rocking his ring? A fat ass ring, might I add. His ass gotta be paid. Surgeon? Hot shot Lawyer? Investor?" Tuscany light brown ass tossed out occupations like she was playing the life board game.

"Tuscany! You too damn nosey," I chastised.

"She's good. Girl, he's neither. And much as Kymani done put me through, I'ma rock this ring 'til I can't no more." I could see a hint of sadness in Quasie's eyes, but she shook it off quick.

"It is a bad ass ring though," Tuscany gloated. I had to agree. It is. Quasie held her hand out in front of her to inspect it before shrugging her shoulders and grabbing her bag.

"Fuck him though. Y'all ready? I hear my song."

It was faint and muffled, but we could hear Throat Baby blaring. I hated the song when I first heard it, but over time, it grew on me. The lyrics are offensive as hell, but the song is definitely catchy. I used a paper towel to unlock the door and immediately was met with the blasting speakers. Before I could step a foot out the door good, I was being snatched up, and a hard gasp escaped my mouth.

My body froze in shock as I was lifted from my heels and carried into a dark hallway. I could hear Tuscany and Quasie yelling and cursing, but I couldn't make out what they were saying. My ears grew hot as my heart thudded in my chest, but fear had me doing the fucking mannequin challenge. I'd come out to have a good damn time, and now I was being carried away like a fucking rag doll. It felt like I was trapped inside my own damn body, screaming and fighting to break free, and every time I tried, I just blinked. After a few more sharp turns in the dark, being carried up a flight or two of stairs, and some forced deep breaths, the shock wore off just as I was placed on my feet. I was prepared to fight for my life. I done been through too much shit to be kidnapped in a fucking club. Naw, I wasn't going out like that so I lifted my arms, ready to duke it the fuck out.

"I wish yo' ass would swing on a nigga." I froze in my tracks. I knew that voice. Had heard it for the first time only a few days ago, but I knew that fucking voice. The hairs on the back of my neck stood straight up as his voice continued to vibrate through my body, although he was no longer speaking.

"Dim the lights," he demanded in his deep rustic baritone. The lights dimmed on command as I fought to get my breathing under control. I could see that I was in an office overlooking the entire club. The walls consisted of fish tanks filled with sharks, and beyond the tanks, you could see down to the lounge. I could even see Tuscany and Quasie, who were arguing with Baguette. If I wasn't so shaken up, I would be amazed.

I turned on my heels so I could face my captor and damn near almost had my breath taken away. The same breath I was still struggling to get on one accord with my body. Goal was standing before me looking like an entire meal. Clad in a cream turtle neck, oatmeal-colored slacks, and Gucci slide-ins with the fur spewing from the insides. His neck, wrist, and ears were frozen in ice. His plump lips were wet as though he'd licked them, and the redness of his grey eyes let me know he was high as a fuckin' kite.

"I should beat yo' ass. Why would you do that? You almost gave me a damn heart attack!" I placed my hand on my chest and walked over to his glass desk, where I sat my purse. I fixed my dress and touched my breasts to make sure the girls hadn't popped out. I was also trying to create some distance between us because this fine ass nigga scared the shit outta me.

"Imagine my surprise when I get to your house to pick you up and you ain't there. Yet, you up in my club shaking yo' ass, showing pussy that ain't even yours to show to niggas that's 'bout to get niggas murdered."

I forgot all about him wanting to take me out. Even if I'd remembered, I had no plans on accompanying him. I appreciated the deal on the house, but that was where he and I ended. Yes, he was fine. The ultimate fine. And he could switch it up. Him being paid wasn't necessary because I had my own bread, but it damn sure was a plus. Still, I didn't need his toxic ass coming in and fucking my boring and peaceful world up.

"Goal? Is that your name? Yea, Goal. I appreciate the discount on the house. I really do. But there is no date. I'm not interested. And if memory serves me right, I told you that. Now, if you would excuse me, I'ma get back to my friends."

I went to pick up my purse so that I could move past him, but this crazy ass nigga grabbed my elbow and backed me into his fish tank that was filled with those big ass sharks.

His hand went to my throat, and I looked at this nigga like he was crazy.

"Why you always putting yo' hands on me? You're crazy forreal! You don't even know me!" I squealed. As dumb as it may sound, I didn't know this nigga, but I was turned on like a motherfucker. He didn't scare me at all. Although a normal bitch would have been done shitted on herself. Now this cold ass glass filled with these sharks? I was afraid of, for sure. The coolness of the glass mixed in with my anxiety with a sprinkle of rich fine nigga all in my face had me vexed like crazy.

"Why you always talking shit? You ain't going no fucking where. Now make that the last time you disobey Papi," he gritted with those icy white ass teeth. Mine weren't yellow, but they damn sure weren't white as his.

"Who? Papi? Get the fuck outta here and let me go. I told you I'm not interested, damn!"

His grey orbs peered through mine as he bit down on his bottom lip.

"Is that ya final answer?"

"I'ma scream."

"Good, that's what I want you to do."

He leaned in, hungrily sucked my lips, and my stupid ass sucked his back. There was so much heat radiating off my body that I felt like I had a fever.

Before I could fully process what was going on, he went from my lips, to my neck and then to my breast.

"Aye, what the fuck?"

I looked down and almost laughed at the confusion on his face. My left breast was on display, but the two long nude strips that ran down the center of them looked to have Goal flabbergasted.

"Fuck is this shit on yo' titty?"

Rolling my eyes, I sucked my teeth long and hard before answering.

"Breast tape. This dress has no support, so I gotta make sure the girls stay in place. And get me off this glass with all these damn killer sharks! What the fuck are you, Aqua man- Ouuuuch, nigga! What the fuck?"

I looked down in horror to be sure he did what the fuck I think he just did. With the way pain was radiating through my body, I knew he had.

"AHHHH! what the hell?

He did the same damn thing to my right titty, and at this point, they both were on fire.

"Shut the fuck up! How the fuck I'm 'posed to suck on 'em when they bandaged up like a patient in the burn unit?"

Goal pinched my pebbled brown nipple, causing pain and pleasure to course through my body, making my crazy ass moan. Had he not pinched my nipple, I would have thought my shit came off with the tape.

"Titties so fucking pretty and they sitting right. You'n need that shit."

Goal grabbed me around the waist, and my legs immediately went around his as he kept my back against the glass. I was trying to wrap my damn mind around this whole damn encounter, but when his mouth sucked in my areola like a vacuum, all that shit went out the window.

"Gooooal-"

Just when I thought he was about to pull that dick out, he pulled his gun out and stood my ass up so fast it made my head spin.

"Why the fuck you in my shit, and who the fuck let you up?"

A dark Hispanic man stood on the other end of Goal's gun, and instead of him cowering, he stood with two buff ass men on the side of him. I was stuck and mad that I didn't have my pistol because Goal was clearly outnumbered.

I tried standing to the side of Goal, but he got right back in front of me. I then noticed my nipples were still out, so I tucked them away.

"AP?"

I whipped my head to the back of Goal's head while trying to control my shaking hands. I didn't know who the fuck AP is, but I guess it's me.

"Go downstairs and enjoy the rest of yo' night, Pretty Pretty. I'ma get up witcha."

I was looking at the back of Goal's wavy head as if he was crazy, but his eyes never left the man nor his gun.

"A...are...you sure?" I was ready to get the fuck up out of there, but I would feel bad as hell if I left the man. Then again, I didn't want to be in the middle of a damn shootout. What if I survived the damn shootings, but the bullets shattered the fish tanks? Then I got daddy shark chomping on my damn leg.

"AP!"

I jumped, grabbed my bag, made sure my breasts were still put away, stepped over the wrinkled up breast tape and scurried past all four men. I turned into a fucking track star real damn fast in the heels, running through the dark. I almost broke my legs trying to get down the stairs.

I hope Goal survived whatever that was back there, but I'm glad they interrupted. How the fuck had my pussy been on lock for half a decade, but the moment I get out the house to celebrate, I almost give it to the first fine ass pretty eyes street nigga I see? This is why I kept my ass in the house put the fuck up. My nipples still burned, and it was still a damn Kentucky Derby in my chest as I eased back into the section. All eyes were on me, including Baguette's. I knew Tuscany had questions, but she knew not to ask in front of her nosey ass nigga.

How the fuck this nigga get them big ass sharks in here any fucking way?

CHAPTER 6

Goal Navarro

"AP?"

I could feel her try to move to the side of me, but I got right back in front of her. I didn't know what the fuck type of time this nigga was on. I wasn't worried about the two on the side of him, but this nigga could be unpredictable.

"Go downstairs and enjoy the rest of yo night, Pretty Pretty. I'ma get up witcha."

Aphrodite snatched her purse up and scurried out of the room, being sure to put a little pep in her step when she got near these damn idiots. She didn't have shit to worry about though. I would shoot it the fuck out with these niggas in a club full of witnesses. Her and I would for sure make it out alive if no one else did.

"That's a pretty piece of pussy, hijo." He ended that death sentence with a smile, showing his fresh set of veneers. The last time I saw this nigga in passing, he had some big ass chompers in his mouth. We were at a gala in New Jersey, and I checked his ass so fucking bad the whole damn ballroom was laughing. I guess he carried his ass back to the dentist and had them shits fixed.

"I suggest you reevaluate what you think is pretty. I would love to turn yo' ass to the Colombian Stevie Wonder. You already got the fucking ponytail. And the next time you address me as your son, you gone be a deadbeat for real. Why the fuck are you in my club?"

This nigga straightened his suit jacket, raised his right hand, and his men left my office.

"You can put the gun down now, Little Navarro. I'm not here to harm you. I'm your father. I brought you in this world; I have no plans on taking you out."

Gilberto Navarro ain't shit to me. Never have been, never fucking will be. If it wasn't for his pops, Gilberto Navarro Sr., I would have ended his fucking life years ago and had his ass floating somewhere in Sparkling City. I had way too much respect for my Abuelo to end the life of his only child. He'd been dead to me since the day I came out of my mother. He was really just a walking corpse.

Gilberto cleared his throat, but his eyes never left mine.

"Fuck you doing in my city for, Gilberto?"

"Well, Jagoda Bay is a beautiful place indeed. I'm simply here as a tourist, hijo. I'm not here to step on your operations."

I had to laugh at that shit.

"You? Nigga, you couldn't even step into the role of your Padre's shoes. The fuck am I worried about you coming into my operations for?" I spat.

Gilberto stood before me with an amused look on his face. This nigga really thought he was untouchable. I would drop his ass in a heartbeat and fold his big, slow ass security guards up quicker than he could blink.

"Son, no need for the hostility. I just wanted to check out your establishment and have a conversation, man to man. If I wanted to harm you, I would have done so already. You see how easy it was for me to get past your security?"

I had to laugh again. This nigga was fucking delusional.

"Nigga, you didn't get past shit. They let you up on my demands. You see, every muthafucka that works with me knows who the fuck you are. They know to give you access to a nigga because they know you ain't no match for a king. I don't want no fucking conversation with you. I ain't never had a fucking conversation with you in my entire life. Fuck I'ma start for now?"

I hated the fucking grounds my pops walked on. This nigga was nothing more than a spoiled ass, entitled bitch boy. When he got my fucking mama pregnant back in Columbia 32 years ago, he never looked fucking back. She was a poor girl, working on his father's coca farm, and Gilberto jr. couldn't stand the sight of seeing an innocent local pretty girl around every day. He fucked her, and had the fucking nerve to try and kill her when she started showing up to work with a growing belly. My Abuelo stepped in, caught his ass dead in action, and shipped my mama to the U.S. For Gilberto jr's actions, he was stripped of the Navarro name but my abuelo still had hope for his only son. It was my Abuelo who took care of us and made sure we lived a decent life, and it wasn't even his fucking responsibility. My mama had to move away from everything and everyone she knew and start a new fucking life as a single mother in a country she'd never been in before.

I'd always known my abuelo was the head of the Navarro Cartel. Hell, we lived too fucking nice for my mama not to ever punch a fucking clock. When I was about thirteen, my weak ass daddy called himself pulling the fuck up on my mama with the same big burly muthafuckas outside of my door. My madre was lonely as fuck, even though she always caught the attention of men wherever she went. Her grey eyes and cocoa skin was a head turner, and 'til this day, my mama is still the prettiest woman on God's green earth. Instead of this entitled ass nigga trying to get to know his only son, he walked right past my ass and took my mama to the back and left. Not even looking my fucking way.

A few months later, her belly began to grow, and I already knew what time it was. Gage was born, and I became a fucking daddy at 14. This nigga dropped his nuts in my mama twice and said fuck us. So damn right, it was fuck him forever.

By the time Gage was three months old, I hit the streets. My Abuelo had bought me a car, nun fancy, but it got me where I had to go. I didn't have a lick of license, but that didn't stop me from constantly driving out to Jagoda Bay. By the time I was 16, I knew the end and outs of Jagoda Bay. I knew all the fucking hustlers and all of their fucking schedules and how they ran their operations. I had no plans on robbing them or no shit like that, so I didn't follow their personal lives. My abuelo kept us straight. I didn't need the fucking money. I wanted to learn the fucking hustle. Watching them niggas in the shadows is where I learned. Little did I know, my abuelo was watching me as I was watching them.

"Como esta tu madre?"

"Nigga, don't ask about my fucking mama. You need to be asking about Gage, your eighteen year old son. Matter fact, run me my bread."

With my gun still pointed, I walked forward, placed the pistol on his forehead, and reached in his fucking pockets. His pants pockets were empty, but the one in his suit jacket housed his wallet. I flipped that bitch open and spotted a black card, his visa, and a few business cards. I snatched the whole damn wallet, even though I'd only be using the black card.

Gilberto held his hands up as his amusement washed from his face.

"All I want is to discuss business with you. With your abuelo dead, I thought that maybe we could negotiate the terms of the Navarro Cartel."

"Negotiate? Nah, ion even know what that term means. I can't even spell the shit."

This nigga lost his fucking mind if he thought I was willing to discuss anything dealing with my fucking organization in the presence of his shiesty ass.

"Hijo, you're young. The cartel is a serious business. Do you really want all this responsibility on your hands? I know there are other things you would rather be doing, like starting a family with that beauty from earlier?"

I don't know what type of powder Gilberto must've sniffed with his coffee this morning, but it had to be some bad shit. For him to come in here and ask me if I wanted to hand over some shit my grandfather left me in charge of five years ago. Some shit that tripled in profits when I took over.

"Gilberto, get yo' tired ass up out of my establishment. I should shoot yo' foolish ass just for interrupting me getting some pussy from yo' grandkids mama. You know what? I'll do you a solid. If you can tell me the position Gage plays, I'll hand the organization over to you right now, no strings."

This nigga tensed up as a perplexed look covered his face.

"Aite, that one may be a hard one since you never even seen yo' baby boy before. Hell, you don't even know what sport he plays. I'll give you another one... What's my birthday?"

"Hijo-"

"Don't fucking hijo me! You a sad ass nigga. This shit not even about you not giving a fuck about your children. The reason why Papa chose me is because I'm a student, nigga! I ain't never too good to fucking learn! And because I was a student, I excelled at that shit and became the fucking master. I learned the fucking game. I know every fucking detail when it comes to my organization! He handed you the cartel even *after* stripping you of the Navarro name and you fucked that up! You were born a bitch ass nigga.

My abuelo left me in charge because he knew I was gone take his shit to the next level. The fucking empire would have crumbled in your soft ass hands, princess. That's why most of yo' fucking clientele came their asses over to me when yo' ass got the boot. Because you ain't about shit. Get the fuck out while you have the chance before you be wheeled out of here in a body bag."

I hated being in this nigga's presence. It made me mad that I really had bitch nigga running through my blood. Like really had the shit coursing through my veins. I needed to do a fucking cleansing or some shit to rid his ass out of my DNA. I would hate to give birth to little bitch ass Gilberto's. The shit skipped me and my brother, so it had to be in one of our future kids. Just the fucking thought made me shiver.

"Okay, maybe another time. I'll go. Can I have my belongings back?"

I looked down at his wallet in my hand and flapped it close before sliding it in my pocket.

"Nah, God gone have to tell me to give you yo' shit back. Gage expensive as a muthafucka. I need all my bread back. He got senior dues and prom and shit coming up. The lil' nigga want a Lamb truck for a graduation gift. Ain't that some shit? I think this black card will suffice."

Gilberto had a look of defeat on his face, but he nodded and turned.

"Oh, and Gilberto, you bet not have this muthafucka cut off either.

I'ma hand this shit to mama when me and Gage finished. I'ma warn you though. She got a nasty ass Chanel habit. Get the fuck out, nigga."

I hated this bitch boy so bad. Just thinking about the day I showed up with my abuelo to snatch the Cartel out of his hands had me grinning. He was mad as fuck that Baguette and Kilo decided to keep doing business with me. I thought the nigga was going to have their ass killed he was so fucking mad. Even though Gilberto was no longer the head, he still had access to the product since he'd built lifetime connections in Colombia. When the rest of the niggas he was dealing saw how snaked out he was, they brought their asses back to me on their knees. Their pockets had to pay for that shit too.

Once Gilberto was out my sight, I went and sat at my desk to watch Pretty Pretty. I had half a mind to go down there and snatch her lil' thick ass up. I'd been all around the fucking world, so I done seen plenty of pretty ass women. But Aphrodite. Pretty Pretty was a fucking ten all across the board. I loved the fact that she had a lil' height to her. Her long torso, small waist, fat ass, and soft features had me in a trance. The only drink I got from Starbucks was a Carmel Frappuccino with extra caramel at the bottom, and her skin tone matched the syrup at the bottom and on the sides of my Venti drink. It had been a minute since a woman had come along and had me ready to put every part of her in my mouth. Aphrodite was that one.

"Aye boss, Daphne tryna get up."

If it wasn't one thing, it was another. Daphne had been blowing me the fuck up since I'd gave her ass a champagne shower. I wasn't fucking with her ass at all, but I guess I needed to show her again.

Daphne walked in but made sure she rolled her eyes at my mans. My dick didn't even brick up at the sight of her. She was in a sheer bodysuit with black pasties on her nipples, and a black thong could be seen through the fabric. Her ass needed to be spinning around a pole with the way she was looking.

"Assume the position."

I didn't have time for no fucking small talk when it came to Daphne. She knew what the fuck it was with me.

Daphne placed her Jacquemus purse on my desk, hit her knees, and pulled my dick out. I gripped her by her hair and could feel all of her blonde tracks that were sewn in. When I felt her tongue hit my tip, and my dick touch the back of her throat, I tightened my grip and let it rip.

Daphne's muffled screams couldn't be missed, and when I felt her try to close her mouth, I placed my gun on her forehead.

"You bet not bite my dick, hoe! Since you can't get the picture that I ain't fucking with you, drink this piss, bitch!"

Tears and snot covered her face as her light skin turned beet red. Piss spilled out of her mouth and onto my pants, but it was all good. I had a change of clothes and a shower in this bitch. I'd been gone off the Henny, so I had plenty to give. Once I had it all out, I let her go with a push.

She began coughing and gagging.

"You bet not throw up in my shit either!"

"You fucking peed in my mouth? Because of a rumor about Wex's fat ass?" She screamed.

"Nah, I gave you a golden shower because you walked in this bitch with my sperm donor. Hoe, I ain't dumb! Get the fuck out and go kiss that nigga with the same mouth I used as a fucking toilet."

Daphne ran her sour ass out. I made a mental note to kill this bitch just because she was too damn hoeish.

CHAPTER 7

Kymani "Kilo" Lantis

"I'm just saying, Kilo. You ain't gotta talk to nobody crazy. I was just about to comb ha' hair. I ain't know you was pulling up." My baby mama, Kaisha smacked her lips with a stank ass look on her face.

"Mane, fuck allat! Her shit 'posed to be combed every day. She a lil' girl. Don't yo' shit be combed?" I looked at the long blonde weave that was flowing down Kaisha's back. It was a little bit too many baby hairs if you asked me, but it was her head, not mine.

Glancing around her home, that was completely paid for by me, caused me to shake my fucking head. This bitch didn't work, and her only job was to be a mother to my daughter. Yet her three bedroom home was nasty as fuck. Not only was it nasty, it was stank. Shit was everywhere. Clothes, shoes, dishes, hair, toys, just all kinds of shit out of place. It looked more like the fucking local dump than a home in the suburbs. Then to make matters fucking worse, my six year old daughter was obliviously laying on the couch, knocked out in the mix of all this shit.

Now, I know how depression can cause you to lose sight of yourself. My grannie always told me one of the number one signs of depression is an unkept living space. But with Kaisha, that wasn't the fucking case. Everything was dirty except this bitch. She was standing in my face rocking the latest Jordan 5's with True Religion jeans jacket and matching pants. House nasty as fuck, but she was fresh to death, smelling like my fucking money. Yet my daughter was knocked out on the couch with a melting blue popsicle in her hands, a nappy head, dusty pajamas on her body, and sticky fingers. *Pathetic.*

I knew coming here today was going to give me a fucking headache. Having kids by motherfuckers that don't value shit but a Facebook like tends to take you out of your element. I shifted my eyes from my baby girl to my baby mama. Her ass was standing there with her nose turned up like I'm the one fucked this house up. I pinched the bridge of my nose, praying I didn't have to lay hands on this girl.

"Kilo, I got somewhere to be. I don't feel like hearing yo' bullshit today. You always trying to judge somebody. Just take yo' daughter and get up out my house." This crazy ass girl had the nerve to dismiss me but was looking everywhere but at me while she was talking shit.

"Kaisha, I been gone five years. Five fucking years ,bruh. Even behind them bars, I made sure you had a spot, a whip, monthly cash drop-offs, clothes, and shoes for my daughter. I even paid Kyma's health insurance! You can't even keep the fucking house cleaned and keep my daughter on point? All that damn name brand in the closet! Do she ever get to wear any of that shit besides on a holiday when you wanna post pics on Facebook and IG to stunt? Hell nah! She don't! You know how many times I done heard my baby out here dusty? But yo' funky, unfit ass stay in the latest!" I roared, prompting my daughter to jump in her sleep.

I looked at my baby at the same time the popsicle lazily fell from her fingers. She was now sleeping with her mouth wide open and her arm dangling down the front of the couch. She flipped over fast as fuck, now laying on her chest with her knees bent and tucked underneath her. It was the same way she slept when she was a baby. Even though I'd been gone all of her life, I was happy to see that she slept just as I remembered before I went in. Since Kaisha didn't make a move to pick up the fucking popsicle, I did so and brushed past her ass into the kitchen to discard it. The kitchen smelled sour, dishes were piled in the sink, and there wasn't a trash bag in the garbage can.

"Aye bruh, where yo' trash bags at?"

I wanted to fucking gag, glancing around the nasty ass kitchen. There were even opened boxes of cereal spilled on the counters. A gnat buzzed by my ear, and I was shocked there weren't roaches on the damn wall.

"In the cabinet underneath the sink."

I opened the cabinet door, grabbed a garbage bag, and tossed the popsicle in it. I couldn't put the damn bag in the garbage can because there was all type of gunk and shit at the bottom of it. This shit is ridiculous.

"So, now I'm funky? I wasn't funky when yo' head was all up my ass, nigga." She folded her arms underneath her B cup breast and rolled her neck as I walked back into the living room. Kaisha is ghetto cute. She's small but got a fat ass and a cute ratchet-looking face that stayed balled the fuck up. One thing that drew me to her sandy skin tone was the fact that she got these pretty ass brown eyes that she passed down to our child. Fine as she was though, bitch kept an attitude, and that shit took away from her looks. No matter how sexy my baby mama is, she's equally trifling.

"Dick all up your ass? Yes. My head? Never. Stop playing with me up in here, Kaisha." It was the truth. I only put my mouth on one female, and she didn't mother a kid from me. *Yet.*

"And who told you my baby be dusty? I bet it was that bitch ass cousin of yours! Tell that Ho-" before Kaisha could finish her sentence I had her by her throat as her size 7 Jordan's dangled.

"Act like you don't know who the fuck I am. Don't disrespect my family! Now, go to the back and get my daughter's coat. Hat too!" I let her go, and she hit the stained carpet with a thud while coughing and rubbing her throat. I gave her ass a look, and she ran to the back to do what I demanded.

Before I got locked up, Kaisha and Ree took me through hell. I was there during the pregnancies because I'm a man before anything, and I was there during both births. That still didn't stop them from causing hell and disturbing my peace. That shit was over with now. I let both them hoes ruin my happiness, and on Jesus Christ, I'll kill 'em dead before I let 'em continue. I'm too damn good to the both of 'em. Bitches like them don't get good baby daddies like me. They lucked the fuck up.

If they wanted to keep living good, they better fall the fuck in line and stand down.

I walked over to the couch and picked my daughter up. She's so beautiful, even in her sleep. Kyma is the perfect mix of me and her stupid ass mother. Even with a nappy head. I was grateful that she had my texture of hair before I shaved my shit bald. It was soft and curly. I don't know what the fuck Kaisha's shit looked like because it stayed in a fucking weave, even back then. Ass probably didn't have no fucking hair left in the follicles, but it was good to see my baby had plenty of pretty ass hair. If my daughter's shit was ate off, I was on Kaisha's ass for real.

Kaisha came back in the living room, still rubbing her neck, and handed me my daughter's hot pink Ralph Lauren coat with the matching hat. Even though it's the first week of March, it's still cold as shit outside. Shit was coming like December.

I snatched the coat and hat out of Kaisha's hand as she held it out while rubbing her neck with her right hand. Them fucking tears didn't move me. Kaisha had been playing with me for five years, and she'd been getting away with the shit because I was in no position to check her.

I inspected the pieces, making sure no fucking roaches were going to fly out of them. Both items still had tags on them, making me wonder if it was because she had plenty of coats or was this shit still new because Kaisha's trifilin' ass hadn't been dressing my baby appropriately all winter. *Dumb ass broad.*

I snatched the shit out her hands and walked up out her spot.

"I'll bring her back in a week and make sho' this fucking house cleaned up! How the fuck can you even live like this?"

I made a mental note to have the carpet taken up because her ass was gone continue to let Kyma eat all over it, so it would get right back nasty. I had to call someone over to clean this shit up too, because I knew Kaisha's ass wasn't going to do it. My daughter needed to be in a clean fucking space. She was gone make my baby grow up thinking living like this is normal. People tend to not value shit they didn't pay for, and Kaisha was a prime example. Here she is living in the fucking suburbs in a house that was brand new when she moved in, as well as fully furnished, and she had this shit looking like nine fucking kids lived here with no adult supervision. Shit was sad. It's sad that I even have to get the carpet taken up instead of her ass getting it shampooed twice a year.

The cold, gloomy air smacked my face as I power walked to the car and placed my daughter on the backseat of my Lamborghini truck. Once she was buckled in, I stood back and admired sleeping beauty. She began sucking on her bottom lip. Something she always did in her sleep and as a baby, it made her skin raw. I was going to have to buy her some cream because my baby too pretty to be 'round here with a ring around her bottom lip.

Pulling out of the driveway, I pulled my phone out to send Ree, my other baby mama, a text. After Lil Nasty done had me step out of character, I didn't have the energy for Ree because she was usually worse that Kaisha. How the fuck I get stuck with two ignorants? I don't fucking know.

Me: *Headed to pick up KJ. Make sure he ready.*

Ree: *He is. I'll send him out; just honk when you're outside. Should I pack him a bag?*

I see this bitch had some sense today. I bet Kaisha had called her. They couldn't stand each other when I was out but all of a sudden, they family and shit. It made me feel like they were just doing some shit to make it harder for a nigga. Bird asses.

Me: *Nah. Just make sure he got his coat on.*

I didn't need my kids getting sick. It was too much out here going on in the world as well as this up and down as weather. I was happy as fuck when I got out a lil' early four weeks ago. I almost lost my damn mind in that bitch. Folk were getting sick and dying left and right, and with limited resources behind those bricks, we had to self-medicate as best we could. Every other day an inmate or a CO had a fucking contagious case of something. I was over that shit.

Once my son was in the car, we chopped it up a lil bit and his ass had me straight tripping. He was only a few months older than his sister, but his ass acted like he was 15. Despite both my baby mamas being ghetto as fuck, I had to admit they were doing good raising them. They both were at the top of the class, could count, read, and write. That's the only reason I ain't took 'em yet. If they kept that bullshit up, I would though.

Ree was so stupid she didn't know my real name but wanted my son to be a junior soo bad, the bitch named him Kaejay. The shit was dumb as fuck, but it fit so we stuck with it. My grannie told me she was trying to name him Kilo, but she shut that all the way down. My child wasn't going to be named after no fucking dope. Despite having a ghetto ass mammy, KJ was my twin fasho. I been behind bars ninety-five percent of his life, but that nigga walked like me, talked like me, and kicked shit like me. He was alllll me. While being locked up, I did allow my kids to see me. I needed them to know our reality. I saw them twice a month every month for five years. They needed to know their daddy wasn't perfect and was paying for stupid mistakes. In the end, that shit will make them wiser. Their pops wasn't no regular man with a regular job. I'm a street nigga and would be till the day I died. I needed them to know and understand that when they are old enough to comprehend it.

Hell, KJ already know what's up. Them being aware of who the fuck I am will save them in the fucking long run. Too many street niggas try to raise sheltered ass children, and that shit backfires every time. I don't want no green ass kids. Do I want them in the streets? Fuck no. However, I do want them to know what living a life like mine means and leads to.

I glanced at my kids again. KJ was in a black and red Jordan set with red Jordan twelves. His hair was in a fresh line up. He used to have long hair until he asked his mama to cut it because he hated getting it braided. He'd even asked her could he have his shit bald like mine. I laughed hard as hell when my grandma told me that story. My boy wanted to be me so fucking bad. That's one thing Ree does have over Kaisha. Ree keeps KJ in his clothes, but the bitch was forever dropping my child off to her people in the projects. That's why the lil' nigga bad as fuck now.

While swerving through traffic, I took occasional glances at my kiddos. Having two women pregnant at the same time was stressful as fuck. I used to selfishly think of murking both them girls with the babies in their stomachs just so my life could go back to what it was. I was a wild ass nigga back then. Ion know what type of high or drunk I was to impregnate these damn girls, but it was the sole reason I got off the fucking drank. I used to pray to God that I would wake up and the reality of two babies on the way would be a damn dream, but when I woke up, I wanted to kick my own ass. I couldn't understand for the fucking life of me why in the fuck would a woman want a baby by a nigga she didn't even fucking know. It wasn't that much money in the fucking world. I had nothing against kids and wanted to be a father, just not from them crazy ass ducks.

Now, I feel bad as fuck being in my kids' presence sometimes just thinking about how I used to wish I hadn't created them. When I was released, they were the faces I wanted to see first. I cried like a fucking baby hugging my children. Them two in the back seat were royalty and would always and forever have it easy in life. I was doing this hard shit so they wouldn't have to.

"Daddy, where are we?"

"Yeah, daddy, is this your new house?"

KJ couldn't stand to see his sister asleep, so now both their asses was up looking out of the tinted windows.

The GPS alerted me that I had reached my destination, and my heart swelled with pride. This crib was the cream of the crop. Sitting on at least an acre of land, it was the only house for miles. *Shirah.* This community was nothing more than trees and dirt roads when I first purchased this plot. Now I see this bitch was coming like the fucking black Hamptons. Muthafuckas was riding in nothing but quarter million dollar whips or better, and the ones that weren't riding foreign, were in fucking golf carts on the damn streets. That's wild.

The home was so big it looked to be divided in several different homes in one. The dark brick gave it a mysterious feel to it, but I loved this shit.

"Yea, it's OUR new home, y'all."

The kids started screaming in the back and hadn't even seen the inside. I parked in the long driveway that led to six garages and let both kids out. I carried Kyma since she was barefoot and held KJ's hand as we walked on the fresh cement leading up to the front door. I tried to open it and of course it was locked. To the right of us was a plant, so I looked underneath and retrieved a key. *I guess old habits never die.*

Once I had the door unlocked, the kids and I were amazed at the layout. This shit was dope, grand, and damn near too pretty for any motherfucker to live in.

"Daddy, this house so nice, mane! On God, I ain't never going home! That's on God!"

"Mane what! On God, daddy! Can I have a princess room?" Kyma blinked up at me with her hair all over her head and blue lips. Seeing my baby like this had me cringing. I was going to have to make a mall run asap.

"Yea, baby. You can have whatever. Come on." Each step I took, I was more and more impressed with the layout. It was designed to the T, and the decor wasn't too feminine or masculine. It met right in the middle. The color theme throughout the home seemed to be grey, black, and emerald green. We stumbled upon a grand door, and I knew my damn ears weren't deceiving me.

"Look, KJ, take your sister to that room we passed with all the games in it, aite? Don't come out no matter what you hear? Close the door too. Understand?" He nodded and took his sister by the hand.

"Can I wash her hands first, daddy? They sticky." KJ balled his face up, looking just like me. I noticed his ass had a missing tooth in the front and knew the one beside it was soon to follow.

"I'll wash 'em. Just head straight to the room. Sticky fingers not gone kill you nor her. Gone."

They took off running, and once I saw they were in the room with the door closed, I removed my pistol from my back.

I slowly opened the door, and the shock of discovery hit me full force. *What the fuck?* I was so fucking confused and badgered, I couldn't speak. My heart sank to the bottom of my size thirteen shoe as I watched my bitch throw that ass back on some nigga. All I could see was his thin ass back and heard the slaps of her fat ass on this nigga's pelvis. Her sultry moans filled the room and had me feeling like I couldn't fucking breathe.

Seeing red, I cocked my fire and sent the nigga a straight dome shot. His body went flying to the side of the bed, and I knew then his ass was outta here.

"Ahhhhhhh!" Boobay screamed while covering up her body with the white sheets that were on the bed.

"Stop all that fucking screaming!" I pointed the gun at her whopped ass wig because she was next.

"Please, please don't kill me. My-wait. Kymani? Oh my God! Kymani, when the hell you get out?"

I chuckled. "You got some nerve asking me when I get out all the while you in here giving another nigga my pussy. I expect that shit from these hoes out here but from you? My wife?"

She looked at me, puzzled and shocked to see me. Quasia was still fine as the last time I'd seen her in person five years ago. Her naked ass body looked like it had a few enhancements, and that shit made her even finer. She almost looked like some shit that was off limits. And she was, that's why the nigga she was fucking is blowed the fuck off on the side of the bed.

"Wait. You think? Hold up." She belted in laughter. I'm talking holding her stomach laughing. She was cackling so hard she had tears coming from her eyes. But all I was doing was standing there pissed that she was fucking another nigga while rocking my wedding ring.

"Do you think a nigga Kevin Hart or some shit? I'ma let you get all them laughs out your system before I off your stupid ass. Go ahead. Let's see if the shit be funny when ya mammy picking out a black dress," I spat.

"Ohhh, and I'ma tell her you said that too."

"You bet fucking not!" I loved Ms. Sherry to death. She checked on me and wrote me more than her damn hoe ass daughter.

"So let me get this straight. You out early on a ten year sentence for murder, and come up in here fucking up my dick appointment trying to go back up the river?" She got out the bed with the sheets still wrapped around her frame, walked up to her robe, and placed it on her body. I was able to get a sneak at that fat wet ass pussy and my dick hardened. Now was not the time for that. This disloyal hoe had to go.

"Put the gun down, Kymani. You in here making a fool of yourself." She waved me off.

"Fuck you mean I'm making a fool of myself? I'm 'bout to send yo' crooked wig ass to meet our maker like ole boy over there." I was steaming, and the fact that her ass was too damn calm for me was what really had me vexed up in this bitch.

"Hold up. If memory serves me right, you packed up all your shit and left me six months before you went and caught that damn charge. Remember? You called yourself choosing what's her face? Dora? Diela? Oh no, it was Daphne. Yes, you chose Daphne over me? How that shit work out?"

She adjusted her wig so that it was now centered, and I got mad all over again at ole boy for knocking my ole lady wig out of place.

"Mane, ain't nobody leave you for that hoe. I left because you wouldn't accept my kids. Kids that were born and weren't going any fucking where. You was constantly nagging a nigga about Kaisha and Ree." It was true. I didn't leave my wife because of no damn Daphne. I left because she made my ass get out, and she wouldn't stop going on and on about my kids. I wasn't even allowed to bring them in our home. What type of shit was that?

She tossed her head back and belted in laughter.

"Nigga, two kids that you HAD OUTSIDE OF OUR MARRIAGE! By two damn cousins at that! Them ghetto bitches made my life a living hell and yours too! Yet you was still sticking your nasty ass dick off in them! Nigga, you're damn right I put your ass out. I said get out, not go live with the next bitch. You know what? Get out. Please. I'm happy you're out so that you can be reunited with your kids and all, but you've got to go. I don't need your toxic ass coming back around and fucking up my peace. Life is good. Great, actually."

"They not cousins. They auntie and niece." I mumbled,

Quasie was my greatest fucking asset. We married young as fuck, and crazy thing is, I'm the one who pressured her into marriage. She didn't want to marry me because she said I wasn't ready. Even though her ass was right, I still put that ring on her finger. I was fucking bitches left and right with no plans to ever stop, even though I was married to my soulmate. I was on some stupid shit fucking two blood related muthafuckas. We didn't do no weird shit like fuck together. I knew Ree and Kaisha were family because they were damn near identical, but I still fucked them. It wasn't enough to fuck. I planted my seed in them and hadn't even planted a child in my own damn wife.

"I brought the kids by so you can see them."

Quasie didn't break eye contact, but a look of sadness showed briefly until it turned into anger and hurt. When Quasie found out about my kids, that shit broke her the fuck down. I'd never seen her so fucking hurt. The wail that escaped her lips had me tearing the fuck up. I did a lot of shit to her, but having two babies was her breaking point. She stayed for a year after they were born, but that year was nothing but her cursing my ass out and refusing to give me pussy. But it's been five years. It was time to let that shit go.

"Not only did you fuck up my nut, you brought your bastard ass kids to my house?"

"Quasie-"

"No negro! Don't call my fucking name! You think because you did some time, all is forgiven? What, I'm supposed to raise your kids as my own because you had them by trifling ass women? I hope that's not what the fuck you thought would happen? Kymani, I love you. With everything in me. But love just ain't e-fucking-nough. Not only did you make a baby on me, you made two. Then, because I wasn't willing to let you pass them off to me, you went and got with the biggest hoe in the city?

You not no fucking man, Kymani! You're a boy! You were never husband material! You got so much fucking street sense but no damn common sense. The playa thing to do would have been to come at me alone, bearing gifts, flowers or something! Have a sit down with me, see where my head is and figure out how we can make this work and slowly ease your kids into my life! Yes, we are still married, but that don't fucking mean I gotta accept your damn babies!"

Tears streamed down Quasie's dark brown flawless skin. My baby was always dressed up like she had somewhere to go and in full glam from head to toe. Although I love that about her, I appreciate seeing her bare-faced and raw. I hurt my wife and violated in the worse way. However, I just ain't willing to walk away.

"I just needed to see you, baby." I felt like my breath was cut off as fear and anxiety churned in my stomach.

Quasie briefly gave me a full inspection from head to toe and then looked off. With the rise and fall of her chest, she then gave me her undivided attention, and the tension was now gone from her face.

"I don't want nor need you. Fuck them kids, and fuck you too."

Her words cut me deep as fuck, I can't even lie. I swallowed with difficulty as I tried to find my fucking voice. There was nothing I could say though. Nothing I should say. I fucked up, and Quasie had the right to feel however she wanted to feel.

"Before you go, I got some shit that belongs to you."

She disappeared in her closet with her robe dragging behind her. I still had my gun at my side just in case her ass jumped stupid. A mad Quasie is a dangerous Quasie.

I heard a click and a clank, and seconds later, she appeared with two black duffel bags.

Tossing them at my feet one by one, she then crossed her arms underneath her breast.

"There. That's everything you left behind."

Confusion plagued my face and Quasie rolled her eyes.

"The moment they picked your stupid ass up, I went to the house you shared with Daphne while she was out sucking the next nigga's dick and cleared your safe. I also cleared the one you kept at the Meshia bitch house too, and the other one at the main trap. You had two fucking babies on me. When you got locked up, I could have easily robbed yo' ass and lived happily ever after with the next nigga. But I'm not even built like that. It's all there. Now take your bastards, and go."

I couldn't believe she did that. I thought I was robbed when I sent my cousin to clear the safes and they were empty. I almost put a bounty on them bitches head but then remembered they never even knew I had safes at their spots. So then I thought maybe it was the police. Whatever the case was I eventually said fuck it because my nigga Big Red, Goal, and Baguette had stepped up for a nigga. It was on account of them that my operations were still able to run smoothly. I should have known Boobay took the money. I never even told her about the stash spot at them hoes house. My wife knew though, because she knew a nigga's patterns.

My expression softened and I lowered my gun. The only reason I'ma spare her life is because she at least did that. I came home straight. Super straight. I'm talking 'bout up up, BUT what was in these bags will really put a nigga up. Three million dollars and almost a mill in jewelry. Before I got caught up, I was a hustling dog. I could out-hustle most niggas, and I put any and everybody on. That was my first mistake. Trying to see everybody eat. In turn, I put a dummy on my team that caught a body with a pistol from my trap. I still don't understand that shit or how it went down, and I guess I never will since the nigga who went and murked his babymama is dead along with her ass. I had been hustling and stacking. Yes, I was flashy, but I saved more than I spent. This money at my feet was proof of my saving. This shit was years' worth, and Boobay had just came through.

"I gotta at least have that nigga cleaned up." I moved toward the side of the bed his ass had blowed off too.

"Ha. Nigga, that ain't no nigga." I heard her ass laugh.

"Fuck you mean? You in here- what the fuck?" Looking down at this nigga, he had half a face, but the funny thing is there was no blood. As a matter of fact, there was no blood on the bed or covers or shit. I was confused like a motherfucker.

"You fucking a damn blow up doll?"

She was laughing her ass off. I looked up at her and back down at him with my mug on. She literally had tears coming from her eyes.

"It's silicone. But yes, I absolutely am. Every night."

I looked down and inspected the damn doll. This nigga shared my skin tone, build, and some more. Then his dick got the nerve to be big. No homo! She in here fucking Mandingo every night, so I know that pussy worn out like a motherfucker.

"So you went out and got a big dick doll to replace me?" I was really fucked up about this shit right now. A doll?

Boobay raised a brow, "Kymani, I hate to say this, but yours is bigger." Laughter spewed from her lips. She wiped the tears from her eyes and placed her hand on her chest.

"Man, that was fuuunnnyyyy. Boy. Get out my house. Forreal." Her ass switched it up real quick.

"Bruh, I ain't going no fucking where." I placed my gun back in my waistband and stood with my arms folded across my chest. This was my house just as well as it was hers. We had this home drawn up a year before I caught the case. It was my gift to her for having those kids on her. We never got to buy the land and get the permits approved by the county, but I see now, she had.

"No, it's not. I used my money. Not yours. This is MINE. I'm happy you're home. I really am. However, that means nothing to me. We are separated. You stepped out on our marriage more than once, and although it hurt back then, I'm past that now. I'm doing damn good without you. It was good seeing you, but now, you need to leave."

I licked my bottom lip and tried to suppress my anger.

"I need to leave? You must forgot who made you? You wouldn't have none of this shit if it wasn't for me. Yeah, I fucked up, had a couple kids, fucked a few hoes, but I always made sure you were straight!"

"Oh really? You bought both your kids' mothers homes and gave them monthly allowances while you were behind bars, and what did you do for me? Hunh?"

"Shit, what you do for me?" I challenged.

"The same thing them bitches did for you! Not shit! Nigga, you left me! So you damn right I wasn't about to be your ride or die! That was your damn fault for catching a charge. I told you to move smart and stop allowing all them folk in your space. That murder charge was your own damn fault, and had that been a real man, you would have caught another damn charge, possibly two."

"You damn right I would have caught a charge. No matter what, I'm your fucking husband! I go to jail; you stand ten toes own! For better or fucking worse! I should beat yo' ass right now for not holding me down! Your ass ain't solid! Once I caught that charge, all the petty shit should have been out the window! But naaaah! You got the fuck on down. Ain't no moving on! I'ma kill everyone motherfucker who look yo' way, and I'll kill yo' ass too before I let you leave me!" I barked.

Tears streamed down her beautiful face.

"Kilo, you're so fucking selfish. I swear you are. You left me. You cheated on me. You had babies on me. You did this to us. You hurt me. And despite all the hurt, I was still down for you. I still went and collected your shit. I could have spent that money, but I didn't. I even went to hire your lawyer but was told he'd already been paid. It's so much shit I did that I shouldn't have! All because no matter what, I love your bald headed ass."

She turned, opening her nightstand drawer. Grabbing a stack of envelopes, she tossed them and they went flying all over me.

"I wrote you. Every week. But I couldn't bring myself to place the stamp on them and send them. You didn't deserve my loyalty. You didn't deserve my peace. You didn't deserve my energy. I wanted you to suffer. Like I did. All the unanswered calls. The texts. The pop-ups. You took me through hell. The moment you were sentenced, it was like a weight lifted from my shoulders. I loved you more than I loved myself, and that shit was driving me insane.

You niggas think y'all can do all the bullshit in the world and soon as shit hits the fan, us women are supposed to forgive all and be your titty to cry on. Nah, I showed your ass fat meat was greasy, and I'm standing on that. You're not healthy for me, Kilo. You never even wore the ring I got you. It was like I was married to my damn self. I can't do this with you. I want you out of my house and out of my life. I'll fuck twenty blow-up dolls before I ever lay down with you again. Take your money and go because I damn sure don't need it."

See, I was gone leave her ass the money, but since she wanted to talk shit, I was taking my shit.

Bending down to pick up the bags I turned to leave, but stopped before I got to the door.

"You wanna at least speak to the kids before I dip?"

Her bougie ass chuckled and blew her nose on a handkerchief, "Take yo' dirty ass kids back to the projects."

I walked out before I slapped spit from her short hair ass. I was all for her Miss Independent spill, but she did too much. I had to admit I was hurting like a motherfucker. I thought all would be forgiven when I came home, but Boobay was singing a different tune.

I gathered my kids, who didn't want to leave, and headed to my grannie's spot. It was time for me to get my head in the game. I needed to get back control of my team, figure shit out with my baby mamas, and win my wife back. She was still wearing her ring, so that had to count for something. I knew one thing, I didn't have room for shit else on my plate. My cousin Kassie and grannie had been flipping houses for me and I knew they were sick of me bossing them around. Now that I had another three mill to put into real estate, it was time to increase the hustle.

Before I left, Quasie had tears and snot running down her face, and as mad as I was, I knew she was right. I had to fall back. I fucked up. She didn't deserve half the shit a nigga put her through. Sadly, back then, them tears didn't mean shit to a nigga. Every time she would cry after she found out about a bitch, I would brush that shit off. It wasn't a big deal. All them hoes got was dick. They didn't get the ring, the title, the money, the status; just hard dick. I made sure my wife wanted for nothing, and all she had to do is sit back and let me be a man. That was how I felt.

A life of luxury in exchange for embarrassment. Then came the baby mamas, who automatically gained entitlement. Now, seeing her boss up on a nigga in five years without my money, or status, or dick made me realize I was the problem. She was doing better than ever now that I was out of her life. A fucking multi million dollar realtor. Boobay was a boss, and although I was beyond proud of her, it pained me to know that her hunger for success stemmed from the pain I put her through. I hurt her in ways that were more than likely beyond repair. Can't blame a nigga for trying, right?

I needed a clear head to figure out how I was gonna get my wife back. But first, I had to make sure all that street nigga mentality shit was out of my system.

CHAPTER 8

Tuscany Payne

W e were all on our third drink and hadn't much said two words to one another outside of *hey*, and *you look cute*. We were all lost in our own thoughts. Clearly each of us had some shit going in and needed this link up.

"I been going through it, y'all." Aphrodite was the first to speak up as she traced the sugar that lined her martini rim. Her hair had been installed in microlinks, which I hoped she kept, and the curls were sweeping down her back. The cream off-the-shoulder oversized sweater with red hearts on it, ripped jeans, and red Ugg boots she was rocking, was simple yet stylish. The sweetheart sweater was one of her best sellers, and she'd already restocked four times. Glad I got mine.

"Oh no, are you not liking your new home? I'll gladly take it off your hands," Quasie joked. Aphrodite hadn't said much about the house since she closed. She even declined my help to come help her pack. I knew when to give Aphrodite her space, unlike Baguette. When she was ready for me to come over, I was gonna be there.

"The house is everything. I love everything about it. This is more so about my sister. I mean, it's other shit too. But I just wanna talk about that right now." She sighed while signaling our waitress. It was about time for us to order food since we'd all decided on what our entrée would be, and our spinach dip had been demolished. My mouth was watering for fried lobster tails and mac n cheese.

"You have a sister?" Quasie asked. Since she was new to the crew, we always had to catch her up on something so she wouldn't feel left out.

Once Aphrodite briefed Quasie on her long-lost sister, the waitress came and took our order.

"My sister could be right here in this restaurant, and I wouldn't even know. That shit is wild."

I nodded my head at Aphrodite as she finished off her lemon drop, worry and defeat in her expression.

"I'm so sorry you keep running into dead ends. Maybe I can help. I have a client that's a retired PI. Maybe he can pull out his old spy bag as a favor to me," Quasie offered. Aphrodite nodded, and I could see the stress ease off her a bit.

"What's been going on with you? You aren't your cheery boujee self." Quasie was my girl and a bad ass, boss ass business woman, but she was saditty as hell. I never seen her ass dressed down. She was always in heels and dressed to the nines.

"So, remember I told y'all I was married?"

How the fuck could a nosy bitch like me forget? I've *been* ready for her to spill the tea about this husband of hers. I even asked Baguette, but his lowdown ass wouldn't tell me shit besides mind the businesses that pay us.

"Yes. Has he reached out?" Aphrodite inquired.

"Girl, he had the nerve to show up with both his babies he had on me."

"Wait a fucking minute now. What type of nigga was you married too, Quasie?" She was so classy. So jazzy. So well put together. I didn't expect her to marry a friendly dick nigga. But then again, these niggas weren't shit out here.

I could see the hurt in her eyes. The kind of hurt that only a nigga you was deeply in love with could inflict on you.

"I met Kymani when we were young. I'm talking young young. So young that we shouldn't have even been fucking young." She chuckled.

"I was the pretty girl that lived in the good neighborhood, which was a far cry from the hood. Since my mama worked not too far from my grannie, I went to school in the ghetto and walked to my grannie's house instead of going to the good schools in our district. I spent more days at my grannie's than I did at my own house, but I was glad because all my mama and daddy did was fuck and fight. Kymani was that bad boy. The one that hated to be called cute because he thought he was too tough. He had to have me though, and I let his ass. Worse ass whooping of my life when my grannie caught us fucking on her day bed in the guest room.

Over the years, Kymani rose up in the streets, and that's when Kilo was born. He had more money and more bitches than he could count. I stayed though. Through it all. Why? Because I was a young bitch in love that was so focused on a nigga that I couldn't even love my own damn self. I ate, shit, and drank all thinks Kilo. Every day I woke up wondering if he had been fucking the next bitch. I was obsessed. The straw that broke the camel's back wasn't even the two babies by bitches that were related. It was the day that nigga went to jail. It was like I woke the fuck up."

Aphrodite placed her hand over Quasie's with teary eyes. I was still stuck on the fact that this damn girl was married to Kilo's ass.

"Kilo, with the bald head?" Aphrodite asked.

"You know him?"

"From the bricks, yes. But damn! I didn't know he was married. I'm sorry you went through that. Being so in love with a man that all you want is for him to love you back, but instead he hurts you time after time, is the worse feeling in the world. It's like you can feel your heart breaking inside of your chest over and over. My ex, Baguette, is such a good man to Tuscany, but babyyy, I crawled so she could walk for sho'. I'm so happy at where he is now in life, but that man hurt me to my fucking core. I was so fucking infatuated. I know how you feel. Every time a bitch came up to me and told me they were fucking my nigga, the thought of what he was doing to me to the bitches made me want to fucking die. No lie.

We are in a good space now, but even if Tuscany hadn't come along, I would never ever take that man back. I'm not telling you what to do; I'm just telling you my truth. Baguette and I weren't meant, but maybe you and your husband are. You said jail was the breaking point for you, but losing my daughter was it for me. It made me wake the fuck up and realize there is more to life than obsessing over a nigga that's dogging you the fuck out every time an opportunity presents itself. Niggas can be so fucking selfish. Because why not just be single in the first place?"

I felt everything Aphrodite was spitting. I didn't have infidelity issues out of Baguette, but I knew what he did to Aphrodite in the past. She didn't too much talk about it, always claiming she was over it, but he did. He told me upfront how bad he was to Aphrodite, and when I met her, I wanted to beat his ass. If I was a nigga had a bitch that looked like her, ain't no way I'm fucking other bitches. Niggas is dumb.

"We spoke our peace. What's up with you?" Quasie asked.

Aphrodite sipped her lemon drop while waiting on me to answer.

"I know you're new to the circle, and stop me, Aphrodite, if I'm overstepping my boundaries, but Baguette and Aphrodite lost a child. Baguette is still grieving, and although I'm doing everything I can to be here for him, it's not enough. We don't even have sex anymore because he is always in his head or daydreaming or having nightmares about Athena."

"Have you advised him to get counseling?"

"I have; he won't do it. It's not even him grieving his baby though. I love Athena like I'd met her. What makes me scared is him possibly wanting a child from me."

Everyone's head snapped up at me, and that's what I expected. Growing up as the oldest of six children, I was always the fucking babysitter. My mother wasn't a crackhead or a drunk nor was she the type to run the streets. Ronnie Joe was a good mother and is now an even better grandmother. However, having six kids by four different men that all ran out the moment she pissed on a stick meant she had to work two, sometimes three jobs. I didn't get to have a normal teenage life like going to school games, movies on the weekends, or spending the night at my friends' houses. I literally had to keep my ass at home and see after my little brothers. Yes, I'm the only girl, on top of being the first-born. I had to cook, clean, and play mama, and I did that shit with a smile on my face. I couldn't even join sports teams at school because that meant after school practice. The moment I graduated high school, I applied at Jagoda Bay University, got in on a full ride, and hadn't been back to Memphis ever since. I still talked to my mother and siblings weekly, but the freedom I got with living on my own in a completely different state without having to care for no one was liberating. My senior year in high school almost took me the fuck out though. That was really the main reason I ran the fuck out of Memphis, but that's another story for another day.

Signaling for the waitress, I ordered crab cakes because I knew it would be a while on the lobster as the ladies impatiently waited on me to elaborate on what I had so casually thrown out. Once I placed my order, I drank up the last of my lemon drop since I'd ordered another one of those as well.

"Bitch, we waiting. What do you mean you're scared he's gonna want a child from you? I thought y'all were going to have children?" Aphrodite asked with a frown on her face.

Being that I'm in a healthy relationship with a fine ass, big dick, paid ass man, folk automatically thought I was willing to push out as many babies his sexy dimpled face ass wanted. Nope. Wrong bitch. I'm good with just us, and if Athena was alive, I would have loved to be the perfect step mama that loved on her while she was at our house but gladly sent her on her way when it was time to go home.

"Ditey, have you ever heard me talk about children? You know I grew up raising kids. I love children and think they're a blessing. Hell, for a while I wouldn't give Baguette no play because he didn't have any living children. I wanted to be with a man that already had kids, so that he wouldn't be pressuring me to have them. I have the Nexplanon in my arm right fucking now and had the Implanon all through college. I don't want no fucking children. Ever."

Quasie nodded her head in agreement as Aphrodite had a look of uneasiness on her face. I knew her reservations because Baguette loves children. Still, my feelings aren't changing. I love being free. I love my sleep. I love only having me to care for, and if that makes me selfish, oh fucking well.

"Speak your mind, Aphrodite. Quasie is in the circle now. I rather you get it all out today than bring this shit up later on."

Aphrodite chuckled and sat up in her seat. She tossed her black extensions behind her back and looked me square in the eyes. We'd both just gotten our lashes filled yesterday morning. This time, she'd gotten hers fuller than usual, and it had her looking like a doll.

"You know that shit not gone work. Yes, he's grieving Athena, and yes, it's been almost five years, but eventually, he's going to want more children. Hell, even just one. Baguette doesn't care if he has a house full or just one baby to love on and spoil. You gotta give that man a child, boo."

Shrugging my shoulders, I glanced out the bay window that was nearest us. It was gloomy as hell outside even though it was only two in the afternoon. I smelled rain last night and knew by the time we got out of the restaurant, it would be pouring down.

"You give us one then."

"Bitch, please. I'm not having no more fucking kids. Especially not from Baguette. What type of shit you on?" Aphrodite retorted in cold sarcasm.

"We all get along. We can work an arrangement out. Artificial insemination or whatever. You get the baby half the week, and we get the baby the other half of the week. IF we can't do it like that, I'm good." I was dead ass serious.

Folks already judged the way we all hung together any fucking way. Us splitting a child wouldn't cause no extra harm.

Quasie placed her phone down. From my view, I could tell she was listening but had picked up her phone to answer an email that had flashed across the screen.

"I love how you all are intertwined and get along, but Tuscany, you got to know how...abnormal that is? I mean, I'm the type of bitch that can give two fucks about what the world thinks, especially these folk in Jagoda Bay. But that right there isn't it. Sit down and talk with him now. Let him know your reservations about not wanting children instead of walking on eggshells, praying he doesn't ask you for a baby. Has that topic not come up?"

"Yes, it has. Baguette been let her slick ass know he wanted a child, and if I can remember, she was all cheesy about the shit. Y'all better figure that shit out though, because my daughter is in the dirt. I did that. Not doing it again. At the same time, he has to respect your feelings. If you don't want no fucking kids, you don't want no fucking kids. It's your body, boo," Aphrodite concluded, signaling the waitress as she brought out my crab cakes.

We all leaned back as the brunette-haired lady placed drinks in front of us since I'd ordered us all another round but this time in raspberry lemon flavor. I loved *Tipsy* because it was not only a vibe, it's low key and has a mixed crowd. Not too bougie, but damn sure not ratchet, and they didn't play no fucking loud ass music either.

"I know, y'all. I shouldn't have lied, but I just feel like shit is good how it is now. We can get up and go whenever we please. I just love my freedom. Being a mama isn't in the cards for me. Stepmama? Yes. Primary mama? Fuck no."

Aphrodite reached across the table and stuck her fork in my plate, making me roll my eyes. She know I hated sharing my food.

"Girl, boo. You keep your hands in my plate. But for real. It looks like you need to be having a conversation with yo' man, boo. May as well get that shit out the way now. All I know is, you need to stay on top of your birth control or make that nigga strap up because I hate to kill his ass for killing you for getting rid of his baby."

I rolled my eyes and continued eating. I no longer wanted to talk about this shit, so I changed the subject.

"Okay, so I was thinking."

"Oh hell."

"Be quiet, Ditey! Anyways, I want to throw a housewarming for you. Before you say no, I wasn't asking. I know you have to get settled and all, so I was thinking we could do it on April sixteenth."

Aphrodite's facial expression softened at the mention of the date. It was Athena's birthday. Since it fell on a Sunday this year, I thought that would make for a perfect day to throw it on.

"I'll cover the cost. I can have the bar make wings and tenders, and I can get a chef for the fancy foods. I already reached out to a party planner, and she's going to hook it all up for us. Please say yes, friennnnnnnd."

Aphrodite humped her shoulders and took another sip of her drink.

"You just better hope I'm settled by then or you'll be renting tables and chairs since you're planning shit."

I clapped my hands and danced in my seat. I'd already paid deposits with everyone and locked in the date, so this was happening either way. Not only could we celebrate Aphrodite, but we could release some doves for Athena as well.

"Well, I'm down. I've been itching to step foot back in that beautiful ass home anyway. Tuscany, let me know if I can help with anything. I'll have my videographer come through. I need the content anyways, especially since this one didn't let me do a traditional closing."

When I heard Aphrodite just signed the papers, I wanted to slap her ass. I was ready to color coordinate and pop bottles and shit. That girl there just don't give a damn about shit.

...

After lunch, I took the long way home because the Ring camera alerted me that my man was there. When the rain started coming down too damn hard, I carried my ass to the house so that my bad eyes ass wouldn't run anyone off the road.

Pulling up to our cream brick, two story home, I saw that Baguette had pulled his old school out of the garage so that I wouldn't get wet. I was glad too because this hairstyle had to last until my appointment in four days. Just because I had the funds to be able to get my hair done anytime I wanted to doesn't mean that I wanted to.

I hated sitting down getting my damn hair done, so I made sure mine lasted. I always ask Ditey how in the hell does she have the patience to keep getting her shit done every week. I'm as girly girl as they come, but I preferred to keep my shit up as long as it looked good.

The sound of rain and the garage closing could be heard as I stepped into the kitchen. I smiled internally seeing my man leg gapped, shirtless, and rolling a blunt at the island. His back was to me, but I could see that he had at least three of his diamond necklaces on. Baguette loved jewelry and was forever buying me pieces that I tried my best to wear as often as he did. The thing is, I have little fine hair on my arms and chest that can't be seen with human eyes, and the jewelry was forever snagging on it. That shit hurt too.

I slapped Baguette on his ass since his navy briefs were showing due to his pants hanging slightly off his ass. Baguette didn't sag, but when he was comfortable, he tended to loosen his belt, and that would make his jeans hang off his waist.

"Aye mane, what I tell you about that shit?" Baguette put his fine ass mug on me as I came around the island, hopping up top and letting my legs hang down the side so that I could face him.

I crossed my legs as he lit his blunt, still mugging me.

"Hey, bae. I thought you would be at the bars all day today."

I graduated college with a degree in Business Management and put that shit to use by opening a slew of bars with my man. They were a hit in every state we had one in and kept us busy. Due to the increment of tourists and new folk moving into the city, we'd hired more staff at both the Jagoda Bay locations, and since we were fully staffed, we didn't have to be at the buildings that much.

"I went by both. I thought the rain was going to make 'em slow, but them bitches packed. I got the fuck outta there before they put my ass to work."

I laughed because the managers at either locations wouldn't hesitate to try and put us to work like we weren't the damn owners. Our bars brought us well over six figures a month combined. In the beginning, we took alot of losses. Even though I had a degree, we didn't know what the fuck we were doing, but we eventually got that shit right. Baguette couldn't believe he could bring in the amount monthly legally doing less work and with no risk as he had been in the streets. He hadn't voiced to me that he was out of the streets, but since I hadn't been seeing nor hearing his burner phone, I knew he was. Baguette was the type that didn't like to tell much, but he showed you what was up with his actions.

"How was lunch?" Baguette's eyes went from the blunt to me. The way his orbs immediately turned into slits as he puffed on his potent ass weed had my pussy thudding. I hadn't fucked my man in what seemed like forever, but he kept me satisfied by eating the lining out of my pussy. I loved head, so that was cool, but I needed to feel the dick. I knew his head was elsewhere, so I remained patient and didn't try to nag him.

"It was good, bae. Girl talk. Lemon Drops. You know the usual. Quasie was with us this time."

Baguette took another pull from his blunt and released the smoke right in my face. If I wasn't already tipsy, I would have joined him. It was too damn early for me to be getting fucked up, especially knowing that I wouldn't be getting no dick to go with the high. Plus, I needed to pay a few bills, do a few rounds of laundry and catch up on my shows.

"That's wassup. Quasie cool peoples."

Baguette never asked about the girl talk, but he damn sure listened when I told his ass. If it was some shit he didn't care too much about, he would shut my ass down by telling me to stop gossiping. I wasn't ready to tell him about our conversation, so I didn't elaborate on in it. I just watched as he smoked his blunt.

"You didn't tell me Quasie was married to Kilo."

I didn't personally know Kilo, but I'd seen him on the town before he was locked up and knew he was friends with my man. I was shocked as hell Quasie was married to his ass. Those baby mamas of his were a hot mess and were forever down my timeline on straight bullshit.

Baguette came around to stand in front of me and reached for my foot. He unzipped both my booties and tossed them on the floor as if they didn't cost a stack.

He separated my thighs and stood right in between them. My arms went around his neck as I inhaled his cologne and weed.

"Shit must've slipped my mind."

"Nahhh, when I asked about her being married you told me to mind our businesses." I smirked.

When I first met Baguette, I couldn't believe a nigga this fine was single. I'd talked to a few men in Jagoda Bay my first year of college, and almost all of them were on some slick shit, so it never went beyond a conversation, and one of them got to fuck. Plus after what I'd been through my senior year of highschool, I was cautious of men in general. After moving here, I learned very early that this unbelievable ass city with all these rich ass niggas was full of fine ass ain't shit niggas. Baguette came along, and I just knew a tall, nice body, hazelnut skin toned, perfect ass, thugged out ass, money getting nigga like him came with a bitch, a wife, and a slew of baby mamas. No matter how much he told me he was single, I just wouldn't believe the shit. He was just too fucking fine not to have a Rolodex of women.

Then when I began to believe him because we were dating and talking too much, I started to think that maybe his dick was small. That was the only answer as to why he was single. When he whipped his dick out and had me climbing up the fucking walls, that exed the tiny dick out the picture. I started to accept the fact that the man was perfect until he brought my ass to what I thought was his house and his house alone, but a bitch too pretty answered the door and had my ass ready to beat his ass.

I called bullshit when Baguette started laughing at my balled-up face and began explaining how Aphrodite was his fucking ex and how they shared a child together. His reasoning for bringing me around was so that she could feel me out. He had brought me to meet his ex before I met his mama. Aphrodite seemed cool enough, but when I excused myself to the bathroom and seen a few of this nigga's products on the vanity, I was ready to jet the fuck up outta that house and never talk to this nigga again. Eventually, their relationship grew on me, and I found myself around Aphrodite as much as Baguette.

"What's on yo' mind, baby? Talk to me."

Baguette put his blunt out and licked his bottom lip. This man is so fucking sexy it's a damn shame. I'd always tried to stray away from the fine ass niggas because they weren't worth the trouble, but this damn Baguette was something serious.

"Nothing, bae. I'm just full of lemon drops," I lied.

My eyes went from Baguette's because he was searching them for the truth. I found myself letting my eyes roam all over his many tattoos that I damn near knew by hard. Athena was tatted on the left side of his neck, and on his chest was Aphrodite. It didn't bother me when I first saw it during sex, but when he took me to meet her ass, and I put two and two together, I didn't answer his calls for two weeks. When he explained their history, I let it go eventually, and after a year of dating, my name was added to his ink. My eyes lingered on Aphrodite's too long, and that prompted him to reach for the zipper of my jeans.

"What you doing, Brock?" I called him by his real name.

"Fuck you mean what I'm doing? I want some pussy."

That revelation would have had me bent over the fucking counter like I don't use it to prepare our meals, but right now, I wasn't even in the mood.

"I don't want kids," I blurted out, causing him to freeze up.

I felt the tension in his stance and put my eyes back on his. I was shaking like a fucking stripper trying to read him. His jaws clenched, and his hands dropped from my zipper. When he took steps back and leaned against the fridge, I sighed.

Baguette's hand went down his face before he stuffed both hands down the front of his pants. His Fendi buckle was hanging from his waist, and I could see his dick deflate. I tried reading him but drew up a blank as I struggled to steady my breath. Baguette tossed his head back, making his Adam's apple peak. As he swallowed, I could see it descend down his throat.

"I went to see the lady today."

When men said anything about seeing "the lady," it was usually bull-shit. Who the fuck is the lady, and what she got to do with me not wanting no more kids?

"The fucking grief counselor, Tuscany. I went to see her today."

I could tell it took a lot for him to admit that he needed help by the uncomfortable look on his face.

"Umm, okay. That's good, baby. How do you feel?"

I'd been trying to get Baguette to talk to someone for years about Athena. Finally, he had, and although I was proud of him, I was still antsy about where we would fall once he realized I was dead ass serious about not wanting no kids.

"Mane, shit was weird. Putting a bitch in my business that I don't know. She asked all of these fucking questions and shit, and I wasn't rocking with it. But then I thought back to the day at the restaurant-"

"Hold up, what restaurant?"

Baguette paused, and a bewildered expression was in his eyes.

"Nothing. Just know that I realized I needed to talk to somebody. It was awkward, but the shit made me feel better. I still miss my baby, though."

The frustration in his eyes had me feeling bad for my man. There was nothing I could do to make him okay. Outside of telling him things were going to be okay, I didn't know what else I could personally do to help him.

"Baguette, I don't want you to forget Athena. I just want you to learn how to deal with her loss. It's killing you, baby. You barely sleep, and when you do, you're crying for her in your sleep. I can see if she'd just passed away, but it's been half a decade. You can miss her. You'll forever miss her, but you can't let that loss fuck with your quality of life, bae."

I never wanted my man to forget his only child. Him crying out in his sleep just scared the fuck out of me. There were nights that he would grab his pistol, and I had to calm him down and make him realize I hadn't harmed her. That shit was terrifying. He needed help. Real bad. Death was consuming him and swallowing him whole. Aphrodite was handling it well, but she'd gone to counseling immediately after her baby girl's death and kept it going for months. Either she'd learned how to harness her pain or she was just damn good at hiding it. Baguette needed help or he was going to fall off the deep end.

"I know. I know that shit, baby. I just miss her so fucking much. How the fuck can I miss somebody I'd only met and saw once? My fucking baby, mane. I killed my fucking baby! Being a fuck nigga killed my fucking baby, Tuscany. You know how that makes me feel as a fucking man? Aphrodite didn't deserve that shit. She 'posed to have our fucking daughter. Doing girly shit like going to the nail shops and hair appointments and shit. It was established that I'd fucked up the relationship. I made peace with that. But my daughter. My daughter should still be here. I did so much to Aphrodite. She put up with so much of my bullshit, and even after I stressed her to the point that it killed our baby, she still deals with a nigga."

Tears streamed down Baguette's face, and I hopped from the counter and wrapped my arms around his waist. He towered over me since my heels were off, but that didn't stop him from bending and snuggling his head in my shoulders. His wet tears had me tearing up. My man was hurting, and I didn't know how to help him.

"I'm sorry, Baguette. I really am. But you didn't kill Athena, baby. Aphrodite forgave you, baby. I wish Athena was here too, but we can't live in the past like that. You gotta forgive yourself. If you don't, it's going to eat you alive."

"Ahh shit!" Baguette continued to cry out. But being the macho man he was, he stood straight, wiped his face, and grabbed his blunt.

"I ain't never cried so much in my fucking life since I got with your ass. Fuck you be doing to me, girl?" Baguette shook his head as he lit his blunt.

"Love you. Be your peace. That's what I do to you."

Aphrodite always says she never seen Baguette cry, but I've seen it more times than I could count, and that shit had me seeing him in a different light. Men often hid their vulnerability from not only the world but their partners. Baguette wore his heart on his sleeve with me, and I loved that for us.

"I know you don't want no kids, Tuscany. You know how many women I've fucked? Every last one of them don' tried to trap a nigga. You're the first one to come along and not mention a fucking baby. I made peace with Athena being my only child a long time ago. You been raising kids all of your youth. As bad as I would love a shot at being a father, I respect that shit."

Baguette took a long pull from his blunt with squinted eyes while I tried processing his revelation.

"So, you cool with it just being us for the rest of our lives, bae?"

Baguette nodded with now red eyes and hit his blunt again. My man was even sexier when he was high. The look he gives me through hooded eyes almost always has me ready to suck his dick on demand. Even now, standing in the kitchen with a puffy face, slightly sagging, and doing something as simple as smoking had me ready to fuck, but it could be that I'm just well overdue since his ass not laying dick.

"Ion got a choice, baby. We gone have to get a puppy or some though. It be too damn quiet in this big ass house."

"Unhhh unhhhh. So it can be shitting all over my floors? No, sir. Maybe one day, Aphrodite can have a child, and we can kidnap her baby from time to time. Goal been sniffing around her lately."

Baguette looked taken aback.

"Tum' 'bout my Goal? The Goal that sold her the house?"

"Yep. He got rid of Daphne's ass, but ion think Ditey studying his ass." I snickered, thinking about how she dissed him at the open house and his club. My girl was so hard on a nigga.

"I guess that's why he snatched her ass up at his club."

I nodded, talking too damn much as usual.

"I'ma have to talk to Ditey. He a good nigga."

My eyes bucked because I wasn't supposed to be saying shit like that to Baguette. Aphrodite was going to curse my ass out for telling her business.

"No, you better not say shit, Baguette. She don't want that man."

"Nah, her mean ass ain't going. Plus, she don't want no mo' fucking kids no way. Was mad as shit I got her pregnant with Athena," he added, telling me something I already knew.

I dropped to my knees and pulled Baguette's dick out. It had been a minute since I sucked his dick, and I was all of a sudden craving it.

I licked the precum oozing from the tip before tossing his dick down my throat, relaxing my throat and gagging a few times in the process.

"Shit! If I can get this uninterrupted for the rest of my life, I just might be aite with just us. Eat this dick up, Tuscany."

And I did just that. Since we were on one accord, I decided to tell him about the housewarming another day. For now, I was about to ride this dick.

CHAPTER 9

Aphrodite "Ditey" "Pretty Pretty" "AP" Greer

"When I get you to myself, it's murda."

"Hello?"

I placed my iPhone down in the cupholder as I tried to control my agitation. I'd just spent the last five minutes searching my mama's four bedroom home, and when I finally got to the garage that I should have searched first, I came to the realization that her ass was gone.

"Mama, I'm at your house."

"Bobby, you ain't have to do 'em like that!...I know that. Ring cameras, boo," my mother laughed out.

"You saw me on the Ring and didn't think to say you're not home through the speaker?"

"Bobby, these young folk said they cutting yo' head out here!... Nope. I keep telling you to stop using the key to walk in my shit. Serves you right. One day, I'll be busting it open on the couch, and I can't wait."

My face balled up as I pulled out of her driveway. I was pissed and agitated because she lived at least twenty two minutes away from me, and today was hot. We still had a few weeks 'til the first day of spring, but Jagoda Bay was unpredictable like that.

98

"Girl please. You ain't got no man. Nobody can weigh up to my precious daddy."

I rolled my eyes upward because I was still salty about not being able to find my sister. My mama still held my daddy up to the highest standards, even though he left her, made a new family, and died. We weren't even invited to the fucking funeral. I didn't understand it for the life of me.

"Girl, fuck yo' daddy. I ain't you. I know how to move on. Just because you hadn't met no man of mine don't mean I never had one. I respected you enough to never bring them in our home. Just know, I gets mine off!"

I damn near threw up in my mouth listening to my mama. She was too much at times, but I loved her to death. I hopped on the expressway, knowing exactly where she was on a Friday afternoon. The schools were just getting out, so I knew there would be traffic. I just hoped it wasn't too bad. I prayed no more damn people moved to Jagoda Bay because traffic was bad enough.

"Mama, don't start. Just because you haven't seen me with a man, don't mean I don't have one," I lied with ease, and the shit didn't even sound believable.

"Honey, please. How the hell you supposed to meet a man with Baguette on your ass everywhere you turn? Don't get me wrong, I love my forever son in-law and my new daughter Tuscany, but that's one damn couple that needs a life. They 'posed to be all over the world humping in foreign places but instead on the couch with you. Y'all the damn three Little Stooges."

I had to laugh at her, even though I didn't want to. I'd been dodging the hell out of Baguette and Tuscany's calls lately. Not because I was tired of them, but because I just wanted some time to myself. She only wanted to talk about this damn extravagant ass housewarming. I'd been feeling a bit overwhelmed as of late, and when I got like that, me time was the cure. I know they were seconds away from popping up, but I hoped like hell they didn't.

"Whatever, Ma. When I get a man, you and them gone be big mad because I'll be unavailable."

My mother scoffed, "I'm not, but Baguette shol' is. It's all good that you don't have nobody, but soon as he sees you moved on, that brother/sister shit gone go out the window."

"Ma, you so fake. You be all in Tuscany face," I taunted.

"Girl, I ain't fake. I love Tuscany to death, and I think she's perfect for Brock but she know what's up. Why you think she always popping up anytime he over without her? Stop playing dumb, boo. I can't wait 'til the housewarming either. I'm bringing Bobby with me, so I hope y'all ready to party."

I hated when my mama talked about this topic. I really had no more romantic feelings for Baguette. We had our thing, but it didn't work. I'm over it. We were always friends before anything, and that's why we're so cool now. When he finally stops playing and marries Tuscany, I'll be right there doubling as the best man and Maid of honor.

I listened to my mama crack jokes until I was whipping my Lexus beside her Lexus RX350. It was only a few years old since I'd gotten it for her fiftieth birthday some time back. Baguette's ugly ass topped my gift by giving her the very house I'd just left with the deed to match it. *Show off*. My mama was spoiled ass rotten, even by Tuscany. I think Tusc missed her own mama, and that's why she was always under mine. Baguette's mama was forever under his daddy and wasn't the friendliest, but she didn't mean no harm. It was the Aries in her.

Since it was kind of warm outside, I decided to dress in a pair of Jeans, Tory Burch sandals, a red silk blouse that was copped, and the matching cross body. I could hear my mama's loud ass from the parking lot laughing at my damn crackhead play uncle dancing. She always made a damn fool out of Bobby.

A few kids on bikes almost ran me over, and instead of cursing them out, I waited on their mama to get off work to do it because I knew she would since they were still in their uniforms. I knew their mama, and she didn't play. Her ass would be off work soon enough.

Looking around the hood, I couldn't help but smile. My auntie lived a few streets over in a new home she had built on my granddaddy's land, but this apartment here in *the bricks* belonged to my Big Ma, and everyone decided to just keep it in the family. It was the hangout spot, and although I hadn't been over here in a while, it still gave me a nostalgic feeling. I got into so many fights in the very dirt of the courtyard over Baguette. I got so tired of bitches claiming they'd fucked him back then that I stopped coming around. All of the holidays were spent at my mama's house, so that's where I hung at most of the time if I wasn't home or at Baguette and Tuscany's.

"Look at my fine ass niece! Aphrodite Greer! Turn around, let auntie see ya!"

I laughed as I did a spin for my auntie, causing my mama to playfully roll her eyes. Bobby was still dancing to the speaker playing Johnny Taylor on the porch and sweating his ass off. He didn't have not one tooth in his mouth, was dressed in overalls and long and ass green Chuck Taylor's with a towel wrapped around his neck. Bobby was dark as night, and I think part of it is because his ass is always in the hot ass sun dancing and shit.

I spoke to a few of my girl cousins and took a seat in one of the empty chairs my auntie had in the yard. My cousin Jainie went to fix me a cup of Strip and Go Naked punch. My auntie made two batches every weekend and had since we were kids. We used to be drunk as hell sneaking it back then.

"Aphrodite, get that shape from me, boo. I was fine as hell when I was yo' age!"

All the women in my family were shaped alike. Wide hips, booty, small waist, average tits. I didn't have no hating ass family members or no shit like that. My cousins were always busy with their men or their children. We got together on holidays and get togethers and hung out occasionally. It was no beef. We were all just grown ass women but make no mistakes, they'd gotten in the mud with me plenty of times against these bitches and vice versa.

"Here you go, boo."

I accepted the cup from my aunt's oldest daughter, Sora, as she sat beside me. She was married to a big time dope boy, had three kids by him, and lived the good life. They were the ones to build my auntie's house from the ground up. Of course she made them build it right here in the hood.

"Girl, we had the same damn shape, so how my only child get anything from you?"

My mama hated when my auntie claimed I got anything from her. It was crazy because I did get my naturally curly hair from my auntie, and Sora got her thin silky hair from mama. Genetics was weird like that.

"I love your shoes, boo."

I looked down and admired Sora's Gucci sneakers. They were cream but had the infamous tan Gucci pattern on the sides and the top. She topped her look off with a tan fitted knee length dress and the matching crossover bag. Her hair was in skinny, long knotless braids. Sora didn't even look like she had kids aged nine, four, and three. We were both pregnant at the same damn time and gave birth a week after each other, so her four year old was soon to be five. She was definitely a shoulder I leaned on during my grief.

"Thank you, boo. If these damn kids keep on riding in the fucking dirt, these shoes gone be going to Litty."

Lydia aka Litty is our cousin that's a senior and spoiled as hell. She was forever in our damn closets and pockets. She's a product of my Uncle Luda. I was sponsoring her prom dress that was costing me fourteen hundred damn dollars, and Sora took on the graduation dress, hair, and makeup. That girl was rotten, but being that she's a good kid and runs anytime I need her to help with the boutique or if Sora needs her to babysit, we make sure she's straight.

"When Litty get done cleaning them, they will look fresh off the showroom floor. Where are the babies? I need my hugs from Rayna."

Rayna is the soon to be five year old and oldest girl. She was forever hugging and kissing me and always in my lap. Rhea is the feisty three year old and Redman jr aka Red jr is the oldest and only boy.

"Girl, with their crazy ass grandma. She had them since Wednesday and won't be giving them back 'til next Wednesday. As bad as I can't stand the messy bitch, she definitely be coming through with her grands."

Baguette's mom was mean as hell and bougie as hell like she didn't come from these same projects, but she was my girl. Sora had the mama in-law from hell. The lady is messy and ratchet as fuck, but she loves her son and grandchildren. There were plenty of times Sora had to curse that damn lady out like she was our age. I'm glad I never had to deal with no shit like that and prayed I never would have to.

We danced and drank until we were toasted. I loved being around my family. For years I felt bad keeping them out the loop when I was always up Baguette's ass. It got to the point where he would show up to the family functions without my ass sometimes, and I would sit my mad miserable ass at home. He would bring my plate home and carry his ass right back out to the streets.

"I know I'm married, and I love my husband to death, but damn, that nigga fine."

I was scrolling through my new orders on my Shopify while my cousin whispered in my ear.

"Umm humm."

"Girl, you not even paying attention to who I'm talking about. Talking 'bout some umm hummm. Look."

Taking another sip from the cup, I finally raised my head, and my face grew warm seeing who it was she was speaking on.

He was across the courtyard, hopping out of a matte grey Rolls Royce truck that matched his eyes. He was fresh to fucking death in some jeans I couldn't make out, but they laid on top of his off-white Jordans. His top had some shit in another language printed on it, and his jewelry was glistening so hard, it blinded me even from twenty feet away. I watched as he slapped it up with another cute dude that I knew from around the way because he used to fuck with Sora's little sister. When he smiled, I saw that his teeth were glistening in diamonds. Not just the bottom row either. The top too.

"Told you his ass was fine. Here's a napkin. Get that drool up, boo."

I slapped the napkin away from my face as Sora doubled over in laughter. We'd shared a blunt, so her eyes matched mine in tightness. I was definitely going to be spending the night or taking an Uber home. Not because I was too fucked up but because I was always lazy as hell when I was lit.

"Girl, he aite," I lied for the second time today.

"Chile, please. It's okay to agree he's the finest nigga in the city. That's saying a lot because my husband is definitely the finest."

Big Red was definitely fine. But Goal's cocky ass was finer. I'd never tell him that shit though.

My eyes never left his until his gray orbs locked in on mine. My scary ass snapped my neck away from him so fast I heard it pop.

"Ohhh shit! Girl, he coming over here! Bitchhhh, he coming over here!" Sora squealed like she didn't have a crazy ass nigga at home.

I was no longer looking his way, but like a fucking magnet, I could feel him get closer and closer. I had to bear my weight down in my seat because I felt like I was about to be snatched toward him, and I'm sure he was still a few feet away.

"Why the fuck is Goal's fine ass coming over here?" I heard one of my cousins ask, but I was fake looking in my phone, so I didn't know who the question came from.

"Giiiiirrrrl, that nigga so fine. He putting all these niggas to fucking shame," someone else added.

I heard a few children scream his name, probably the same ones that almost got their ass beat in the courtyard for having their school clothes still on.

"Keep them grades up."

"Thank you, Goal!'

That exchange of convo let me know he'd passed out dollars, and knowing these begging ass kids around here, more were going to follow soon.

I smelled him, and then I felt him standing over me. My eyes traveled from my phone to his shoes that were inches away from my feet. *Damn, he smell so fucking good.*

A million butterflies took motion inside my belly, their gossamer swings stroking my soul. Then, he spoke, and every one of those happy butterflies went still.

"Hey, how y'all doin'?"

Those four words were enough to turn my cheeks rosy, and he wasn't even speaking to me. My mom, aunts, and cousin replied with a "Heyyyyyyy." and an array of snickers.

I didn't want to sit here like an idiot, so I locked the screen of my phone just as a call came through from Tuscany and let my eyes travel up his tall frame.

Once I settled on his eyes, the smirk on his face, revealing his diamond fronts was enough to make me cum right there in my chair in front of my whole damn family. I tried to be discreet about the shit, but obviously he caught on because his smile deepened.

"Wassup witchu, Pretty Pretty?"

Crossing my legs, I cleared my throat and ignored all the eyes that were burning a hole in the side of my damn head.

"Hey."

A sparkle went off in his grey eyes, and the sun was about to set. This man is too damn sexy for his own good and got the nerve to be slightly bowlegged. He was nothing but trouble, and trouble was some shit I didn't need.

"What's your name, young man?" My mama spoke up. I tensed my shoulders because she'd had one too many cups of punch, and her ass was a light weight. One cup was all it took for her, and she had the nerve to have four.

Goal's grey eyes went from me to my mama as he held his smile.

"I'm Goal, pretty lady, but you can call me son in-law or son. I rock with either."

That shit had my cousins laughing their drunk asses off.

Sora slid me a piece of gum on the sly that I chomped down instantly and pulled out a travel size perfume and stood but was spraying my ass with it secretly. It got in my damn mouth though, forcing me to cough.

"I'm headed to get me a cup of punch. Welcome to the family, cousin in-law."

"'Preciate that. Tell that nigga Big Red to get at me."

Sora nodded and scattered off.

"Do you ladies mind if I borrow my future? She been running from a nigga like I'm contagious or some."

I wanted to kill his ass dead.

"Aphrodite, get yo' tail up. You hear the man."

Goal held his hand out, and I hesitantly placed mine in his.

"Uhh, I'll be right back, y'all."

"Don't bring her ass back, nephew in-law."

Goal nodded at them again and turned to pull me away from my family. I shot them all the look of death as Sora came back outside, bending over and twerking as her sister play hit her from the back. I couldn't stand their asses. My mama was smiling like I was headed off to prom.

Pulling me to his side, Goal tossed his arm around my shoulder, and that shit had chills creeping down my spine.

"Was good, baby? You looking good out here."

"Preciate you looking out, Goal."

"Goal! I see ya, my guy!"

"Goal, can I have some money!"

"Yeah, me too!"

We were only halfway through the yard and Goal had already stopped six times to slap hands with folk. He'd only removed his arm from my neck to pull a knot from out of his pocket, peel off twenties and hand them to about ten children. Instead of putting the wad back in his pants, he slid it in my purse and placed his hand back around my neck.

When we finally made it to his car, he ushered me to the passenger, and before he could get to the driver's, he'd stopped and talked to three elderly ladies that were cheesing in his face. While inhaling the cherry mixed with new car scent of his vehicle, I watched as he pulled another knot out and passed the ladies a few hundred a piece. They were smiling their asses off. Hell, it made me smile. I'd grown up in this hood and had never seen Goal, but now, everyone was acting like his ass God. He was definitely well-respected in the hood.

The door opened before he could get to it, and when he slid in the driver's seat, I cleared my throat and turned to face him.

"Mr. Popular."

"Mrs. Popular. What you been on?"

I could get lost in those eyes of his, and that shit is what made the nigga bad for me. I bet he could get off on a fucking murder charge with one damn gaze at the judge. He was too damn pretty but in a thuggish street type of way. I knew a lot came behind dealing with a man like him. Lucky for me, I wasn't in the market for the male species.

"Nothing. Just work." I shrugged.

"You supposed to be moving. But I see the house still empty. After I let you bust me up for a little of nothing, I thought yo' ass would be running to move in."

I was taken aback at him knowing I hadn't even moved a hanger in the house. I'd been in my head, and since my lease isn't up for another three months, I figured I'd take my time.

"How you know I haven't been there?"

I hoped like hell this fine ass nigga wasn't a stalker.

"Because I came through trying to eat some pussy, and that shit was a ghost town."

There he go again, making me squirt in my fucking jeans. The look he gave me was one that let me know wasn't a hint of sarcasm in his tone. Then he had the nerve to finish the statement off with the lick of his lips.

"Well, if I was there, wouldn't nun' of that be going on," I lied for the third damn time today.

"Yeah, aite." He laughed cockily.

"Why you wanna fuck me so bad anyways? You not interested in getting to know me or no shit like that? Just straight to the pussy? I'm not Daphne, Goal."

This was the same nigga that was just pouring champagne on a bitch at ten a.m. Now he was ready to jump up and down in my tail.

"Have you seen you?"

Have you seen you?

"Okay, I look good. But so does most the bitches in Jagoda Bay. Do you wanna fuck me just because of who I'm tied to?"

Niggas used to always try to get at me back when I was with Baguette. Mainly his opps or niggas he thought was his friends just to have one up on him. Hell, they still did try to this day, and although we weren't together, I respected him too damn much to ever fuck with an enemy of his.

"Who the fuck you tied to?"

"Baguette. My ex."

"Ion mean no harm and no disrespect to that nigga Baguette, but I could give a fuck who you were tied to in the past. The moment my eyes landed on you, any tie you assumed you had, was clipped and burned."

Cocky ass nigga.

"Oh really?"

"Yeah, really."

"You still want me, and you and Baguette are friends? No loyalty to the bro code?"

Goal licked his bottom lip and pulled off from the parking lot. My orbs went across the dusky courtyard to my cousins, and they were smiling still.

"That nigga know when I want some shit, ion give a fuck about who had it before me. He knew when he sent yo' ass my way, it was a wrap."

I wanted to comment on that but decided to keep my opinion to myself. I would beat a bitch blue if she was in my face, turned around, and fucked my EX. I didn't have any friends outside of Tuscany, my family and now Quasie, but I could never see myself going after any one of their niggas or niggas they dealt with in the past. That's just some shit you don't do, but I guess it was different for men. Hell, Daphne had been one of the reasons I left Baguette, and here go Goal buying the bitch million dollar houses. Men just got their own fucking logic in shit.

I pulled my seatbelt on and looked out of the window. The hood was live as hell, and everyone was still flagging Goal down as he sped down the street. I said a silent prayer that no one would shoot at our ass or something. I know how niggas in the Bricks can be, and no matter how much you fuck with the hood, it's always that one that will take your ass out. Plus, I was still thinking about those men that busted inside of Goal's office. He had some type of beef it seemed. I didn't want no parts nor did I want to be caught in the crossfire.

"When you moving in though?"

I humped my shoulders.

"Ion know yet."

The car grew quiet and Goal pressed the steering wheel prompting Sonder's *What You Heard* to play softly in his speakers. This was one of my favorite songs, and I was shocked that his ass was listening to it.

"What you know about Brent Faiyaz?"

Goal took me for a rap guy. I would have never guessed he listened to my boy.

"What's the word? Tell me whatchu heard. Don't tell me what to do, just tell me when it hurts. When I getchu to myself, it's murdaaahhhh."

I tossed my head back in laughter as he sang the lyrics. What was crazy is this damn thug ass nigga actually had an amazing voice.

"You can sing? I would have never guessed. What can't you do?"

"Get yo' mean ass."

"I hear ya."

"That's real shit. You giving a nigga a hard ass time. I told my mama I'ma have to lock yo' pretty ass up and throw away the key. Real shit."

"Unh, no, you did not tell yo' mama about me."

He gave me a look before pulling his phone out and gliding his thumb across the screen. *Madre* was plastered across the screen, and a picture of a woman with eyes as grey as his popped up.

"Hey, son. I miss you," she cooed.

"Wassup, ma. I miss you too. What you doin?"

I could hear pots rattle and water running. Goal toggled his focus from the phone to the road and then me. The simple and normal shit this man was doing had me squirming in his leather seat. *Looooord*.

"Cleaning the kitchen. Your brother keeps dishes in the sink but never wants to wash them What are you doing?"

Goal cut his eyes over at me and licked his lips.

"That nigga eighteen now, he need to be cleaning up behind his own damn self. But I'm not doing too much of nothing, I just snatched up your daughter in-law. You gone let me stash her in the basement 'til she get some act right?"

I gasped and playfully hit his shoulder.

"If you don't unhand that lady. *Dejala ir*! Heyyy, Aphrodite! How are you?"

I gave him a sidelong glance in utter disbelief, and his ass was just cheesing, showing all of his diamond teeth. *So fucking fine.*

A small voice that I barely even recognized escaped my chords, "Hi! I'm good. How are you?"

I didn't know what else the fuck to say. This crazy ass man really had told his mama about me.

"I'm good, sweetheart. I'm hoping to see you soon. I need to meet the woman that my stubborn firstborn can't seem to stop talking about."

My cheeks grew warm, so I turned my head to hide them from him.

It was a damn shame how the basic ass shit this man was doing around me had me smitten. *Crazy.*

"Aite now, mama. I'ma call you in the morning. I love you."

"Don't end the call now! Give her my number so we can do lunch soon. *Te amo, hijo* and be safe. Enjoy your weekend, Aphrodite."

"Enjoy your weekend as well."

Goal ended the call and continued to cruise the streets.

"You gotta stop doubting yo' nigga, baby. Ion gone tell you no lie."

"Whatever, Goal." I dismissed him, but I couldn't stop smiling.

"You have a little brother?"

"Yeah, Gage aka Big Gator. That nigga in his last year in high school and a senior and shit. He play football, so that's why I try not to be on his ass so much, but he be on too much hothead shit. I'm tryna figure out how the nigga spoiled and a fucking hothead? Shit don't go."

"Y'all did it to him, though. I don't have a little brother, but I have a cousin that's also a senior, and she be in our pockets hard. It's cool though. She not out here on no fast shit, and she do what her dad expect so I don't complain too hard. She lost her mom when she was in elementary so all the women in the family try to play our part. She graduating Salutatorian."

Hearing Goal talk about his brother had me thinking about my own long lost ass sister. I hadn't completely given up the hunt, but I was strongly thinking about taking Quasie up on her offer to reach out to the PI.

"Back to yo' move-in date though. What's the holdup?"

I could see one of Jagoda Bay's many lakes come into view. I hadn't been to this particular one, but the view was breathtaking even now at night time. It's crazy how it was so close to the hood, yet far enough away for it to feel like it was across the city. Even the houses we'd just passed coming here were a sight. Jagoda Bay is like that though. The hood can take up about five streets, and the sixth street will have three hundred thousand dollar houses, clean parks, and fancy restaurants.

"You asking a lot of questions. Howe you know I trust you with that type of information? Bad enough yo' bitch know where I stay." I rolled my eyes.

"First off, that ain't my bitch. Secondly, you trust me with yo' life, girl. Stop it."

"How you figure that?"

"Because you haven't questioned the destination once since you stepped in the car."

There go that cocky ass smile again.

"I knew we were going for a ride. Plus, my family saw me leave with you. I knew you weren't going to do anything crazy. My cousin's husband knows who you are. He would have retaliated if you'd done something to me." I honestly spoke.

"If I wanted to do something to you, ain't a nigga on earth, let alone Jagoda Bay, got the balls to come at me sideways about it." His eyes bore through me as he spoke with so much conviction I almost believed him.

Goal parked right in front of the lake and rolled the windows down, as well as opened his panoramic roof. The moonlight shined down on us, giving me a perfect view of his perfect face. The burbling water in front of us instantly calmed me. *I bet I would get the best damn sleep out here.*

"How come everyone seems to know you, but I'd been in the hood my whole life, and I've never seen you?"

Someone like Goal would have stuck out like a sore thumb. He couldn't have been from around here.

"I'm the type of nigga that didn't want to be seen until I was ready. But I'm not from here. I'm from Sparkling City. I'd always visit though. I got folks I fuck with tough out here."

Made sense.

"What's on yo' mind though? Talk to Papi."

"Papi?"

"Yeap."

I didn't have shit else to do, so I reached in my purse, around the wad of money and grabbed my gloss. I plumped up my lips, and Goal sat in admiration.

"My problems are mine. I'll be aite."

Lately, I'd been harboring my emotions because I just didn't want to talk about it to the people around me. Problems were just that. Problems. Most of the time there weren't any solutions. When there was a solution, it's always one that you don't want.

"Nah, that's where you wrong. With me, you ain't got no problems. I'm that nigga that's gone move hell in order to find a solution, and if I can't find one, I let the money do it for me. So again, what's on yo' mind?"

Tossing my gloss back in my bag, I let my head hit the seat and sighed.

His question was a stab in my heart. My stomach clenched tight, and as I closed my eyes, it was impossible to steady my erratic pulse.

"The death and birthdate of my daughter is approaching. When this time of year comes around, I get like this. I know she died almost five years ago, but it's like, my life has moved on, but my daughter is stuck in a grave. My child was supposed to outlive me, but she didn't. She was only on this earth one day and left. That shit fucks with me.

I try to be strong for Baguette because he takes Athena's death so hard, but when I'm alone, I break the fuck down. I don't feel right moving in a home big enough for twenty five people, and it's just me. My daughter is supposed to be running around it, drawing on the walls, and putting her sticky handprints on my refrigerator. I've been scared shitless to move, honestly."

When Baguette talks about Athena, I try my hardest to shrug it off, but I be holding back my fucking tears. I carried that girl for nine damn months. Had her room set up, felt her kick every damn day, read to her, prayed for her, and anticipated her arrival.

"Ain't nothing wrong with missing your baby. You ain't gotta hide that shit to try to be strong for Baguette. He's a grown ass man, and he has a bitch to lean on. Who you got, Pretty Pretty?"

I didn't answer the question because I was too busy fighting back tears. I wasn't about to cry in front of this damn man. Nope!

"Life isn't fair."

"Nah, it ain't. But, you still gotta live. You don't have to be cooped up in the house, afraid to live your life because you feel guilty your baby girl gone. She would want her mama to have a life. A damn good life. Let her live through you, Pretty Pretty. Want me to go up to heaven and tell that nigga big God to send her back? I ain't above that shit."

Laughter broke through, and at the same time tears rushed down my face.

Goal beat me to wiping my face, and that nigga was aggressive as hell with it too.

"You gone be aite. You stronger than you think."

"How you know?"

"Because my wife ain't no weak ass bitch."

"We gone skip the friends, dating, and lover phase, huh?"

"Hell yeah, you did that shit already. We got plenty time to date after you rocking my last name. I know what the fuck I want, I'm just waiting on you to catch up."

"I haven't been in a relationship in years. How you know of all the men in Jagoda Bay, I want you?"

"When I put a hunnid on yo' finger, niggas gone be too intimidated to step to you because they know they won't be able to come correct. Plus, you'll be rocking another quarter on yo' shades, so you ain't gone even see them otha' niggas."

I bit down hard on my bottom lip as he gritted his diamond fronts. They were glistening harder than the moonlight on the fucking lake. Whew, it was getting too damn hot to trot up in here, and suddenly his spacious truck felt too small for the both of us.

"Goal, you really want to get married one day? I don't believe it."

My way of thinking may be a little ignorant, but Goal is just the type of nigga that's too damn handsome to be married. I mean, not saying ugly niggas be married because lord knows I done seen plenty of fine ass married men. Goal just screamed *playa* and *fuck bitches get money*. I couldn't see him being anybody's husband. ESPECIALLY not mine.

"Hell yeah, I do. Not one day, but the day yo' ass stop playing. I want kids too. Plenty of 'em."

"Well, that scratches me off the list. I'm not having any more children," I stated with finality.

"Yea, you are. Athena want a sister. Brother too. We gone grant her wish too."

"You just got it all figured out, don't you Goal?"

"That's my job, Pretty Pretty. We gone have a lit ass life together. Nasty ass baby making sex too."

There go my kitty purring.

"All you want to do is fuck."

"Come 'ere."

Goal's strong ass pulled me into his damn lap, scaring the shit out of me because I thought I was about to hit my damn knee on his middle console. Thank God these jeans were more like jeggings because I would have been uncomfortable as hell straddling him. My pussy was thumping so damn hard, I was praying he didn't hear it. It's like the coochie and heart were in a race to see who could pound the fucking hardest. I didn't know what to do with my hands, so my lame ass just wrapped them around my waist. *Damn, I hope I'm not too heavy.*

Goal grabbed my chin, and our lips were so close they were damn near touching.

"I do wanna fuck. I want to fuck the shit outcha. I'ma fuck yo' face, fuck yo' pussy, but before I do either of those, I'ma fuck yo' mind up. I'm a real nigga, baby. I see you hurting. I see you holding on to some shit that I want you to let go of before I enter yo' body. So while I know I'm gonna fuck, I'ma wait that shit out and be the real nigga you need to lean on."

"I will never let my daughter go."

"You better not."

"Baguette isn't going anywhere."

"I know that. I'm not intimated by him. That's my nigga. I'm talking about that hurt, baby. You gotta let that shit go. Can you do that for Papi?"

Without hesitation, I nodded my head.

"I have an interior decorator I sent my mood boards too. I'll move soon enough."

Goal's hand went from my chin to around my neck, prompting him to plant a wet kiss on my lips. Instead of pulling back, he latched onto my bottom lip and sucked it in his mouth. Heat radiated from my center, causing me to moan.

"I told you all I had to do was get you to myself."

"And I told you I like my steak medium well," I gasped.

"I ain't no regular nigga. When I take yo' ass on this date, don't be crying 'bout I did too much."

"Do the most. Impress me, Goal."

"Say less."

The rest of the night, we chilled, blew each other guns, kissed nastily, and talked about this imaginary future Goal had planned for us. Instead of talking against his plans, I pictured myself with him and how much different my life just may have been if I ran into him when I was fourteen instead of Baguette.

CHAPTER 10

Quasie Lantis

I t's been a few weeks since Kilo called himself showing back up from whatever fucking cell he crawled out of, and I'd been in my fucking feelings ever since. With the way my brokerage is set up, I couldn't afford to be in my fucking feelings. Not only did I have clients beating down my line waiting for approvals, I have an entire team that included seven agents, two assistants, a closing attorney, inspectors, contractors, builders, and so many more to name.

I jumped into real estate over seven years ago. Back when Kilo was slinging dope, I had my head in the books. I wasn't always this multimillion dollar realtor with an elite brokerage housing top-earning agents. Back then, I was lucky if I sold three houses a year. That was cool at the time because I was the wife of a dopeboy, and all of our bills were paid by my man. The money I made was play money, and selling houses was literally just something to do. I also knew the risk of being with a man in the streets, so I wanted something for us to fall back on if or when the police came knocking.

Pain had a way of changing you, and I guess that shit turned me into a beast. Dealing with Kilo in the beginning was refreshing. He wasn't my first, but he was the first guy that came along and showed me something different. Kilo wasn't shy about what he wanted from me. We got together at seventeen and eighteen and by twenty, he was ready to get married. We were young as hell, and Kilo was making so much fucking money we had no idea what the hell to do with. With money came street fame and groupie bitches to match. I heard the whispers, but since I was reaping all the benefits, I let the shit roll off my back.

Kilo insisted we get married at only twenty years old and although I stressed that he wasn't ready, he insisted. It seemed like the moment I said I DO, Kilo's dick said I DON'T. The whispers turned to full-on proof, but through it all my cheating ass husband still kissed the fucking ground I walked on.

Constantly being cheated on had a way of fucking with your self-esteem. I began dissecting the women, trying to figure out what the fuck they had that I didn't. What did my husband seek in other women that I couldn't provide for him? Tired of getting my feelings hurt playing detective, I decided to get up off my ass and do something with myself. The more Kilo dogged me out, the harder I went at my goals. By the time he brought two babies to our doorstep, I was nearing one million dollars in sales. Now, that didn't mean I earned a million dollars. I'd sold real estate estimating around a million dollars, so that meant I'd made 50k for that year. Kilo wiped his ass with 50k, but for me, that was a dream.

When Kilo brought his kids home that were the same age by related women, I cursed his ass out, beat his ass or at least tried and cried my heart out. He real deal had two newborn ass babies in a carrier in each of his hands. One boy. One girl. I was fucking flabbergasted. Kilo tried to get me to forgive him for a year. After he saw I wouldn't budge, he left me high and dry. Kilo is damn stubborn. He had the nerve to be mad because I wouldn't accept his illegitimate children. So, he said damn me, damn our future, damn our plans, and went on to do what the fuck he do.

After that, I went harder than ever. When Kilo settled into a new relationship, I'd done two million in sales, and by the time the judge slammed the gravel on the charge he caught, I was at three. I went from a dumb ass dopeboy's wife to a six figure bitch. Jagoda Bay was steadily growing, and since social media is where we all spent most of our time, I gained a healthy following by always posting pics and videos of me dressed to the nines during my sales. At the time, I was only being me.

Fashion has always been a hobby of mine. Doesn't matter if I'm at the gym, my workout clothing match, and my hair is still laid. I documented damn near everything on social media, except my dog ass husband and my family. That had the people eating out the palm of my hands. My promo and lifestyle alone had my DMs blowing up with clients. I went from Jagoda Bay's top-selling realtor to opening my own brokerage and having everyone wanting to be apart of *Dream Team Realty*. I'm so damn highly requested I have to pass clients on to my agents.

It felt so good to build something organically from the ground up without the help of a man. Yes, Kilo took amazing care of me while we were together, but I took my own damn money and invested in my own damn dreams. There were times I could have used Kilo's money to invest in my business, but I refused. The only thing I did was swap his bills out for updated ones and put that shit in the safe. I don't need a man for anything, and that right there is my biggest flex.

Real estate is my life. With selling so many homes, I felt like I wasn't giving other realtors outside of my company a chance, so after a while I scaled back from being in the field and focused on training my agents and building my brokerage. After I had that under wraps, I grew bored, missing the hustle and bustle of selling property, so I jumped back in.

I'd known Kymani was getting out any day for some time, but still, I was shocked at his sudden arrival. I hadn't even told him I had the house finished. Even though the man was cheating every chance he got, I was still planning our future together. We drew up the plans and bought the land before he revealed he had the babies. Just 'cuz he was jammed up didn't mean I wasn't going to finish building my damn dream home. The moment I had the money and the credit score, I secured a loan with the bank and had my home built. All I had left to pay was about one hundred and eighty seven thousand dollars, and the deed was mine. That was good, considering the loan I'd secured it on was about seven hundred thousand dollars.

I live well and dress to impress, but I'm about what I be preaching to my clients and agents. Most realtors don't even own a home of their own, and while I understand everyone is not ready to purchase, you can't expect a potential client to be able to trust your expertise if you haven't even gone through the process personally. If my agents don't own a home, I advise them to pretend they do or at least have it in their five year plans.

I take a chunk of my earnings from every other sale and put it towards my principal balance. My seven hundred thousand dollar home was soon to be paid off, and it had already doubled in equity, and was worth one point four million dollars. Not only that, the community of Shirah that I'd had it built in was now thriving and flooded with professional ball players, young CEOs, and rappers, so the area was highly sought after. Jagoda Bay's properties are skyrocketing in value because the market is rapidly growing, and the demand is greater than the inventory. I could almost ask for whatever I wanted when it came to my property, and I would most certainly get it. I always tell clients and potential clients not to wait for the market to crash because it may not ever. The time to buy is now because it's for sure an investment.

Today had been a day. My office was in an uproar because not only did I have two closings tomorrow, four of my agents each had a closing as well. We spent the day making calls, getting paperwork together, ensuring we had keys to all the properties, and assuring clients their big day would run smoothly. I'd reached out to both of my clients so that we could be on one accord with the wardrobe. The Jensen family wanted to wear navy, while The Kodas family preferred cream. I had two perfect navy and cream sets, one a striped skirt and the other color-blocked pants. I just had to go home and decide on which one. I was going to combine the two colors that way I wouldn't have to go home to change and risk being late to the Kodas' closing since theirs is second.

I still sent both families texts to see if they wanted me in a skirt or pants. If they both gave opposite answers, I would just bring both fits to the office and do a quick change. I always think it's cute how my clients love to match me. My followers ate it up every single time in the comments. Plus, it made good content because I for sure had my videographer following me for the day.

I was now pushing the basket down aisle four of Publix, trying to grab seasoning for the salmon pasta I'd been craving. I had every ingredient in the basket already, as well as a bottle of Stella Rose black, but I needed onion powder, garlic powder, lemon pepper, and Cajun seasoning. The salmon pasta wasn't going to take me long, and I planned on drinking a very large glass of wine while I waited for it to cook. I normally meet with agents to get dinner or a few of my girlfriends from college, but today I didn't want to be out late since tomorrow will be so long.

"Excuse me. I am so sorry."

Turning to the left, I ran my basket right into someone. I was too busy trying to fish for my ringing damn phone, which I'm sure was only a client. My team knew not to call me when I was no longer at the office.

"Excuse me. Uh, Quasie?"

I turned my nose up at the guy, and not because he wasn't good looking. Dressed down in a pair of grey sweets and a Nike hoodie, he was definitely fine, but I didn't know him. True enough, I had a large following, but I wasn't no celebrity. I didn't like when people, especially men, approached me in public over social media shit.

"My bad. Let me start over. I'm Eleven."

What the hell type of name is that? And also, I don't know where this nigga's hand has been. I wouldn't dare shake his hand. So I looked his stretched-out hand it as if it were shit on it, and I damn sure didn't miss the tattoos on his knuckles. There wasn't shit a nigga marked up like the side wall of a corner store could do for me. Been there, not gonna do that again.

He smiled and lowered his hand. Unfazed at me bluntly dismissing his ass. Usually, this was the time men called me a stuck-up bitch under their breath, but my resistance seemed to amuse him.

"Do I know you?" I squinted my eyes, trying to figure out if this was a man from Kilo's past.

Even though most of the men he ran with got ghost on his ass when he was locked up, I'd still sold homes to a few of them They never mentioned my husband, so neither did I. That street shit had nothing to do with me.

"Nah, my bad. I ain't mean to freak you out or no shit like that. My sister is always on your page and shit. Just wanted to speak. But uh... skirt. You enjoy your night, beautiful."

Stupid ass name Mr. Eleven walked past me carrying his light scent with him. He didn't have a basket in his hand, but my eyes still followed him to the fridge where he grabbed a gallon of milk. *What the hell he mean skirt?* I looked down at the olive-hued skirt I was rocking and figured he must've been paying me a compliment. My phone vibrating again had me successfully retrieving it from my Givenchy bag. Seeing that the number was one that I didn't recognize, I declined the call. I already knew it was Kilo's ass. I didn't have time for his bullshit. Not tonight, not ever really. I wasn't the same Quasie from back then. You fuck me over once, I pay you dust for a lifetime. Kilo had fucked me over twice, so it was fuck him forever. He can take his jailbird ass over to his two damn baby mamas.

...

My first closing went by smoothly. I gifted The Jensen family a Hermes throw blanket to show my appreciation. That was another thing that had clients begging to work with me. I always give luxurious gifts. The higher the sale, the more I spent on the gift. It was a marketing tactic that had realtors all over the world copying. After walking the Jensen family through their fully renovated three hundred and sixty two thousand dollar home, taking some pictures and videos with the photographer I'd been using for the last two years, I still had two hours 'til the Kodas' closing, so I took my ass home, had a shower and still decided to change into an unauthorized outfit. I felt like I'd sweat some, and since my next client's home is a brand new Modern Transitional luxury six bedroom, four point five baths on two acres, seven thousand square feet, I wanted to pull out something specifically for the closing.

My client closed on this home at one point five million dollars, and this is a cash purchase. My commission is seventy five thousand dollars, so damn right I was changing and meeting her color preference. We hadn't met in person just yet, but I'd been doing Zoom calls and Facetimes with her to show her the properties. The process was so smooth because she agreed on the second home she virtually toured. She lived and worked out of state but would be flying in this morning and staying for good. I knew she worked in the hospital because every time we Facetime, she was in a full mask, so I barely knew what the damn lady looked like. My assistant handled all the paperwork, so I hadn't had a chance to even look at the copy of her license she sent over.

After getting dressed, I grabbed the four Louis Vuitton bags and made my way out the door.

My client requested that all paperwork be signed at the property, and since I got the notification that the wire had been successful, I happily made my way to her home. The neighborhood wasn't too far from Aphrodite's and was nestled in Crystal Cove as well. She was about nine minutes away from here. I hadn't heard from her in over a week, but I did place a huge order on her site last night. Her new arrivals were the bomb, giving all the tropical feels. I didn't have not one vacation planned, but I needed those pieces. My agents were deep in work just like I am, and my girlfriends from college are all married and always traveling the world with their husbands. I needed me a damn life and asap.

"You have arrived at your destination."

Siri alerted me that I was here, so I parked my Maserati truck on the curb but not directly in front of the home so that the videographer could get good pics. Her car was a few inches down from mine, so I knew she had beat me here and was more than likely already shooting videos.

Grabbing the bags from the back seat, I gave myself a onceover as best as I could. I was rocking the hell out of this damn outfit and almost changed because I didn't want to appear too sexy. The upper half of my dress was long-sleeved and fitted. Right at my bottom, the dress went from bodycon vibes to asymmetrical ruffles. I loved the way the dress hugged my body, but since this ass done got colossal, I tried to stay away from skater or ruffle skirts. All the wind had to do was blow my way, and my business would be on display.

This all-cream number I effortlessly rocked was topped with a thick gold rope necklace, gold Versace pumps, and the matching clutch. My hair was in its signature black banged bob. I'd even touched up my makeup and added an ombre red matte lip. Walking up to the white and black home, I smiled. The driveway was lined with luxury cars, including a Ferrari, an AMG, and a Bentley coupe. To my understanding, Ms. Kodas wasn't from here, but the tags of the cars in the driveway concluded her guests were.

My phone rang in my purse, so I paused in my stride to retrieve it.

"Hey, Kassie. I'm here now at the Kodas closing."

I knew my assistant was making sure I wouldn't be late. When I told her I was going home to change, she wanted to rebut so damn bad. Kassie is Kilo's cousin, and I loved my girl to death because she was right there cursing her cousin out when he was dogging me out. We made our money. She didn't bring his name up and neither did I over the years, and for that, she was the highest paid assistant in Jagoda Bay.

Kassie knew it could take me forever to get ready. This was a big closing for me, so I wouldn't dare be late. I've sold multi-million dollar homes plenty of times before as well as I've assisted out-of-town buyers with purchasing, but this was the first client I dealt with one hundred percent virtual. I was proud of that.

After ending the call, I pulled on the handle that replaced the knob on the black steel door. That simple touch alone let you know that this home was next fucking level.

"Helllooo," I sang out as I stepped into the home and bent down to grab a pair of slippers to put over my heels. I had this basket put here for the fucking contractors that loved dragging their muddy ass work boots all across the floors.

"Girl, ain't no need for those! Hiiii, how are you?"

I stopped in the middle of sliding the first slipper on and was taken aback at the face that matched the eyes I'd been facetiming for the last month.

"I'm Earis Kodas! It's sooo good to see you in person, and babyyy, you're just as pretty as your Instagram! I'm loving this outfit!"

Tossing the slippers back in the basket, I blushed at the compliment. Earis was the opposite of what I'd expected. I mean, I'd only seen this girl's brown eyes for over a month. I had no idea under her mask would be a whole damn Lori Harvey stunt double. Not only was Earis drop dead gorgeous, she's young too.

I leaned in and gave her a hug since her arms were out and inhaled her Jasmine fragrance.

"Come on in, I already signed everything electronically through your lovely assistant, but I took the liberty of bringing dummy contracts to sign for the camera. OMG, girl, you are just too pretty and bossed up. Come on, my family is waiting."

Earis pulled me in the direction of the kitchen, and I had to clear my damn throat. Standing around the massive island was a whole damn family of Cullens. You know, the fine ass attractive family from Twilight? Well, these folk were the black version. Every single one of the five people that were standing around smiling and conversing was dressed in cream, slender built like Earis with good hair and brown eyes. One set of eyes I locked in with particular was familiar, and when I noticed where I knew him from, my cheeks grew warm.

"Everyone, this is the amazing Quasie! I couldn't have chosen a better realtor! Quasie, this is my youngest brother and his twin, Earah and Earren. This is our mother, Eya, and my big-headed older brother, Eleven."

Her mother gave me a warm hug that reminded me of my own mother, and the twins tossed out a wave and a head nod.

"Damn, I drop two mill on you, and I'm the big head brother? You know Earren got a watermelon under them nappy ass dreads."

Everyone laughed, even the mother. This family was really fucking attractive. I was at a standstill gazing at all of the good genes floating around the room. I know folk liked to say I was my mama's twin but damn.

"Thank you so much, brother. I love you, and I appreciate you."

Earis was speaking with her brother, but his eyes were still on mine. I shook how good his ass looked from my thoughts and got right into realtor mode. We signed the fake papers for the camera, and even though we were flexing at this point, Earis, her mom, and sister made it fun. The photographer got plenty of pics and videos. When HE pulled out a bottle of sixty thousand dollar champagne and shook it up, I stood back but laughed along with everyone else as it spilled onto the floors. Caterers came in and served fried lobster tails, mac n' cheese, and asparagus. They'd even set up tables and chairs for us to sit. I hadn't planned on staying long, but I was really enjoying myself.

By the time I was full and tipsy, it was time for me to go, but Mrs. Kodas and Earis talked me into staying until a few pieces of her furniture were delivered. My schedule was clear for today, and since my agents didn't need me, I agreed.

I'd had a little bit too much champagne to drink, and it was weighing on my bladder, so I excused myself to tinkle. Earis let me know she had tissue in the bathroom as well as soap. I wasn't worried one way or another because I had wet wipes and sanitizer. I usually came prepared at home closings because I knew the homes weren't furnished. After handling my business and moisturizing my hands once they were dried, I walked out of the bathroom and ran into something solid.

"You got a habit of not watching where the fuck you going, hunh?"

A frown covered my face as I looked up into the eyes of the person I'd been trying to ignore the entire closing. He was looking too damn good in a cream bomber jacket with black hardware and a black zipper, cream leather pants that fit his body nicely, and black and cream Rick Owens. There was even a black chain hanging from his pants but not in a crazy rockstar type of way. His medium walnut-hued skin matched that of his mother and siblings. His hair was in a low fade, but I could tell the hair on his head was just as good as his siblings. Next to the outer corner of his eye was a small beauty mark that I thought was a tattooed tear drop at first, but seeing his sister Earis shared the same mark, I knew it was genetics. His face was void of facial hair, yet he still looked like a grown ass, fine ass man.

"No, you're just always in my way," I sassed.

He looked down at me with those brown eyes of his and licked his lips. I had to look away because the kitty was dripping, and Kilo's dumb ass had killed my mannequin hunch buddy.

"Maybe being in your way is where I wanna be."

I swallowed hard.

"I see you wore that skirt."

I snapped my neck at him at the revelation of what he meant when I ran my basket into him yesterday at Publix. I suddenly felt like shit for being a bitch to him.

"Yeah, I should take some of that commission back for you being mean to a nigga yesterday. But I won't because ion like mine friendly no muhfuckin' way."

"Could you please excuse me, Eleven?"

I needed to get away from this man because it's no way that damn statement should have me turned on like this. No way.

"Could you please let me have you?"

Any other man I would have cursed out and then mated, but with Eleven, I was internally screaming yes like he'd asked my hand in marriage.

"I'm married."

I flashed my ring in Eleven's face. Never mind the fact that my husband is no longer my husband and a cheating ass jailbird with two project princess ass baby mamas. Eleven didn't need to know all that. I just needed to throw something out there to get him the fuck out of my face. With the way this man's expression didn't change, I could tell my truth didn't move him one way or another because he was still blocking my path.

"I'M M A R R I E D," I spelled out.

"Okay, and I don't G I V E A F U C K. That's that nigga's problem, not mine. Now, can I have you, baby?"

My lips parted in surprise while the smile in his eyes contained a sensuous flame. Eleven's expression stilled and grew serious. While his eyes were like summer lightning.

"I... can't." My voice was fragile and shaking.

"You will. But I ain't tryna wait. I want you and I want yo' fine ass now."

I swallowed hard, trying to manage a feeble answer. I'd never had a man make an offensive ass statement sound so sexy. I was real life sitting here testing the idea instead of pushing his ass out of my path.

"This is your sister's house."

Eleven rubbed his marked hand down the lower half of his face before taking the same hand and placing it on the wall above my head and leaning in.

"I bought this muthafucka. A gift for her becoming a nurse practitioner. I know who the fuck house this is. If I don't know, my bank account damn sure does. You done threw out the fact that you got a bullshit ass husband that I could care less about and pointed out our obvious location. Now, I need you to get on one accord with that pussy and hand it over, I want you in these heels too."

Lord, why does he have to look and smell so damn good? The rise and fall of my chest was moving so rapidly one would think I was about to have a damn panic attack.

"Can I have you?"

"Ye-"

"Quasie! The first truck here!"

Saved by the good sister! I sighed with relief and went to walk around Eleven, but he grabbed my arm.

"Hold up, we choppin' some business up!"

Eleven bit his bottom lip and backed me into the bathroom that I'd just left from. It's like I snapped into my damn senses when that door was locked behind him.

"Eleven, I can't. I'm... married," I stammered.

His eyes were trained on me and I could tell he was undressing me with them.

"Unfortunately for yo' husband, I'm 'bout to beat the pussy up so good, she ain't gone even drip for him the same."

I stood there feeling like I was bagged into a damn corner because I most definitely was.

"Eleven-"

"So, you telling me no?"

The passion and intensity in his eyes sent shivers down my spine. I hadn't folded for another man in five years. True enough, I knew it was over with for me and my husband, but he'd hurt me so fucking bad I preferred toys over niggas. My focus went on my career completely; a man wasn't even a second thought. I'd sold homes to mostly all of Jagoda Bay's most eligible bachelors, and many, if not, all had tried my hand. The married trick kept me safe from them because no man wanted a woman that was committed to another man. Their egos won't allow it. But Eleven just don't give a fuck.

"No."

"Aite then, come 'ere. You scared?"

I nodded as I stood in place. There was no reason for me to lie. I was terrified. Here I was, behind a locked door with a man I'd just met today, but was having thoughts about him as if the ring on my finger was from him. I was scared of what the hell I was willing to do since the sexual tension was so damn high. I swallowed hard and tried to blink away the uneasiness I was feeling in the pit of my belly, but that didn't seem to work.

Eleven laughed, and that had my knees buckling.

He grabbed me by my waist, making my chest crash into his. Eleven began walking backward and when he sat down on the toilet with the top down, his hand rubbed up the side of my leg and grabbed my ass underneath my dress.

"Pull that dick out."

A sense of urgency drove me, so with shaky hands, I pulled at his belt buckle as he continued to rub my ass. He looked me over seductively, and when I got down to the cloth of his briefs, he lifted up a little so I could pull his pants down. When I had the dick out, I jumped back. A cocky smirk covered his face as his honey eyes lowered.

"*Now* you need to be scared."

Eleven pulled a condom from his pocket and sheathed his impossible ass monster dick with it. Kilo's biggest issue outside of being fine was not only the money but his big ass dick. Every bitch wanted to take a test drive on it, and the nigga let them too. Eleven had skated past Kilo by a hair, and I didn't even think it was possible.

"Eleven-"

He snatched hard at my fifty-dollar underwear and placed the ripped fabric in his pocket.

"Sit on this dick."

Not giving me the chance to do so on my own, he snatched my ass up again and lifted my dress above my head, almost taking my wig with it. He placed my dress on the sink and used one hand to unhook my bra. Now, here I was ass naked sitting on his lap with his long dick up against my stomach. *How in the fuck did we get here?*

"You so fucking sexy. I knew that body was fire up under them threads, but ion know the shit was perfect. Raise up for me, mama."

I hesitantly rose up while gripping his shoulders. At the same time, he removed one of his chains, the biggest one, and placed the cold jewels around my neck. The necklace was cold as hell as it hung in between my surgically enhanced breasts. Two years ago, I'd gotten a boob job as well as lipo, and I was damn happy about it. Seeing the way Eleven's mouth was watering at the sight, I could tell he was enjoying every penny of the nineteen thousand that had been spent on my body.

Eleven's hands gripped my waist as he guided his dick to my opening. I tossed my head back as he fought his way through.

"Ohhhh...Elevennnnnn!"

The way his meaty member had me stuffed, I had to bite my lip and blink back tears. His dick was so wide it had my ass hole spread.

"Fuuuuck! That nigga in trouble fasho'. This pussy gripping like a muhfucka."

Eleven grabbed my neck and began sucking my breast as I slowly bounced in his lap with my head still tilted back. The warmth of his tongue with the mixture of the coolness from his ice felt so damn good.

When his free hand found its way between us, thumbing my clit and heightening the experience, a squeal escaped my lips.

"Yeah, cream on this dick, mama."

What the hell did he say that for? The grip he had on my neck tightened, and just as my walls clenched, he pulled me into him, and covered my lips with his. My thighs shook, and I came so fucking hard my body went limp.

"Shit, girl!"

He began fucking me from the bottom, long and hard.

"Elevennnnn! Oh my God, Elevennnnn!"

His hand that he used to thumb my clit with was now covering my mouth as he smiled at me screaming so loud I'm sure the neighbors heard it, and the damn house was sitting on two acres.

I was still screaming, but now my sounds were just muffled. This man was beating my fucking kitty up like it had run away from home. I'm glad the contractors had the toilet put in good or else we would have fucked the caulk from around it.

"Fuck, I hate I strapped up! I'm 'bout to nut!"

Those words were music to my ears because there wasn't much more of Eleven that I could take. Feeling his nut fill up the condom caused me to cum again right behind him.

"Ohh, and she a squirter."

That million dollar smile had me smiling shyly. The dick was so damn good I couldn't even be embarrassed right now. I was on a damn dick high.

Eleven kissed the side of my mouth and pulled his beast out of me. Once I was standing, I opened my purse that was sitting on top of my dress on the sink and pulled out my wet wipes. Eleven pulled his clothes up, but I kept my eyes on the blue plastic packaging in my hands. When I felt him behind me, I tensed up. His hand grabbed my hip while his other arm was in between my titties and choking my neck again. He forced me to look at him in the mirror as I held the wipe in my hand. Whew, good Lord, this man is unreal. Fine as hell with dick so good I risked my damn license for a few minutes of it.

"I want you, Quasie."

Our eyes were locked through the mirror, his gaze as soft as a caress.

"You just had me."

"Nah, I had that good ass pussy. I want you."

"I'm m-"

"Married? Yeah, you told me that shit a total of four times now. Stop fucking playing with me. Ain't nobody been inside that pussy in a minute. As a matta fact-"

Eleven took my hand and slid my ring and band off.

"Don't put that outdated ass shit back on no mo'. Here."

He dropped it in my purse.

"What's wrong with you?"

"Pussy whipped already. I'm going to New York this weekend. Come fuck with ya boy. Can I have this pussy overlooking the Big Apple?"

I was so fucking turned on like I hadn't been to New York a few times.

"I can't."

"You can. And you will."

"I have a business."

"I know that, But ain't no banks open on the weekends. If you got showings, let yo' team handle that shit."

"Eleven."

"My name sound so good, especially with my dick in you."

"I-"

"Can. All I wanna do is show you a good time, mama. Let a rich nigga take a pretty girl and buy her what she wants. I know you got it, baby, but I got it too, and I want you to use it the fuck up. Can you do that? Can you use me up for dick and bread until you get tired?"

Ohh shit.

Eleven grabbed my wipe and began wiping my pussy without breaking eye contact. He even spread my ass cheeks and got in there. I prayed it wasn't no damn sweat in them. When he was done, he grabbed another wipe and repeated the process, and helped me in my bra and dress.

This man was fire, and the smoldering flames I saw dancing in his eyes told me to run the opposite fucking way. But, like a moth to a fucking flame, I was drawn and would sadly be getting bent over the balcony while rats roamed freely on the ground below us in NYC.

CHAPTER 11

Kymani "Kilo" Lantis

After a long day of securing my paper, having my baby mamas blow down my line, and just now stopping by to check on my kids at both their houses, my fucking head was hurting. I loved the fuck out of my seeds, but the worst decision I could have made was getting their mothers pregnant. They got on my fucking nerves all fucking day, every fucking day. Especially when they saw that I wasn't handing out no daddy dick. God couldn't pay me to stick dick in either of my baby mamas. I wouldn't fuck them bitches if they was the last hoes on earth. On God.

Being gone so long, I left my cousin Big Red in charge of my operations. We weren't blood-related, but my granny was best friend's with his granny, so we grew up together and gave ourselves the cousin title. Big Red was doing so fucking good at the shit that I left him in charge. He handed me a bag when I touched down, so that plus what I'd gotten from Quasie had a nigga super straight. I hadn't bought shit outside of a few outfits and a new whip. Quasie still wasn't fucking with a nigga, but I had hope that she would let me in. So instead of going out to get me a new spot, I was staying with my grandma.

I'd bought her a house right before I went in, and outside of when out-of-town family visited, she lived alone. I had three bedrooms to choose from but had still been finding myself in the basement on the couch most nights, deep in my thoughts. Most niggas that would have come home from jail to a few M's would be ecstatic. Me, on the other hand, was feeling like I was missing something. That something is Quasie. I logged into my old IG account, and her face was the first one that popped up. Scrolling her page and seeing all of her success had me smiling from ear to ear. Being locked up, I'd heard all about how my wife was killing the real estate game in Jagoda Bay, and although I was proud as fuck of her, a part of me was bitter because I wanted her at my side.

"I know you bought it, but make this your last damn night sleeping on my couch. This is a four bedroom house, and three of 'em are vacant. Pick a bed. That damn cousin of yours already be bringing her ass over here and sleeping on my living room couch. I'm 'bout sick of both y'all."

My cheeks met my eyes as I glanced at my grannie. Haddie Lantis is the fucking light of my life. I didn't call her much when I was locked up, but she was the only person to consistently send me letters. My mother had passed a few years before I got locked up, but her and I were never really close. She had a whole other life and children in Cali while I was right here in Jagoda Bay, a grandma's baby. My cousin had also lost her mama during childbirth, so my grandma took on the both of us.

"I don't even be sleep, Gran. I be up watching tv. Catching up on everything I missed out in half a decade."

Haddie humped her shoulders and started dusting invisible dirt on top of the fireplace. My grannie was in excellent shape and health at seventy years old, and I prayed to God he granted her seventy more. I would easily shave off years of my life and give them to her. My mother is the spitting image of her mother, down the slender cheeks and short frame. Thank God I got my height from my pops because my grannie was barely five feet while I stood at 6'3.

"You ain't too much missed out on nothing. Especially nothing in these streets or on that there television."

"Easy for you to say, Gran."

We had access to damn near everything in jail that one did on the streets, but I never wanted to fall into those habits. I wanted to do my time and make it as easy as possible. I didn't have a phone, nor did I fuck them ran through ass CO's. I didn't even watch the fucking TV in the rec room. I occupied my time with reading books and putting plans in motion. I'd been running the streets so fucking long that sitting my ass down in jail gave me time to really reflect on life and just fucking think.

"You off work today? I keep telling you them folk work you too hard. They need to watch their own fucking kids. You raised yours."

My grandma had picked up a job as a nanny to keep her from going crazy after I got locked up. I didn't know anything about the family, but I'd met the two kids she kept, and while the lil boy was bad as fuck, the little girl was too loveable. I found myself buying them shit every time I bought my own damn kids something. My grannie had been caring for them since the girl was born, but the little boy had his sister by a few years. Although the family paid her well, I didn't like that shit. I didn't even allow Ree and Kaisha to drop off KJ and Kyma on my grandma. I mean, every now and again she got them, but on her terms. I don't know why folk automatically felt like grandparents were in-house babysitters. My kids were going to have a rude awakening because when I get old, I'll still be running these fucking streets. I won't be no babysitting ass grandpa, hell nawl.

"Ole hush. I enjoy it. It's better than sitting in this house. I get free meals since they have a chef and free vacations on their private plane. I love it there."

"Who are these people again?" I raised a brow.

"None of your damn business. Now back to what I said. Stay off my couches."

I chuckled as my grandma went to the bar and began wiping it off and put a Hennessey bottle that I'd been sipping back in place.

"When my wife stops acting crazy, I'll be out of your hair."

I can't believe Quasie was real life not fucking with a nigga on no levels. I was trying to give her some space, but my patience was getting thinner by the day. I missed the fuck out of my wife.

"Who? Chile, you may as well play eenie meenie miney moe with them two ghetto hot messes you done procreated with. Quasie is not taking you back. She a damn fool if she do."

My fucking heart dropped from my chest to the soles of my Jordan 7's.

"How you gone say some like that, Gran? You not rooting for us?"

134

She scoffed and twisted the top tight on the Hennessy bottle.

"You want the truth or you want me to pacify your feelings?"

When I didn't give her an answer, she kept going. "Well, I take it that you want the truth. Hell no, I'm not rooting for y'all. I'm rooting for Quasie. If that means her living her life without you, I can live with that."

My grannie had always told me to do better by Quasie, but she never told Quasie to shit on me, not to my knowledge anyway. Maybe the reason my wife is acting funny is because Haddie's ass has been putting a damn battery in her back. Or maybe it was my cousin since she did work for Quasie.

"Don't ball your face up at me. I haven't encouraged that girl to do nothing, and neither has Kassie. I have always minded my business when it came to your marriage. I didn't stop just because you went and had two babies and got yourself locked up. I'm a woman before anything, son. I told you you weren't ready for marriage. Hell, Quasie told you. But you were so scared another man would snatch her that you married her prematurely. I've watched you dog that girl out so bad that it made her physically sick."

"Damn, Gran, you making it seem like I beat on her or mistreated her. I always treated my wife with respect and took care of her."

Gran tossed her rag and propped her hand on her hip while the other rested on the marble.

"No, you didn't put your hands on her. If you had, I would have took you out myself. But physical abuse is just as worse as emotional abuse-"

"I never emotionally abused her-"

"Let me finish! Not in the aspect of tearing her down or belittling her, but every time you laid down with another woman, serving her the same penis you served your wife with, it killed Quasie emotionally. No woman and I mean, no woman, wants to think of their man with another. All the things you did to her, doing to another woman." Haddie shook her head.

"Gran, I never put my mouth on these bi- I mean, broads."

"You think that makes a difference? Sex is sex! Your young generation kills me! Just because you're not pleasing a person orally doesn't mean a damn thing. Y'all try and say, 'oh, because I'm not giving her head as y'all call it or kissing them, it's all good.' Wrong! What good is that when you still serving raw peen? Quasie done became a hot shot realtor, is looking good and running circles around any bitch you've had or ever will have. You messed that up."

I rubbed my hand across my bald head and down my face as the truth of Gran's words stuck me like a knife.

"Not only did you cheat, you went out and made not one but two damn babies! How the hell you give the next random a child before you give your wife one? Then you did the shit twice! No woman on earth deserves to have that type of pain inflicted upon them. You were wrong!

When you got locked up, you didn't even look out for your wife. You bought those heathens houses that they don't even take care of while leaving your wife out here to dry. So, not only did you give them something to throw in her face with the babies, you bought them homes and cars and whatnot, to add insult to injury. I wouldn't have bought their asses a rusted kettle."

"Okay, and? She didn't do nothing for me! Not a letter, not a dime on my books."

Haddie waved me off. "Don't sit up in here and lie in my face. Just cause she broke up with your ass don't mean she broke up with me. That girl tried to pay for ya lawyer, kept money on ya books, and held your money. She even made sure your cousin Kassie was employed, and that shit helped get her off the streets! Some shit you couldn't do. She better than me though, because I would have spent it all, down to the last penny."

"She knew better," I scoffed bitterly.

I did feel bad for not making sure my wife was straight, but my anger was misdirected toward her. I couldn't do shit about it now though.

"You did so much dumb shit; you're a damn fool if you think that lady taking you back. I hope and pray she gets a man that treats her like the Goddess she is. You got a better chance at winning the lottery."

I stood, tired of the conversation because the truth was taking my fucking breath away.

I walked over to my grannie, kissed her temple, and turned to leave.

"Lucky for me, I am the lottery, Gran."

"Sadly for you, she is too."

...

After grannie whooped my ass with the truth, I found myself walking around the neighborhood until I got sick of the white ass neighbors looking out the windows. I hopped in my whip, drove across town, and had been sitting on the side of Quasie's bed for the last three hours.

I heard her heels echoing through the halls and when she stopped, I looked up into the disgust on her face.

"Stop breaking in my house, Kymani!"

Quasie looked good as fuck in a blue jean jumpsuit that accentuated her curves. On her pretty ass toes were a pair of gold pumps, and her normal short bob was curly now. Just gazing at my wife had my chest tight. She was and is the prettiest woman I'd ever had the fucking pleasure of laying eyes on and dick in. Quasie never had bad days. Dressing up was a fucking sport for her, and she was the MVP of that shit. Grams was right; only a dumb ass nigga would fuck up with Quasie. I was that dumb ass nigga. Even sitting here in her home that looked like some next Level HGTV type shit had me fucked up because she was living better than I could imagine, and she was doing that shit without me.

"I swear to God I hate yo' ass got out," she spoke in an annoyed ass tone.

She walked into her closet, and from where I was sitting I could see a glimpse, and that shit looked like a damn designer store. A few minutes after going in, Quasie walked out barefoot and void of her jewelry. Once she grabbed her gold MacBook from her light wood dresser, she opened it and began typing with one hand while holding it with the other.

I had every intention on coming here to beg for her forgiveness until she let that jail shit slip from her lips. Quasie was just begging for a nigga to turn up on her ass.

"So what you saying is, you was happy a nigga went to jail? You know what the fuck I went through behind them walls? You really ain't gone forgive me?" my jaws clenched as I gave her ass a look that could knock her the fuck out.

"You know what the fuck I went through when yo' ass was free? Slanging dick to every bitch that bats a faux lash at you? You damn right I was happy yo' ass was in jail. Jail meant my dick was put up! I was fucking EXHILARATED! You want me to forgive you? Hunh?"

She removed her eyes from her laptop and placed them on me.

"Mane, you on that bullshit"

"No. Answer me! You really want me to forgive you?"

"Ain't that why I'm here?"

"Honestly, I don't know why the fuck you here because you damn sure not welcomed. It's giving stalker, but okay, cool. I can forgive you only if I can do to you what you did to me. EVERYTHING. I do that, and all is forgiven."

"What?"

"As a matter fact, I already got the perfect candidate. He's young, fine, rich, and got a big d-"

"Yeah, let me get the fuck up outta here before I catch another murder charge."

I stood ready to leave her fucking house before I was back in federal prison. This was Quasie and I's problem. She couldn't let the hurt go for five minutes in order to have a conversation with a nigga. All she did was throw insults and push every fucking button I have.

"Yeah, you do that, Kilo. Just remember you're my ex and I done exed your ass out of my life a long fucking time ago. But when you ready for me to forgive you for real, get at me. 'Cuz ole boy damn sure ready for me to bust a move."

Licking my lips to stifle my anger, I chuckled at her sarcasm. It took me about seven steps to be face-to-face with Quasie, and her expression never wavered. *Hate.* She looked at a nigga with so much fucking hate that if I didn't think she forgave me before, I knew now. The same Quasie that used to go to war behind a nigga was ready to go to war against a nigga. There used to be so much fucking love radiating from her pores anytime I was near. Now, I couldn't feel shit but coldness.

"So you really gone throw all those years away because I had kids?"

Quasie shook her head. "You just don't fucking get it, Kymani. But since that's what you want to hear, yes nigga. I did. Either you smoking the crack you sell or you can't comprehend. I told you this the last time you popped up unannounced."

A laugh escaped my lips but wasn't shit funny.

"You know what? You's a stuck up, lonely ass, miserable ass female."

Quasie was drawn back by my insults, but I didn't give a fuck.

"You make all this fucking money, yet you still walking around this bitch with a chip on your shoulder about your husband stepping out on you. A real boss ass bitch would have either forgiven her nigga or moved the fuck on. You're supposed to be with a nigga that's shitting on my whole life. Yet, here you go still sporting a tarnished ass ring I put on yo' finger! You think yo' shit don't stank when in reality, you the fucking daughter of a side bitch. No matter how many fucking followers you got, how many fucking houses you sell, this crack slanging ass street nigga got yo' ass in a chokehold." Spit hit the back of her laptop as I hit her ass with straight fucking facts.

Quasie took a step back and smiled.

"Don't speak on my fucking mama. The same mama that's been keeping your ass leveled-headed while you were behind those walls. You can't get mad because those BeBe's kids aren't mine. I don't want you. I don't want them. Stay the fuck away from me. That chokehold was released forty eight hours ago, boo. You two days too late. Go get Keke and ReRe. Good luck with them bitches making you miserable the rest of yo' life. Baby mama drama don't go with my aesthetics."

With the slap of my hand, her fucking computer went crashing to the floor, and since she didn't have carpet in here, it broke in half.

"Get the fuck out!"

"Gladly! With yo' uptight miserable ass."

I stepped right over the pieces of what used to be her computer and took my time walking out of a home that should have been half mine. I had to get the fuck away from my estranged ass wife before she had me away from my kids again. I couldn't afford that because one thing for sure, her ass damn sure didn't give a fuck if they ate or starved. *Fuck Quasie.*

CHAPTER 12

Brock "Baguette" Cherman

"**B**rock, in order to get you through your grieving, you have to give me more than one word answers."

Sitting slouched on the plush grey velvet couch, my eyes moved from that of Ella Dorsewood's to the tan silk blouse resting on her shoulders, down to the chocolate skirt hugging her curves. Her hair was what I called the jazzy lady style. The one where they went to the beauty shop and got rollers put in and came out looking all silky and flowy. I could smell vanilla permeating off her skin, and it added in with the lavender fumes igniting from the candle on her desk. Ella was easy on the eyes even as a BBW. Had she been fifteen years younger and came across my radar when I wasn't shit, I would have for sure took her ass down. No matter how good she looked, the scowl on my face hadn't moved. She didn't seem to be fazed by the shit though.

This was my third session with Ella. After the first time, I swore I wasn't coming back. Then, I told Tuscany I'd come, so I owed it to her for a follow-up. The second session wasn't as bad as the first one. Or should I say, it wasn't as awkward as the fucking first one. Maybe because I knew what to expect the second time around. After the second session, I didn't have a dream about my daughter for a week, so here I was at the third session.

"Truth be told, this shit uncomfortable as a muthafucka for a nigga. The only women I've let get in my business besides the woman that birthed me is my woman and before her, the mother of my child."

Ella nodded and scribbled something in her grey book that had silver flowers engraved in it.

"I understand how venting to a person, or in this case, a woman you don't know can be uncomfortable, so how about this."

Ella placed her notepad down on the small end table beside the accent chair she'd been planted in for the last ten minutes and placed her undivided attention on me. During our first two sessions, she asked me a few things about my daughter and my life. All of my answers had been short. Ella came with a thousand dollar an hour price tag that I almost had my bank dispute until the dreams stopped.

"I want you to forget I'm a counselor. I'm your ex, the mother of your late child. I'm Aphrodite. I want you to narrate the day she went into labor. Speak it as if you're the author and Aphrodite is reading the novel."

I licked my bottom lip, rubbed my palms down the front of my jeans, and exhaled. I didn't want to talk about this shit. I didn't want to remanence. But, for the sake of my fucking sanity, for the sake of my woman, I had to try. I had to let this shit out and try to gain knowledge as to how I could deal with this shit.

"Aite....

"Ummmmm, shiiiit! Fuuuuck, Baguette!"

Using my thumbs, I spread her ass cheeks apart since my nails were already buried in the flesh of her hips. Seeing the rubber covered in her juices had my dick growing a few more inches longer.

"Ohhhh damn, baby! You fuck me sooo good!"

Her essence began spitting out of her, dropping down to my balls that were pounding against her pussy, and that shit felt too good. My phone vibrated in my pocket for the hundredth damn time, but being that I had three, I didn't know if it was personal or business. And the way this pussy is hitting, I really don't give a fuck.

"Shit! Come catch this nut. Good pussy ass."

I snatched out of her, slapped her ass, and watched in amazement as she used her hands that housed long ass ghetto nails to pull the condom off and expand her throat so that I could glide in with ease. Tears burned her eyes as I emptied the fucking clip down her throat.

Once she sucked me for every last drop, I used the towel she'd soaped and wiped my dick and hairs off before pulling my briefs and joggers back up.

"You gone come through tomorrow?"

Without giving her my attention, I pulled my business phone from my pocket and scrolled the call log. In ten fucking minutes, I'd missed more money than most folk made in six months. I called myself diving in pussy during the afternoon since my mornings and nights were busy, but today, niggas needed to re up after lunch hour seemed like.

"I'ma call you."

I pulled out my knot, peeled of five hundreds and tossed them on the bed. I could hear her fucking smile from across the damn room, but she knew I always broke her fine ass off. I was getting too much money not to be paying for my nuts. A couple hundred ain't gone make or break me, and paying for it helped me skip past all the extra shit. The courting, the lying, the finessing. I didn't have time for none of that. Give me a nut, and ya light bill or car not paid for the month. Give me several nuts, then you just might get hair, nails, and mall fare on top of ya bills getting paid. If you don't run ya fucking mouth, a bag it is. Not no Chanel or no shit like that, but I'll fuck with 'em on a Gucci.

Since my business here was done, I snatched my pistol from the night-stand, and placed the hood of my hoodie on my head. Ole girl lives on the north side of Jagoda Bay, and her neighbors mostly consisted of old mutha-fuckas since she inherited the house from her grandparents. I didn't know too much about her, but one of the many times when she was supposed to have a mouth full of dick, she called herself trying to give me her life story. I only remembered because I was wondering with the kitchen looked like some shit straight out of the fifties.

Once I was in my whip with one eye on the road and the other in my phone, I scrolled through the rest of my mist calls, trying to prioritize who I was going to serve first. I'd already scratched three muthafuckas off my list because I knew their impatient asses had moved on to the next. Just as I'd made up who I was about to pull up on, my phone rang in my hand.

"Fuck you keep calling me for, Daphne?" I answered with a mug on my face.

Daphne's fine ass was the last fucking straw that broke the fucking camel's back when it came to my relationship. My folks kept telling me I couldn't place the blame on her because I shouldn't have given her the dick, but fuck all that. She was on so much messy ass social media shit, putting up slick pictures and shit of a nigga knowing my girl was lurking on her pages since she'd heard through the soggy ass Jagoda Bay grapevine that I'd been fucking on Daphne. The shit was true, but the fact that Daphne continued to put our business out and had my bitch leaving my ass for good, granted her a spot on my opp list.

"Damn, a bitch gotta call you a billion times just for you to fucking answer the phone?"

I couldn't stand this bitch, but my dick bricked up at the sound of her sultry ass voice. Daphne messy as fuck, but the pussy is immaculate. The dick sucking is out of this fucking world. Not only that, she knows how to fucking cater to a street nigga. After a long day of hustling, instead of taking my ass home, I would find my ass at Daphne's doorstep. She would answer the door in some sexy ass lingerie, have blunts rolled, and dinner ready. Before she got on her bullshit, she was fasho' a nigga's peace, and that shit had me doing more for her and with her.

I found myself taking her ass out of town just so she could blow the malls down and we could be affectionate all in public without a muthafucka reporting back. I was smitten with her light bright ass. A nigga was dead ass wrong for letting shit get so far with Daphne, but I let her fat ass, slim waist, and pretty face take me clean off. It's not like my girl ugly or had slaw pussy. She's actually killing Daphne on her worst fucking day and the only woman that can fuck me into a coma.

The reason I was pushed over to Daphne was because Aphrodite and I had been together since we were fucking kids. Even though I loved her more than life, I did a whole lot of fucked up shit to her. Cheating being the whole lot of fucked up shit. Getting money too young can give a nigga the big head. I was having my way still having my way, but that shouldn't have given me the right to shit on my bitch. I did though, and instead of loving on me, Aphrodite was going upside my damn head and nagging every chance she got.

Daphne was the nail in the coffin for us. All them other bitches I'd cheated on her with didn't go so far as blasting it on social media. Aphrodite left my ass after a year of Daphne antagonizing her, and while I tried to force her ass to stay, my mama sat me down and let me know I had no one to blame but my damn self. All the shopping trips, raw dick, pussy eating, and wifey privileges I'd given Daphne made her feel like she had one up on Aphrodite. I had to eat that shit.

Aphrodite left a nigga and didn't look the fuck back. I was sick as a dog behind that shit. Balled up and cried like a fucking baby at my mama's feet. I was begging her to help me figure out a way to get her back. I hadn't cried since elementary but Aphrodite leaving me had a nigga throwed the fuck off. For a month, I couldn't fucking eat, sleep, or shit. All I did was make my money, blow Aphrodite's phone up, and try to figure out where the fuck she'd moved. I was on my parent's couch because being at home was too fucking painful. Her smell was every fucking where. That shit was suffocating a nigga.

Six weeks after she'd left my ass, she popped up over my folks' house. Seeing her for the first time in six weeks had me kicking my own ass. Aphrodite's skin was fucking glowing. Baddest bitch in Jagoda Bay belonged to me, and I lost her ass because I let the next bitch shit on her. Even though Aphrodite looked pretty as fuck in her sun dress and naturally curly bush on her head, her eyes told me everything I needed to know. This wasn't a rekindle visit. Eyes that once held so much life and love was void. Cold. Expressionless. Knowing that I'd caused her so much hurt and fucking pain gave me the will to accept that she was done with my ass.

That day, Aphrodite told me and my parents she was pregnant and keeping it. She made it clear that we were not together, nor getting back together. Although I wanted her, I respected her, but was present every day of the pregnancy. I was there to hold her hair behind her face as she threw up her insides. I was there to feel my baby's first kick. I was there when the doctor told us we were having a girl, and I was there serving dick up when Aphrodite's hormones had her craving sex. Best fucking pussy I'd ever had, on God.

No matter how much I sucked and fucked her, she kept her stance. The last two months of the pregnancy though, I'd made my way back in Daphne's bed. And the moment Aphrodite caught wind of that shit, the pussy privileges were revoked again. So, Daphne on my fucking line again when I cut her ass off weeks ago had me ready to pull up and smack the shit out of her messy ass.

"Damn right, Ion fuck with you, G."

I'd pulled into the neighborhood of my serve but was stopped due to children crossing and shit since school had just let out. Thinking about my baby girl one day going to school had a nigga smiling when I should still be frowned up since this broad was still on my line.

"Nigga, please. You love me. You just mad right now."

"Fuck off my phone. Daphne." That shit struck a nerve because I really used to tell this bitch I loved her. When in reality, I just loved the idea of her. Only woman I love outside of my creator and family is Aphrodite.

"I loved the way you ate my dick. That's it."

"Just like I love when you suck the cum out of this pussy. But I ain't call you to argue. We both know you'll be back. Anyway, when you start fucking on Fee?"

I pulled the phone from my face and looked at it. How the fuck she knew I fucked Fee? Especially since I'd just been in her bed not even fifteen minutes ago.

"Ain't nobody-"

"Save the lie for yo' baby mama, nigga."

"Daphne, stop calling my phone before I hurt yo' fucking feelings, real talk. Keep Aphrodite's name out yo' fucking mouth. You worrying about the wrong shit," I spat. I wanted to fire up a blunt so bad to calm my damn nerves, but I was riding dirty. Soon as I got all this shit off, I had to smoke and go rub Aphrodite's belly and feel my daughter kick.

"No really, nigga. Save the lie for yo' babymama. She in labor. I just got off, but I saw her walking in bent over and in pain. Congratulations, baby. Can't wait to meet my stepdaughter and-"

I hung up on Daphne and went straight to my call log and, at the same time I did a 180 in the middle of the street. The crossing guard was cursing my ass out, but I didn't give a fuck.

126 MISSED CALLS -MY BABY

"Fuuuuuuck!"

Sweat beaded on my forehead and broke out on my back as I swallowed hard, listening to Aphrodite's phone ring with no answer. I hung up and called again. I repeated the process seven more times before a video came through. It was from Daphne, and seeing the video her ass snuck of my baby doubled over in pain as she screamed for help, had me pressing the Challenger to its limit. I should report this bitch to HIPPA, but she got a pass for telling me Aphrodite not only was in labor but at the hospital she worked at. We had plans to deliver at Jagoda One, but Central was closest to Aphrodite's house. She liked Jagoda Once better because it's private and newer. Plus, her OBGYN delivered there as well.

Luckily, I was only ten minutes out, but I continued to ring her line. I called until I got to the hospital. Once I was parked in the handicapped, I hopped out, still with the phone to my ear. Busting through the emergency doors, I saw that the waiting room was packed with men, women, and children. The stench of throw up, piss, and sickness permeated the air. I hated county ass hospitals. I walked up to the counter and noticed another junt I'd knocked down working it.

"Where the fuck you been, nigga? Aphrodite is here in labor!" Gia scolded me.

Gia was this cool lil' Italian chick that I rocked with. Unlike Daphne, she knew her fucking role, but she cut a nigga off once she got married. It was no hard feelings on my part because she was just a pretty fuck to me.

"Fuuuck! I know. What room, Gia?"

Gia shook her head as she typed on the computer. When she turned her back, I was about to curse her ass out until she came back and snapped a band around my wrist.

"She's on the other side of the hospital, so you have to go through the double doors, make a left and walk straight down the hall. Bust another left, and you'll see a set of elevators. Take it up to the eighth floor. Labor and delivery-"

I sprinted off, repeating her directions in my head.

"She's still in labor. Hurry up! Room 800!"

I heard Gia yell at my back just as I got through the double doors. It took longer than I expected to get to the damn elevators. Gia didn't tell me the long ass hall walks you to a whole other building. After getting off the elevator, I ran fast as I could to room 800, and when I bust in the room, my heart was in the pit of my ass.

"Aphrodite, baby. I'm so fucking sorry!"

Aphrodite was in her hospital gown with a doctor and a nurse on the side of her.

"Ummmmmm."

"She's having another contraction. Are you dad? Here come take her hand."

I took the nurse's place and let Aphrodite squeeze my hand. Her face was damp and covered in sweat and her eyes were closed. She hadn't even opened them when I walked in.

"I'm sorry, baby. You doing good. What can I do? Can I help?"

"Ahhhhh, fuuuuuck!"

Aphrodite screamed loud as fuck and was squeezing the shit out of my hand. I see why the nurse handed her ass off.

The doctor was unfazed by her screams as he looked over papers that were coming out of the machine.

"Just breathe, baby. Breathe. I know it hurts, but you about to meet our pretty ass daughter soon. Y'all will be spending all daddy's money dressing alike and shit. Just focus on that."

Aphrodite let up on my hand but kept her eyes closed. Her contraction must was over. I'd watched a few live births on YouTube, so I knew a few of the terminologies, but this shit was still all new to me. I wasn't prepared to see the woman whom I love more than life look as if she was on her deathbed.

"She can't have shit for pain?" I snapped at the white fat doctor as the heavy set Hispanic nurse went to the opposite of the bed and rubbed Aphrodite's head. She'd gone and got individual braids a few days ago in preparation for her due date but our daughter still had two weeks to bake.

"Her blood pressure is spiked high, and the baby's heartbeat keeps dropping. No, she can not have anything for pain." This muthafuckin' doctor had the nerve to snap.

"Bitch ass-"

"Ohhhh fuuuuuck! It hurt's so baaaaad! Oh my God, please get her! Get her out of me!"

"Okay, well y'all need to prep her for a c-section, don't it? Who the fuck is you anyway? You not her doctor!"

I sized this Santa Claus-looking muthafucka up. His white coat was dingy as fuck, and he wreaked of cigarettes. This nigga was the last damn person I wanted to deliver my child.

"Dr. Phine is on vacation and not set to come back 'til the end of the week. We reached out, and he's willing to end his trip, but his flight will take at least a day. She was fine when she came in, but all of a sudden, her stress levels caused her blood pressure to spike. She's crowning. It's time to push. "

"Fuuuuck!"

I didn't want her doctor to deliver the baby either, but he was better than this nigga. When Aphrodite brought me to her first appointment, and I saw her damn doctor that looked more like an NBA superstar, I almost lost my shit. But, the nigga was smart and came from a doctor. Since he knew his shit and was one of the best in the city, I let her rock. We knew he was going on vacation the entire pregnancy, but according to the calculations, we were hoping the nigga would be delivering the baby with a tan.

"Baby, you gotta push with this next contraction. You hear me?"

Aphrodite nodded her head as the doctor and the nurse pulled the bed apart and propped her legs open.

"Okay, here we go. Push in your chest and not in your face."

Aphrodite sat up and buried her chin in her chest as she pushed.

"One..two..three..four...five...doing amazing! Her head is out! So much hair.. seven...eight-"

"Ahhhhhhhhh! Fuuuuuuck Help me, Brock!"

Tears burned my eyes, knowing there was nothing I could do. I couldn't imagine pushing a fucking baby out. Women are amazing.

"Ohh.. keep going, mama! Keep going. Don't stop!"

I was too scared to look, so I kept my eyes on Aphrodite instead. She was pushing so hard, her face was red.

"She's out."

No cries filled the room, and an eerie silence took over. Aphrodite still had her eyes shut, but her head was now to the ceiling as tears spilled down her plump cheeks.

"Wh...wh...wh...Hold up! Where y'all taking her? Fuck she not crying for?"

The nurse ran over to the steel cradle that was posted near the door. I could see my daughter in her arms, bloody and small as fuck, but she wasn't moving.

The doctor jumped in front of me, still with blood on his gloves.

"Please go be with Aphrodite. I just delivered the after birth, and she didn't tear. Let us do our job."

"Nigga-"

"Brock. Please..."

I gave the doctor one last look before rushing to be at Aphrodite's side.

Just as the doctor and nurse pushed my baby out the room, two other nurses came in and began cleaning Aphrodite up.

The scene of what just happened made the back of my neck tingle as panic clawed at my throat.

"What.. what the fuck just happened?" I was trying to wrap my mind around this shit, but I was completely fucking stuck.

"What are they doing with her? What are they doing with my fucking baby?"

"The cord was wrapped around her neck, so she came out not breathing. The doctors are doing all they can for her."

One of the two Hispanic nurses answered. Fuck is up with all these damn Mexicans?

"How the fuck you know? You just walked in!"

The nurse didn't respond as they continued to clean Aphrodite up and put the bed back together. Once they were gone, Aphrodite finally spoke up.

"I woke up from my nap, and you were gone so I went to get me some tacos. It started raining so I ate in. When I got home, I tried laying down and was feeling pain. I called you, but you didn't answer. I shook it off, thinking it was Braxton Hicks, but when my water broke, I drove myself here. The whole time, I kept calling you. Over and Over. Over and Over. No answer. I get here, your bitch is at the reception desk. Then I turn my back, another one of your bitches is recording me. No biggie though. I ignored them hoes and got to a room. I can't even focus on shit the doctors saying because I'm calling you. I must've called yo' ass two hundred fucking times. Then, before I could call two hundred and one times, I get a DM. A bitch is live while being fucked. Guess who's doing the fucking? The father of my fucking daughter!"

Aphrodite's eyes were now open and bloodshot red. I looked off and grabbed the back of my neck as I stood, suppressing a wave of nausea.

"Aphrodite-"

"No, Brock! I pushed out a dead fucking baby because my blood pressure went through the fucking roof! I did this! No fuck that! You did this! My fucking baby is dead! A baby I carried for eight months is dead!" Spit flew from her mouth as she screamed.

The whole world seemed to be moving in slow motion. I felt like I was standing in a dream world- a horrific, nightmarish dream world.

"Why...why the fuck would you say that? Our daughter ain't no fucking dead!" I choked out. Spasms racked my muscles until it seemed my bones would snap. No one had touched me, nor had I given birth, but I was in fucking agony.

I jetted out of the room and ran right into the doctor. A look of sadness covered his face, and I knew then, my daughter had died.

After that, I went numb. A few hours after she'd been born, they brought her to us. She was so fucking tiny. She didn't even feel real. Her eyes were closed, her lips sealed, and she was dressed in the pink crotched outfit Aphrodite had packed. Seeing her howl in pain as she held our daughter had a nigga feeling lower than life. I'd been fucking another bitch while Aphrodite needed me. Had she not seen the video of me fucking another bitch, my baby would be right here today.

We called our parents up to say their goodbyes. They took pics of Athena and was just as heartbroken as us. The grief was so thick it suffocated me. Watching Aphrodite at her lowest., The lowest she'd ever been in her life had me feeling like a fuck nigga. I knew the relationship was done. There was no coming back from what I'd done. I knew that. I also knew I'd done her wrong, so I had to make it right.

"And that's why I put her on a fucking pedestal. Aphrodite will never have to come second to no bitch on this earth!"

Salty tears entered my mouth as I banged my chest.

"I killed my daughter! I'm supposed to be at daddy-daughter dances. I 'posed to be nursing scraped knees, collecting teeth for the tooth fairy, shopping in girly ass sections, and shit!

Ion got that! Aphrodite don't got that! It's all because of what? Another bitch? I miss my daughter! I need my daughter! Tuscany saying she don't want kids but guess what? I don't give a fuck! I don't want them bitches either since I can't have my fucking Athena! I did this! I fucked up! I gotta live with this fucking pain. Nobody knows what this shit feels like except me and Aphrodite!"

The counselor removed her glasses and used her napkin to dab at her tears.

"I don't give a fuck! I fucked that girl's life up! And still, to this fucking day, she love a nigga. She let me lay all my fucking problems at her feet, when in reality she is supposed to hate a nigga! I took so fucking much away from Aphrodite! I gotta...I gotta make sure she gets the best of everything. Not even on no sexual type shit because we passed that. We beyond that! I love Tuscany with everything in me but ain't a bitch on this earth harder than my baby mama. If that means I gotta take care of her 'til my dying days, I will. Cars, houses, vacations, whatever! She can get it! I'll give that lady my last, on God! I fucked up!"

I'd never been an emotional or vulnerable nigga. I was raised with so much fucking love in a two-parent household, but being in the streets turned my heart cold. Aphrodite thawed it out anytime I was in her presence, but when I was in them streets, it was right back on Frozen. Losing my baby turned me into fucking mulch. Here I was crying in front of a fucking stranger. I was so sick of crying about this, but I didn't know what the fuck else to do. I was stuck. Stuck in a dark ass room with no fucking way out. The sounds of my baby girl calling my name have me constantly running into a brick wall to find her. That's how the fuck I feel.

Ella placed her hand on top of mine.

"This is me speaking as a woman. Not as a Psychiatrist. I understand your pain. I feel your pain. You don't have to forget your daughter. But, you and this relationship with Aphrodite. Be her friend. I think that's amazing that you all can co-exist with each other. However, in order to make peace with your daughter's passing, you have to make peace with what was. Aphrodite isn't your assignment. She's your ex turned friend. Your family. Not a project that you have to handle with care and nourish. In order to accept the loss of your child, you must grieve the relationship you once had with Aphrodite."

I heard what Ella was saying, but I wasn't hearing her. People didn't understand us and that was okay. I knew one thing though, this was going to be my last fucking session.

CHAPTER 13

Aphrodite "Ditey" "Pretty Pretty" "AP" Greer

A cold glass of Giulia wine did nothing to calm my nerves, but it did take the edge off a little. Brent Fiyaz played from the Beat speaker as I looked down at the two outfit choices I had out. One was a ruffle mini dress with layered bell sleeves, and a corset bodice with a deep v-cut. It was sexy and soft, but the flowers on it gave it a girly feel to it. The second dress I was calling the mummy. It had a crochet look to it, but it's a long sleeved bodycon dress. What makes the dress unique and sexy is the fact that it looks almost crotchet all over. In a few areas, it was completely showing skin. I would have to wear an ivory bra and thong. Although I loved it and couldn't wait to put it up on my website because I knew it would sell out, I didn't want this man to be thinking I was on my hoe shit.

I hadn't been on a date in five years. Really almost six. When Baguette and I used to go out, it was mainly because his ass was trying to make up. There was no thoughts, no just because, no I just want to date you because I love you. Now here I was about to go on a date with a man who I shouldn't even be given a second glance. I blame his mama and daddy though. Goal's parents created something magical when they fucked around and conceived him. With a demeanor, looks, and stature like his, I'm sure no one said no to Goal. Hell, look at my dry ass, standing ass naked in front of the bed with a glass of my favorite wine in my hand, debating on an outfit.

Not sure if it was the wine of me really knowing when I put this outfit on, not only was I going to make an impression ,but I was guarantee to sell all one hundred and twenty pieces I'd ordered. Since I now had a fucking two thousand dollar mortgage, I'd increased the quantity. I needed all the money I could get. While I wasn't hurting and had a nice stash, if I wanted to not dip in my savings, I needed to work my ass off. Plus, I'd had a meeting with the interior decorator a few weeks ago, and with the one hundred and nineteen thousand dollar price tag she came with, I needed to hustle. She'd met me at the property and did a walk through. That was my third time in the house, and I hadn't been back. The second time was the closing that only my mama and Quasie were present for, and I was in sweats.

Goddess Wears also had seen a high increase of sales lately. Don't get me wrong, I sold out every single week, but usually when I sold out, I would put a few pre-orders out just to see how many more of that item I could sell before ordering more. My clothes came straight from the manufacturer overseas, and shipping was high as fuck. For the last few weeks, I'd been selling out of not only the drops, but the pre-orders as well. I wasn't complaining, but my mama was because her ass had been the one helping package and distribute since my baby cousin Litty hadn't been feeling well. Mama got paid good too, but she still fussed.

After drinking the rest of the wine, I moisturized my body with body butter and then went over it with Baccarat body glitter. I loved this stuff and had shamelessly bought two more bottles for the summer before it sold out again. Most of the shit I bought was used for my business, so things like body oil went fast. When I say I dress my pieces up like I'm really about to head out the door, I mean that. Sometimes I do get ready with me on IG and Tik Tok; with that, they love to see what moisturizers and fragrances I used. Most of the time, I would take that shit right off after I had my content and hit the couch with a glass of wine.

Once my body was glowing, I clamped on an ivory bra that had the girls sitting nicely and a matching thong. My doorbell sounded just as I was about to step in my dress, so I turned to look at the phone that was on my dresser. Typing in my passcode, I went to the Ring app and rolled my eyes at who was on the other side of my door.

Instead of talking through the speaker, I took my time getting my dress up my hips. I didn't want to pull it over my head because I didn't want to smear this one hundred and fifty dollar makeup I had done, and my braids were still tender. Since the next few weeks, I had vacation pieces and dresses that could be worn for Mother's Day, I swapped out the tape-ins and booked braids. These shits took all damn day since I had them extra small, but they were so worth it. For the curly pieces sprouting from the braids, I used human hair to ensure it wouldn't tangle on me. My lashes were freshly filled, and once I added my jewelry and shoes, I was going to be good to go.

Remembering I had an unwanted guest at the door, I made sure my dress was in place, tossed my braids behind my back, and headed to the door.

Snatching the door open without looking since I already knew who it was, I turned back on my heels so that I could finish getting dressed.

"Aw shit, I should have stayed where the fuck I was at. I didn't know you was doing a fucking drop. Ion got time to be the damn cameraman."

I made it back to my room with Baguette hot on my heels. Stopping at my dresser, I picked up the gold earrings I'd gotten from TJ Maxx and laced them in my ear.

"That's a swimsuit cover up, ain't it?"

Once my earrings were in, I fastened my gold Rolex on my arm and slid my feet in my Bottega pumps.

"For your information, this is a dress, and I'm not doing a drop today. I'm going on a date, but since you're here, you can definitely take my pics."

Once my shoes were fastened, I walked over to the floor length mirror to admire myself. I looked damn good and knew I was going to have to order at least four hundred more of these damn dresses.

"Fuck you and Goal going? To the beach?"

"Uh no, nigga. I don't know where we going. Speaking of Goal though-"

I turned to face Baguette, who was sitting on the side of my bed, still looking at my damn outfit.

"How do you feel about us going out? I mean, I know y'all hang out and stuff, and you know I'm not on none of that Daphne shit. I'm not trying to run through the whole clique. Really I was just chilling, but this dude won't leave me the hell alone. If you not comfortable-"

Baguette offered me a lazy smile.

"Ain't no issues on my end. Goal a good dude. We grown. You grown. If you like him, go for it. I think y'all a good look. Real shit."

Hearing Baguette give his blessings eased all of my tension and anxiety. I know I shouldn't care what he thought, but I didn't want to disrespect him or make him uncomfortable. Baguette had done a lot of shit, but to my knowledge, he'd never fucked anyone close to me. I didn't want to do the same shit to him. I had too much respect for him and our friendship as a whole.

Although Baguette had given me his blessing, there was some other shit on his mind. I had been dodging his calls still, and I knew he was going to pull up soon. Usually, he fussed at me about not looking out the peephole first before opening the door and went straight to the kitchen. He had this faraway look in his eyes, and I could feel how off his energy was.

Instead of trying to jump on the bed beside him, I leaned against the dresser in front of him.

"What's wrong, Brock?"

He chuckled and looked off.

"That obvious, hunh?"

Baguette unzipped his teal Nike tech jacket, revealing a wife beater. On his feet were a pair of cream navy, teal, and orange Nike dunks that I was going to order as soon as I got back home.

"Yeap, I know you better than you know yourself. What's going on?"

I'd hoped like hell he wasn't here to cry about the fact that Tuscany didn't want children. I wished my girl would reconsider because I feel like every woman should experience pregnancy at least once, but he had to respect the fact that the girl didn't want a kid. Hell, if I would have raised kids all my damn life, I wouldn't want any either.

"How you feel about Tuscany throwing the housewarming on Athena's birthday?"

"I mean, it's cool with me. She said something about a balloon or dove release," I answered Baguette's question with a shrug. I was cool as a cucumber on the outside, but internally, I was sweating, and my heart raced. Not tonight. I didn't need thoughts of Athena plaguing me. I wanted to have a good time and not be sulking in sorrow. This week had been tough, and I had to take a few melatonin to get to sleep. Today, I woke up in good spirits, and I wanted to stay that way. But of course, I couldn't tell Baguette that.

"How the hell you having a housewarming in a few weeks but you haven't packed a sock yet?"

Baguette looked around and shook his head. Hell, I was wondering the same damn thing myself.

"I miss her. How the fuck can I miss her this much, and I didn't even get to know her?"

Baguette dropped his head just as his eyes began to water. I'd never seen this man cry before, and the shit had my fanning my face and blinking away my own tears.

"Brock, I know I don't act like it, but you know the Leo in me have me trying to face everything with my chest out. But the truth is, I miss my baby every day. Every fucking day. It's okay to miss her, and I think it's just getting the best of us because her birthday is a few weeks away. Losing my baby was the worst thing that has ever fucking happened to me, but it also made me look at life differently."

Baguette kept his eyes closed as he pinched his nose.

"I just...some shit don't feel right. Some shit just don't feel right."

I looked at Baguette with a confused expression. I wanted to console him, but again, the Leo in me almost didn't know what the fuck to do for him.

"Brock, what about the counselor?"

"Mane, fuck the counselor!" Baguette yelled as he lifted his head with red eyes.

"Some shit just don't feel right! Like when I go to her fucking grave, it's like I'm talking to my damn self. The shit just feels...empty! I think back to that day at the hospital, and so much shit had went wrong. It was like that shit was a planned fucked up ass day. We'd been doing so good. You did everything right. Even yo' pretty boy ass doctor was adamant the baby wouldn't come while he was on vacation."

I'd definitely done everything right. I didn't stress much during my pregnancy, and I ate by the book. However, I started feeling funny midday, and the pain was too damn intense to drive. I had to go to the nearest hospital, and from there, shit just went from bad to worse.

"Brock, you do know sometimes shit just...happens. There is no explanation. As bad as we wanted her here, she wasn't meant to be here. We have to learn to live to be okay with that."

Baguette shook his head.

"You not hearing me. Some shit not right, Aphrodite. You know my intuition is what kept a nigga out the way for so long. Ion know why this bitch done started speaking out almost five years later, but some shit not adding up. I think I seen-"

My phone rang, and Goal's name plastered across the screen. He saved his shit on my phone the night we chilled by the lake, and added a contact picture of him gripping my ass as I straddled him.

I tried snatching it up before Baguette could see the pic, but seeing the smirk on his face, let me know he'd seen it.

"Go enjoy ya'self. I'ma chill here for a bit, if that's cool."

Instead of answering the phone, I waited for it to stop ringing so I could send him a text. He was due to pick me up, and I knew he wasn't outside because the Ring didn't alert me.

"He can wait. You said you seen who?"

Baguette gave me another onceover before reaching out and pinching my stomach.

"Nothing. You look good. I'm happy you getting out and shit. You deserve some happiness."

"I appreciate that. I still don't feel ready, but I'ma give it a try. It's only one date."

The Ring camera alerted me that there was motion at the front door, so I grabbed the bag that matched my heels.

"You sure you good? I can stay with you if you need me to. I don't mind. We can cry together and eat ice cream all night."

Brock smiled, "Nah, I'ma be good. I just need a minute. Go have fun. Tell that nigga to strap up. Ion need him getting my baby mama pregnant and shit."

I hit Baguette on the chest and he stood as he dodged my lick too late.

Baguette grabbed me in a hug, causing me to inhale his masculine scent.

"I love you, kid. Forever."

"I love you too, Baguette. Forever."

He released me and followed me to the door. I didn't think about how it would look with Baguette being at my house while Goal picked me up. Now since Goal was outside, I could feel my armpits began to sweat.

Baguette opened the door and all but pushed my ass out since I'd tensed up. The cool evening air kissed my cheeks, and now I was wishing I'd worn the other option. A black Ferrari was parked in my driveway next to Baguette's navy G-wagon.

When the door let up and Goal stepped out of the car, I damn near fainted. I was standing on the porch like Summer Walker when she was on stage receiving her awards.

"Wassup, Goal? You looking good, baby."

Goal smiled at Baguette, and he had them damn diamond fronts in that I loved so much.

"You beautiful as fuck, Mrs. Navarro. What's good, B? 'Preciate that."

Goal was rocking the hell out of a green Gucci bomber jacket with red stripes at the wrist, matching shorts, and Gucci sneakers. His jewelry was heavy on his neck, fingers, and wrist, and of course his mouth. Everything down to his fresh haircut was on fucking point. He walked toward me and pulled my stiff ass in for a hug. I melted in his arms as I felt an eagerness of affection coming from his body. When I pulled from the hug, he placed a kiss on my lips and led me to the passenger side before headed to the porch.

My face grew warm as I watched my ex and my – well, I don't know what Goal is – talk. I couldn't make out what they were saying because the music wasn't loud but too loud to make out their conversation. They both looked at me briefly and then started back talking.

I took that time to pull out my phone to send a text.

Me: *Mama could you please come by the house (old one) to check on Brock? He isn't acting like himself.*

Mama: *Brock got a woman, and it isn't me nor you anymore.*

Me: *Please!*

Mama: *I'm sick of all three of y'all asses. I will go by after my damn plans.*

Me: *Plans?*

Mama: *Yess, you not the only one getting some tonight, boo.*

I fake gagged and tossed my phone back in my purse just as Goal was making his way back to the car. His cologne filled the space before his ass could get in the seat good. Both doors closed and he pulled out of the driveway.

Goal licked his lips as he drove, and I didn't miss his obvious examination and approval.

"You so damn gorgeous."

I knew before the night was over, my cheeks would be hurting from smiling and blushing so much. This is my fourth time being in this man's presence. Each time, he was complimenting me every hour on the hour.

"Thank you. You're sooo handsome. But you know that though."

Goal placed his hand on my thigh, and that gesture alone opened the flood gates.

"I'm aite. You the prize though. Remember that shit, Pretty Pretty. Put ya seat belt on; shit 'bout to get kinda swift."

Goal wasn't lying because he was doing every bit of one hundred on the dash. We drove for about an hour with me gasping here and there the whole time. Although he was driving like a bat out of hell, there was something about his hand on my thigh as he switched lanes that calmed me.

"We here."

We entered an empty lot, and just when I was about to ask what we were doing here, the car started lowering into the ground. I jumped hard as hell, and Goal began to laugh.

"Chill out, Pretty Pretty. I got you."

Once the car stopped, Goal began driving through straight darkness.

Before I could worry, light came into view, and I saw that we were in a parking garage. There was about four other vehicles present. Goal parked right up to a glass door, and I was trying to figure out where it led to because this garage was all concrete slab.

The doors went up, and Goal hopped out first and made his way to my side. He removed my seatbelt and pulled me from my seat. His arms went around my waist as he pressed his pelvis into my stomach. Even in my heels, he was still towering my frame.

"I love this fucking dress. They got more colors?"

"I'll have to ask my vendor. Thank you. I designed it myself. It will be apart of my next week's new arrivals."

Every now and again, I told my vendor what I was imagining, and she made it happen. I wasn't no fashion designer, but I knew what the ladies liked. This one came in plus too, and I couldn't wait to see my curvy boos in it.

"Real shit? I fuck with this. So that mean you gotta take hella pics inside so we can sell you out."

"I do that anyway but thank you."

Goal smiled and gripped my ass.

"I heard that shit, Pretty Pretty."

Taking me by the hand, he led me to the glass door, and once we walked through the tube like hallway, I stopped in my tracks at what we were in.

"Oh my God, this is beautiful!"

Goal's skin now had a blue glow to it because we were standing in the middle of the damn ocean. Above our heads, all around us was nothing but aqua blue waters and sea life. A big ass whale went over our heads, casting a shadow that made the room dark for a moment.

"Come on, you ain't seen shit yet."

I wanted to pull my phone out and record so bad. The lobby area was so large it looked to be able to hold at least two hundred people. A wedding or any type of event could be held in this very entrance, and I swear it would be magical.

With my clammy hand in his, Goal led me to a doorless entry and down iron spiral steps. He took his time going down the stairs, and I was grateful because I didn't want to bust my ass. These heels were comfy, but there wasn't much support or grip to them. Once we hit the bottom stair, I couldn't hold my excitement. I'd just been looking at underwater restaurants on Tik Tok and to be standing dead in the center of an empty one had my mouth wide open. My hand went from his palm to my face. I was acting like a damn kid on her birthday, but I couldn't help it. I'd never been anything like this ever in my life, so I just had to stand there and take it all in.

"This is truly breathtaking! How-how in the hell are we underwater of a damn ocean? I mean, Jagoda Bay has plenty of lakes and bays, but I didn't know we had a whole damn sea! This is so damn beautiful!"

Goal smirked cockily at me as he stood back, admiring me admiring the setting.

"That's because we not in Jagoda Bay."

Confusion took over the shock as I wondered what the hell he meant by us not being in Jagoda Bay. We hadn't gotten on a damn boat, plane, or train. Last I remembered, we took his Ferrari here, and I know that underground garage didn't lower us to a whole new damn realm.

"We're in Sparkling City."

"That's impossible. Sparkling City is three hours away," I stated the obvious.

"Yeah, but when you doing two hundred plus on the dash, it's way less than that. We sitting over here."

Goal pulled me to our seat, which was dead in the middle of the restaurant. Although the restaurant had an open floor concept, the way the different tables were sitting, and due to the fact the only lighting came from the waters, it provided plenty of privacy. I mean, we didn't need any privacy because we were alone, but I can see this place being the number one spot to come through. I didn't even know the name, nor did I know anything like this existed even in Sparkling City. I had to bring the girls back one day. We were going to have to get a room though, and make it an overnight trip because the three hour trip back wasn't ideal.

Once Goal had my seat out and back in place, he went to his seat, and a chef came from nowhere.

"Good evening, Mr. and Mrs. Navarro. To start here is Maryland Blue crab dip and our signature sauce drizzle. For you, Mrs. Navarro, I have our smokehouse lemon drop, and a bottle of Giulia wine will be served chilled with your main course. Enjoy."

I smiled at the chef as he left just as fast as he came after placing the food and drinks on the table. This man was telling everyone with ears that I was his Mrs. At the moment, I was on too high of a cloud to care. My jaws were hurting from how hard I was grinning. I'd told this man several times how I liked my steak, but he done brought my ass to a whole fucking under the sea spot.

I bowed my head and said a quick grace before hitting my hand with Bath and Bodyworks sanitizer and scooping a piece of French toasted bread in the dip. Once the food hit my tongue, I had to close my eyes to savor the taste.

"Ummm, this sooo good."

Goal had a few bites of the dip. Of course he had me feed his nasty ass, and that shit turned my thongs creamy with the way he was sucking on my fingers.

"You pretty as fuck."

Goal ended his statement by placing his short round glass to his lips that was filled with dark liquor. I blushed hard as hell every time he told me I was pretty, as if it was the first time I'd every heard it before in my life. Hearing it from Goal just did something to me.

"Thank you. You're not too bad looking yourself."

"We gone make some gorgeous ass babies. Know that shit."

This man was determined to make me a two time baby mama. I enjoyed being in his presence and looked forward to him taking me down in the near future, but babies were not on the table. Neither was marriage, but I just let him dish every piece of game he had at me. Sitting across from Goal's fine ass had me in a haze. His clean and manly scent was a mixture of rich nigga, and Baccarat, and each time I inhaled, I felt drugged.

How in the fuck could one man be so fine? Like, God did his big one with this man. Initially, I'd been turned off by the way he handled Daphne, but he was proving to me that different bitches bring out different sides of niggas.

"Here is the main course. Surf and Turf featuring Alaskan Lobster tails on twenty two ounce steaks. Both medium, of course. For your sides, we have prawn mac n cheese, and asparagus, and I brought out king crab per Mister's request. Is there anything else?"

"Nah, we good. 'Preciate you, my guy." Goal dismissed the chef while I damn near drooled at the mouth looking at the spread in front of me. The steak was so big I could eat on it for three days, I know. Cutting into my steak, I bit into it, and the flavor burst into my mouth. This food was incredible.

Having all the different schools and species of fish swim above and on the side of us heightened the experience. This was most definitely the most epic date I'd been on. Hell, if this is what I'd been missing out on in five years, I should have been let a nigga take me out.

We ate in silence while constantly stealing glances at each other. I was good and full and tipsy by the time the chef came and cleared the table. I hoped like hell he was boxing the food up because my excited ass barely ate. It was going to hit good tomorrow.

"This place is everything. Thank you for bringing me. How did you find it?"

Goal licked his lips and stared me down through hooded eyes while reaching in his pocket. When I saw that he'd pulled a blunt and a lighter out, I began looking around frantically. This place was too damn nice, and even though he'd rented the place out completely, he would be dead ass wrong if he fired up that blunt.

"You about to smoke? In here?"

Goal stood, "Come on. You got pics and shit to take. I got the perfect spot too. I want my photo credit and shit when you sell out."

I followed Goal through the restaurant as he led me to the opposite direction of where the chef had been disappearing off to.

We stepped into another room, and the view of this one was even better than the dining area. The room was empty, however, but the ambiance was still on ten.

I saw where the lighting was perfect and pulled my phone and gloss out. Once my lips were back on point, I handed Goal my phone, and he proceeded to take my pics. He was patient as fuck and even encouraged me to take pics from the back and bent over. I was skeptical at first, but when I saw the images, I almost wanted to tell his ass I needed him for all our pics.

He asked me for my phone again, and I handed it to him without hesitation. Goal walked up on me, wrapping his arm around my waist and pushing us through the restaurant with his body.

When he snuggled his face in my neck and began singing, I bit my lip to stifle my moan. I could feel his dick at the top of my ass, and the nigga was packing.

"Is it the kisses for me, is it the kisses for me...she like ooh, she like oooh."

This was my second time hearing Goal sing, and I was just as shocked as the first time. This man could really hold a damn tune. It tripped me out and turned me on at the same time. I felt a shadow over our head, so I looked up, and not only was there a shark, but Goal had my phone angled, recording us. I was still biting the corner of my lip while he was walking us with his body and singing in my neck. He let my hip go, reached in front of him and pushed a door open. A soft frame white bed sat in the middle of the room that was small enough to be an office and nothing else.

Suddenly, all that courage I had slipped away.

"Umm.."

"Nah, ain't no fucking um. I told you when I got you to myself, it was ova'."

Goal walked around me and plopped down on the bed while firing up his blunt. I chewed the inside of my jaw while I stood there feeling dumb and scary as hell.

"Do you.. think we might be moving too fast?"

I was just at my home, skimming through houses, and now I was in the damn deep blue sea, owned a million dollar home, and in the presence of the finest nigga I'd ever laid eyes on. Now we were in this room about to do all types of nasty shit to each other, and I barely knew five things about the man.

"Why you smoking in this place, Goal?"

He inhaled his potent weed that made my mouth water and blew it out the side of his mouth.

"Hell nah, we ain't moving fast enough, if you ask me. Time waits for no man, baby. Plus, this my shit. I can blow sixty blunts down in this bitch if I want."

Hearing Goal owned this beautiful hidden gem, was impressive and made my heartbeat pound through that pussy.

"But we don't know each other like that."

Goal continued to smoke his weed while lustfully eyeing me.

"Aite, ask me some shit, and I'ma ask you some shit. Let's get to know each other, as you say."

I cleared my throat and turned my head, watching a few stingrays pass by. I still couldn't believe we were in a place like this and weren't out of the country. I'd been sleeping on laid back ass Sparkling City.

"Okay, uh. Your favorite color?"

He chuckled, "Green. Money, baby."

Figures.

"Mine is-""

"Orange."

I gave him a wondering look, and he hit his blunt again.

"Every time I've been around you, your nails have been a different hue of orange. That's your favorite color."

"Okay, you got me. What is your favorite food?"

"Yours is seafood. You always eating a fucking crab boil on ya socials. Mine is pussy so come put that shit on my face."

I moved toward him, impelled involuntarily by my own passion. Before I could push his ass back and sit on his face, I stopped myself.

"Last one, when is your birthday?"

He put his blunt out on a shark-shaped ashtray near the bed. I wondered if he had this bed brought in just for tonight or was it here all along. I hoped he hadn't fucked Daphne in this fucking bed.

"I haven't fucked no other bitch in this bed. You wear your emotions on ya face, making it easy as hell to read you, Pretty Pretty. You gone be the first and the last up in it."

Goal reached for my thigh, gripped it, and pulled me to him. My pussy was right in his face, and I knew he could smell my arousal. Even though his hands appeared to be big and rough, his touch was oddly soft and caressing. My body tingled from the contact.

He slowly lifted my dress up my thighs and then above my hips until it gathered at my waist.

"Pussy so fucking fat, and she smell so good... But to answer your

166

question, It's April sixteenth that's my born day."

Same as Athena's.

His finger traced the lining of my underwear, and in one swift motion, he had me on my back, my legs spread, and my panties ripped off.

Since we were here, I went ahead and pulled my dress from over my head, while he salivated at my body. Then, my bra came next.

"Next time, let papi handle that shit for you, Pretty Pretty."

"Okay."

He slid out of his shoes, unzipped his jacket, and pulled his shirt over his head. It was no surprise that Goal's body was ripped the fuck up. I'm talking eight pack, fuck six pack. The nigga needed to be on the front of an Urban fiction book.

"I feel bad as fuck for the way I'm 'bout to fuck the shit out of you."

"Goal-"

He snatched my legs up, tossed them behind my head, and before I knew what the fuck was going on, he planted a fat wet kiss on my kitty and traced his tongue down to my ass crack. Goal went up and down my ass a few times, causing me to squirm beneath him. Once he made his way back to my pussy, the slurping noises he made as he munched filled the room. My mouth was stuck in an O shape, and all I could do was stare out into the water and watch the sea creatures swim by. Goal was eating me so fucking good that I was at a loss for words. His grey eyes pierced through mine as he sloppily and skillfully ate my pussy down to the gristle.

My legs began to vibrate, and when my stomach caved, I knew I was about to cum.

"Ohhhhh sshiii...shiiiii.. Gooooooalllll! I'm 'bout to... hold up! Moveeeee!"

I was no stranger to squirting. I wasn't a fan of the shit, although I knew it drove men crazy. It wasn't something I did often, I had to be extremely turned on.

"That pussy 'bout to squirt?"

"Ye..ye..yeeeesssss! Moveeeee!"

My words came out choppy as I tried to force my body not to wet this man's face up.

"Wet a nigga up. Cum, piss, ion give a fuck, don't resist that shit. I'm drinking up whatever come up out yo' sexy ass." With that, he applied pressure with his tongue, causing me to grip the sheets and wet his ass up. I came so fucking hard, it really did feel and sound like I was pissing, and his nasty ass just latched on, sucking me dry.

"Damn, my baby a freak. I'ma have some fun with you, Pretty Pretty. Can I have you on all fours?"

I nodded, and he flipped me over without effort. He even helped me assume the position because I was lazy as hell behind that nut. I could feel my essence all over the covers while my ass was tooted in the air. I made sure my back was in the perfect arch and braced myself as he lined his dick with my hole. He tried easing in, but I was so damn snug, and he was too damn big.

"Uuuuummmmm! Shhhhit, Goal!"

He broke his way through and was filling me up.

"Breath...Pretty...fuuuuuuck! This pussy feel untouched. D...d...daaamn!"

Goal rocked in and out of me while my chest was flat on the bed and my ass tooted. Goal most definitely had the dick of a porn star. This shit needed to be on display somewhere instead of fighting it's way into my pussy.

Once he was able to break me in, Goal gripped my hips and pounded into me as I whimpered. I was in here real life crying because the shit hurt so fucking good. I'd never cried during sex, so this was a first, and the shit shocked and scared the fuck out of me.

"You gone have a nigga gone off this pussy, Pretty!"

The pleasure coursing through me was pure and explosive. With the way my face was buried in the sheets, I knew my makeup had ruined these covers. I tried throwing my ass back to meet his rhythms as he stroked my walls because I could feel my orgasm building in the pit of my belly.

"Yeah, throw it back, Pretty. You 'bout to cum?

"Yee...yeeessss, Papi! I'm...ohhh shit! I'm 'bout to...cuuuum! Please don't stop fucking meeeeee! I looove this diiiick!"

"I love you too, baby. Shiiiiiit, I'm 'bout to nut!!"

We both released at the same time, and it sent fireworks off in my body.

Goal pulled out of me, making me twitch, and pulled me on top of his chest. His heart was beating fast as fuck as he caught his breath.

When he opened his eyes, he looked at my lips, and I reached in. We shared a sloppy, nasty ass kiss that turned into to me straddling him and his dick sliding right back inside of me. I tossed my head back, making my braids sweep the top of my ass while he pinched my pebbled nipples. This dick was so big, so filling, add in, it's fine ass owner. I had to look up because if I looked in this man's face, I was nutting.

"Come 'ere. Keep riding that dick just like that."

Placing my palms flat on his bare chest, I kept riding his dick as I leaned onto him. Goal grabbed my neck, licked my lips, and separated them with his tongue. Our kiss was just as sloppy and passionate as the first one, making me so wet I was sliding every which way. When Goal moaned in my mouth, I lost the fight and came all over his abdomen. I could feel him stiffen, so I went harder until he was gripping my hips and fucking me from the bottom.

"Ahhhh shiiiiit! You gone make me... cum...agaaaaiiiin! I'm cumming!"

It was crazy the way this man had the ability to pull nuts out of me back to back. Usually, I had to recoup.

"I'm cumming too, Pretty."

We both came, and I collapsed on top of him. When I had my breathing under control, I rolled off his chest and snuggled at his side. Goal had the best sex I'd ever fucking had in my life, and I was mad as fuck about the shit too. It was no way I was gone be able to walk away from this nigga now. He done woke up the damn Lioness in me.

"As much as I would like to stay here and fuck the shit out you all night, it's one more part to our date I need to get you to."

I wanted to oblige, but I was so dick dizzy I stood up ready for whatever this man had to offer. Long as I can get that dick and mouth again, sore pussy and all.

Goal stood and helped me up, and even with him being on soft, his dick still had length and girth. My dried-up juices left a white cast on his tool, and it caused shudders to flow through me. I went into the bathroom in the room that I hadn't noticed before and wiped myself as best

I could. I had to free ball it since my panties were ripped, thanks to Goal. Once I was cleaned up, I limped through the restaurant, still gushing over the views.

"Is this really yours? This restaurant," I asked as we walked up the stairs.

It was hard to come to terms that he owned this, but then again, he's the same man that has an aquarium themed club. Goal has so many damn layers that it made my head spend.

"Yes, Pretty Pretty. It's not finished just yet. My interior designer had to finish another... project. It's expected to be done by the end of July. Shit gone be dope once it's done."

We reached the top of the stairs and was out of the restaurant.

"Well, maybe I can spend my birthday here."

He placed his hands on the small of my back as we approached the car.

"Nah, we gone be across the water somewhere for yo' G-day."

It had been a minute since I took a trip for my birthday. I'd been out of the country with Tuscany and my mom a few times before, but simply weekend trips just to get away.

Goal grabbed my waist, planted a soft kiss on my lips, and it sent electricity through me. Everything this man did turned me on. It was too damn ridiculous.

The entire drive, Goal hummed and kissed the back of my hand while he swerved through traffic. Now since I knew how fast he was going, I tensed up every now and again, but for the most part, the ride was smooth.

About fifty minutes later, I noticed familiar settings and not just because we were in the city I was born and raised in.

When I turned to face him once the car came to a halt, his facial expression was blank. He licked his bottom lip and slapped my thigh.

"Why are we at my home, Goal? Let me find out you shouldn't have sold it to me. You seem to come by here more than I do."

No lie, seeing the floodlights against my home, something I had no idea was there, but it looked good. It made the house look bigger than what it was, even though it was definitely huge.

"Come yo' pretty ass on. Just trust yo' nigga."

Goal turned the car off and hopped out once the doors extended. Once I was out of the car, he wrapped his arms around my waist and used his body to push us toward the front door. I really eyed his ass once he typed a code in on the keypad, and the door popped open.

"Goal-"

My sentence was cut off and followed by a yelp because he swooped my ass up in his arms and carried me bridal style across the threshold. This man was just too damn strong to be carrying my heavy ass as if I weighed nothing.

Goal walked near a wall and hit the switch, causing me to get out of his arms and look around in disbelief. I had to blink a few times to make sure it was real. The home that I'd purchased for a little of nothing, was no longer a blank canvas.

"Goal... how-"

"Remember I told you my interior decorator paused on the restaurant. Well, turns out it's the same one you had a meeting with."

"How...how you know though?"

I bent down, pulled my shoes off because I didn't want to scratch up the floors and walked through the foyer, touching the artwork. When I met with the designer, I let her know I wanted to go with neutral colors meets luxurious. The taste wasn't for many because it was extremely light, down to the couches, but it was the vision I had for this home, especially with there being so much natural lighting. Everything we'd talked about was in place. The home looked exactly like the mockup she'd done for me. The railing on the catwalk that overlooked the living area had even been changed from charcoal to black. It really pulled the space together.

I gave myself a tour, seeing that everything was exactly what I wanted and more. She created three different mocks for me, and I'd chosen the cheapest one, but seeing the fixtures and designs, I saw that Goal chose to go the more expensive route.

After going through the front of the house, I skipped past the guest beds and went right to my bedroom. The custom tuff bed almost took over the entire wall. And the bamboo dresser gave it more of a nature feel. Even the bathroom felt and smelled like a spa due to the eucalyptus plants hanging from the shower head.

Goal was sitting on my white comforter when I walked out of the bathroom, smoking another blunt.

"I told her to go crazy and her ass did just that. This shit most definitely a vibe." He nodded.

"Goal, why did you do this? I can't believe you did this. I was going to-"

He stood and was in my face faster than I could blink.

"See, that's what we not doin', Pretty Pretty. Don't tell Papi how to spend his money. My bitch not doing no payment plans and shit. You wanted your shit decked out, and now it is. All I want you to say is, I love it, Papi, and I can't wait 'til you eat my pussy in the shower." He ended his statement by pulling my body to his and blowing me a gun.

I swallowed the smoke and exhaled it as a delightful shiver of wanting ran through me.

"Thank you, Papi, and I can't wait 'til I suck your dick in the shower." I smirked.

Goal's grey eyes went a shade darker, and he reached in and licked my lips.

"You eat Papi's dick up like I know you know how, and I'll buy you two more fucking houses. I gotta show you one more thing."

I was so overwhelmed with the night I couldn't take anymore, but I followed him. He walked me directly across the hall to a closed door that I'd thought about turning into a distribution room. Along with the master, there were three more bedrooms, an office, and a work out room. The other bedrooms were upstairs, along with a bonus that I told her to turn into a movie room. I hadn't made my way up there yet, but being we went with the expensive option, I knew it was everything and more.

"She said y'all didn't really go solid on what this room would be, so I took the initiative and gave her the idea myself. If you don't like it, I can have her ass over here in thirty, changing it to whatever you want."

I held my breath as he opened the door and stumbled back once the room behind it was revealed. Athena was in gold Greek-like letters above a gold canopy bed with white sheer tied against each pole and a green vines around the top.

"G-Goal?"

He pulled me into the room, and it was hands down the best room in the house. The two dressers and nightstand were all gold, and there was even a small sitting area with a white chair tucked in the corner. New to the chair was a few shelves of books and in the opposite corner was a gold Toy chest. This room was to die for.

"I know she not here, but I wanted to do something to honor her memory. Now every time you thinking about her, you can come in here and sit and talk to her and shit."

I ran my hand across the dresser. I was at a complete loss for words.

"This...is...wow. So beautiful."

Tears rapidly fell down my face as I admired my baby girl's room. Goal had outdone himself, and now I was wondering if I should have let his ass design the entire house.

"Grab that envelope off the bed."

I walked over to her bed, still shaking and crying, and picked up the manilla envelope. I opened it, turned it upside down, and three folded papers as well as two sets of key fobs, slid out. I opted to read the thickest of the papers first and couldn't even get past the first line before I broke down. Goal caught me before I could hit the damn bed, and I cried like a baby in his arms.

"There was never a fucking bank loan or none of that shit. The house is all yours and had been since the day I first saw yo' fine ass. You got the deed, and what's a new crib without wheels? Papi got you two sets. A truck and a coupe. I told you I am the fucking bank."

I don't know what the fuck I did to deserve this shit, but I was so fucking grateful. I was expecting a date night, and I get my house fully furnished and paid off, plus cars? The nigga hadn't even sampled the pussy yet prior to tonight. That's crazy as hell. Daphne out of her fucking mind if she thinks she getting this nigga back, because I'ma turn him every which way but loose.

"Thank you so much." I kissed his lips.

"Thank you! I love this! I can't believe you did this! Like... this is crazy. The house. The cars. It's too much!"

"Well, you got yo' father in-law to thank for the cars."

"Oh, okay. Wow. He bought me two cars? I'll have to thank him. He hasn't even met me."

"Nah, ion fuck with that nigga at all. We ain't thanking him for shit. But his black card knows you grateful."

Goal pulled me out the room, closed the door and then groped my ass. I loved when he did that. I shook the confusion out of my head about his dad.

"Nah, you ain't seen crazy yet. You 'bout to shit on every bitch in JB, that's word to my mama. Now, can you do that thang you said you was gone do?" He smirked with a sparkle in his grey orbs.

Grabbing him by the hand, I led him down the hallway and to the kitchen so I could suck his dick, just like he said I would the day I met him.

Goal's day started early like at six a.m., so after he fucked my no good pussy 'til it squirted again, I had him drop me off at the old house so I could finally start packing. When I walked through the door, light snores filled the living room making me stop at the couch.

Laying on his back was Baguette's tired ass, and on top of his was Tuscany. They were fully clothed, and seeing as the way Tuscany was shaking, I knew her ass was cold. I removed her Ugg boots from her feet and tossed a blanket on them both before walking to the back. My damn mama was in my bed and on my side at that.

"I know one thing, their asses won't be sleeping on my new white ass couch," I murmured as I walked to the bathroom and started my shower. I was glad all their asses were here because I was definitely putting them to work.

Mr. Navarro: *I have movers coming at 8. Just stand back and show them what to do.*

Me: *Really, Goal?*

Mr. Navarro: *See you tonight, Pretty Pretty. I need a 3peat.*

A notification flashed my screen from IG, so I clicked on and smiled at the new post I didn't make on my page. Not only was it the pic of me at the restaurant, there was also the video of him singing to me, another video of him slapping my ass as I walked, and a picture of the two key fobs in my hand. I don't know what I was going to do with Goal but he damn sure knew what to do with me.

CHAPTER 14

Tuscany Payne

Today was finally the big day. I spared no expense when it came to my bestie's housewarming. Even though she didn't want it, she was glowing this morning when I Facetimed her. As this day neared, I began having second thoughts about throwing this on Athena's birthday. Baguette seemed to be in a better headspace these days, and I didn't want this celebration to throw him back in a funk. I can't even lie the unlimited dick he'd been slanging had a bitch feeling like I was on cloud nine. I just hoped and prayed this party wouldn't put him back in his funk.

You have entered the parking lot of your destination.

I put my Benz in park once Siri alerted me I'd arrived. These last few weeks, I'd been busy at the bars and had even traveled to two of the out-of-town locations. I'd hired the best of the best to plan this event. Even though I'd sponsored it, I still had carts full of shit I wanted to get my girl. Everything came wrapped in a bow except this damn comforter set. One day a few months back, while we were at the ghetto ass South Bay Mall, Aphrodite fawned over this twelve piece bedding set out of Macy's. I kept telling myself I was going to get it for her but kept putting the shit off. Seeing how Goal done came in and decorated the shit out of her place, the comforter the interior designer had in her room worked well in the space but was sort of plain.

I immediately went to find the damn seven hundred dollar ass comforter, but it was sold out online. The only store that had the set in stock was Macy's on Merchant Rowe near Harbor area. It was a thirty minute drive from my house, and I was due at Aphrodite's house in the next hour. I'd gotten my girl every cooking utensil and appliance you could think of, and it was all wrapped in lavender paper. This was the final piece to my gift.

Locking my door, I pulled the cream jumpsuit I was rocking out of my crotch and let my Lavender YSL pumps carry me to the front door. Since it was Sunday, the parking lot was empty. Being that it was a little after eleven a.m., I'm sure I would be the only one in the store. I didn't frequent this side of Jagoda Bay often, but the smells of the lake couldn't be missed. It was beautiful out here, but mostly the extremely wealthy and retired lived out this way.

Once the electronic door granted me access, soft tunes and the smell of fresh linen hit my nostrils. Luckily, this Macy's was free-standing. Meaning it wasn't connected to a mall, and the front entrance was the home and décor section. I loved these shoes, but they weren't exactly walking shoes. I already had to host in these bad boys all evening, so strutting through a mall wasn't on my list of plans.

My phone vibrated in my purse as I followed the signs to online pick up.

"Wassup, bae?"

I had half a mind to ask the employee that was making a display bed if I was going in the right direction because all I saw ahead of me were more display beds, but I decided to keep walking.

"Aye, you want me to bring all these gifts in the foyer? You ain't forget shit nowhere else, did you?"

My pussy thudded hearing my man's voice on the other end of the line. He came home last night and fucked me so hard with my legs pinned to my ear. It had my happy as fuck our neighbors were a mile apart from us.

"No I didn't forget anything else. I'm actually picking up the last gift."

Finally, I could see the pick-up counter come into view.

"Damn, you don't think you bought enough shit? Did you leave room for anybody else to buy some?"

Baguette's voice rose an octave higher, indicating that he was smoking his afternoon blunt. I knew he would smoke at least ten more today, especially since it was Athena's birthday.

"Whatever. Look, I'm in this store, and my feet already starting to hurt. Make sure you wear cream and lavender. Those are the colors. I'll see you at the party. I love you."

Once Baguette told me he loved me too, I ended the call just as I made it to the counter.

"Hi! I have an online pick up under Tuscany Payne. Here, I have the barcode."

I went to my photo album and showed the middle-aged, slender black woman my screen so that she could scan it and retrieve my item. Once she did, she excused herself to the back, so I walked near the curtains to browse, since they'd caught my eye on the walk up. I didn't use an interior designer for our home. Baguette and I did it ourselves, and I was still adding things to it every day. I had curtains up for my dining room but were looking to change them, so every time I saw a curtain section, I browsed it.

"Nah, these are too-"

"Hi! You are pretty!"

I looked down at the killer satin pumps before turning my gaze to the small voice who dished out the compliment. My stomach clenched tight as the fear of apprehension coursed through me.

"Thank you..."

I came to an abrupt stop, dropping my hands from the curtains as my heart jumped in my chest. The tight knot that formed in my throat was begging for release, but I was stuck. Bright eyes stared at me. Familiar bright eyes that matched ones that I'd seen every single day.

"Donde estas? (Where are you?) What did I tell you about running off?"

Frightened anticipation touched my spine as every fine hair on the nape of my neck stood. As he came into view, I gasped, panting in terror, but my instincts took over, and I gently shoved the boy child behind my back. Of all the days. Of all the fucking days I leave my pistol in the car.

A smile spread across his face and reached his ears, revealing a new accessory I see he'd gotten. Didn't matter though. All the new teeth in the world couldn't turn the world's most evil fucking man I knew handsome.

"Tuscany. It's been a while."

"Papa, what's going on?"

I heard behind me, and it pained me to my fucking core to hear that word come from the little boy's mouth.

"He is not your fucking father! Don't call him that shit!"

His smile never wavered, and I hoped this man didn't do anything to me in this store where there were not only witnesses but cameras too.

"Tuscany, I did not expect to find you here, but now that I have, come. We have much to discuss."

With all of the spit gathered in my soul, I released it into his face, and a glob hit his left eye socket.

"We don't have shit to discuss!"

Pain ripped through me as his hand went across my face, causing me to see the fucking stars and the moon. He backhanded me so hard I went backwards. I had to balance myself so I wouldn't fall on the child at my rear who was almost as tall as me.

"Now, let's try this again. Come the fuck here, you black ass bitch! I've let you run around long enough! It's time to bring your ass home!"

Tears blurred my vision as he snatched me from the curtain section down the long aisle that led to the lobby and out of the store.

"Ma'am, I have your order!" I heard behind me.

"Have it shipped to the address on the order," he answered for me.

I was trying my best not to break my fucking ankle as he all but dragged me out of the store. I could feel the young boy behind me, but I still didn't have sight in my right eye.

It was like no one said shit because they were allowing this man to pull me out of the store and not a soul called the police. When we got through the double doors, I held in my wail as I caught a glimpse of my pink car parked in the handicapped. Knowing this man, this would be my last time ever even laying eyes on my baby. I was shoved in the back of a Maybach, and before I could try and go out the opposite door, a gun was placed in my temple.

"Unless you want to die, I suggest you sit the fuck back and enjoy the ride."

Swallowing hard, I removed my hand from the handle and slowly sat back. My phone began to vibrate in my purse, and in my heart, I knew it was Baguette. He snatched my YSL bag from my arms, rolled down the window, and tossed it out into the parking lot.

"Cheer up, my love. I've missed you. Son, climb to the front seat!"

The little boy looked off and did as he was told.

Hot tears fell down my face as I closed my eyes and thought back to the day I ran into this fucking monster for the first time. Back then, he was the answer to my young ass problems, but if I knew then what I knew now, I would have never gave his ass the time of day.

"Tuscany! We hungry!"

"Yea, I don't want no more bologna sandwiches!"

"Me either!"

"Mane, what! I can't wait 'til mama get paid!"

I ignored my little brothers as I finished washing the dishes. They were always complaining about food when they never went hungry. Rather it was noodles and bologna for a week or cereal for breakfast, or me going without, they ate if nothing else.

Once the dishes were cleaned and organized on the rack to dry, I moved over to the white bowl I had the ground beef thawing in. Poking my index finger into the three pound pack, I saw that it was ready to be cooked. Going into the cabinet above my head, I pulled out three beef stroganoff Hamburger Helpers, seasoned salt, black pepper, and onion powder. I then moved to the fridge to retrieve the milk, but when I saw the gallon was empty, my eyes zeroed in on Tulscan. He was the cereal eater of my brothers, and I knew he was responsible for drinking the half full gallon down to nothing.

"What! It was no more beard left! I had to eat! My stomach was cramping!"

Storming past my brothers, I walked into the living room and reached on the shelf above the tv to retrieve my mama's foodstamp card. She didn't get her stamps 'til the twelfth. That was two weeks away, but I prayed there was at least three dollars on the card to get some milk. I would hate to have to eat the Hamburger Helper without it because the taste was funny, but if it came to that, oh well.

"Lock the door! Watch them 'til I come back, Tunan!"

Tunan was tuned in to the tv and was the oldest under me. Even though he was tuned in, I knew he would hold it down while I walked a block up the street to Save A Lot. Even though we lived in the hood, the best thing about our house was that we had a corner store on one end and a grocery store on the other end. The Save A Lot was brand new, and I hoped the crackheads didn't run it out of business. It had been a godsend for my siblings and I because soon as the stamps hit my mamas card, we were at the grocery store in a single file.

The heat smacked me in the face, and I knew if it was this damn hot in early June, the summer was going to be treacherous.

After ignoring catcalls from the same boys and men that tried me every day from the moment my hips and ass began to spread, I finally made it to the lot of the grocery store. It was crazy how these niggas was on the corner selling dope and shooting dice and all had cars, but nobody ever offered me a damn ride. I fell for one fine ass dude in the hood and ended up with a wet ass and broken heart, never again. My main focus was my brothers and getting through this summer so that I could finish off my senior year strong. I couldn't wait 'til I walked across that stage. I was taking my ass to college and getting the fuck up out the hood. My brothers were old enough to now look out for each other while my mother worked her double shifts. I was going to go to school in the city, so I would still be here in a sense, but I hoped to bring in enough scholarships so that I could stay on campus. I needed a change of scenery. The cramped up three bedroom house we all shared wasn't cutting it for me no more. Since I was the only girl, I had to sleep in the bed and share a room with my mother.

Walking into the store, I went straight to the dairy and grabbed a half gallon. I didn't want to risk not having enough due to buying a whole gallon. Once I had the milk, I stood in line, and when it was my turn, I groaned at the cashier's response.

"I'm sorry. Your card declined."

I recognized her because we took a few classes together. She'd even told me she would put in a good word for me with her boss, but my mama didn't want me to work. She claimed it was because of her wanting me to focus on school, but I knew better. She needed me to be with my brothers.

Blinking back tears and the sting of embarrassment, I grabbed the milk to take it back, but someone grabbed my elbow before I could get out of line good.

I looked at his hand as if it were shit on it, and when my eyes met his, my expression softened a little.

"I'm sorry. I didn't mean to frighten you. But let me buy this for you."

I gave him a half smile and shook my head.

"That's nice of you, but no thanks. We get our stamps soon, so it's okay." I shrugged.

"Nonsense. I will take care of this for you. As a matter of fact, you grab a basket, and I'll grab one. Come, let's load it with what you need. No strings. Call it my good deed for today."

Looking into the eyes of the dark Hispanic man, I tried to think of a way out of this. He seemed harmless with his long ponytail, handsome features, and sharp suit, but he was a bit older, and older men could be fucking creepy. I'd been around them my whole life and, luckily, hadn't had to fight one off. My mama worked a lot, but she didn't play about her baby girl.

Thinking about how the last pack of meat was floating in a bowl, I threw caution to the wind and walked to the front of the store with the baskets. There were two long weeks between now and the twelfth and I knew my mama had to pay the light and phone bill when she got paid this week. Plus, with gas, that wouldn't leave her with much to buy groceries. I knew she would make something happen, but free groceries were just too hard to pass up. I slowly grabbed a basket that was parked at the front of the store, and he was right behind me doing the same. He encouraged me to grab everything I needed, even tossing steak and shrimp in the baskets when I was fishing for the cheapest meats like chicken legs and pork chops.

An hour and light conversation later, seven hundred dollars had been spent, and my siblings and I had enough groceries for two damn months, maybe three.

Once we were in the parking lot, I faced another dilemma, how would this shit get home? I appreciated the groceries, but I was not about to get in the car with a damn stranger.

"I can see the look on your face, so here. My car is right there. I have a driver, however, he and I will stand out here. After we load your groceries and you can drive them home and bring the car back to us. That way, you're one hundred percent comfortable."

The sincerity in his eyes had my naïve ass nodding. Plus, when I saw the fancy car, I was itching to get behind the wheel. I got my license in driver's ed this past school year and rarely drove unless one of my siblings had a doctor's appointment and my mama needed me to take them.

Once the groceries were loaded, I cruised down the street with all the damn windows down, gaining the attention of everyone in the hood. Kids were even screaming bingo to the car. I was flexing, but it had me feeling good. I made it home, yelled for my brothers to get all the groceries, ignored all their questions, and headed back to the Save a lot. He was standing out in the hot sun with his driver as he said he would be, and I was smiling like I'd hit the lottery.

"Thank you sooo much for everything. You don't know what this means for me and my brothers. I owe you. I don't have anything to give, but I owe you."

He licked his lips and eyed me lustfully. Instead of me trusting the eerie feeling coursing through my body, I stood there, heart racing.

"I know I said no strings attached, but you're too beautiful to pass up. Let me take you out. I'll make it worth your while and make sure you and your siblings want for nothing."

That should have had my seventeen year old ass saying fuck no, but I damn near bit my tongue agreeing. I was tired of struggling, and if this man dropped almost a thousand dollars on me and had barely had a conversation with me, I knew he was going to spend big if I gave him a little coochie. Hell, I'd given it to a nigga for free, may as well give it to a grown ass man for a fee. Little did I know I had signed my soul to the fucking devil and endured a whole damn year of ass whoppings, rape, and degradation. All in the name of feeding my fucking siblings.

When I was able to escape this man, I did that shit and never looked back. I never told him of my college plans or anything like that, so it was easy to get the fuck on when the time came. I was lucky to still pass my senior year with a three point four GPA. I applied to college here in

Jagoda Bay and hadn't looked back. I didn't give a fuck who I was leaving behind, I had to get away.

The car came to a halt, and it was no surprise to me that the house was bigger than mine and Aphrodite's put together. He was always grand and extra in anything he did. I was snatched out of the car, scraping my knee on the concrete as he dragged me to the front door. I turned for the boy, but was yanked and pushed into the house.

"How long has it been now? Twelve? Twelve fucking years! Bitch, you're out of your mind running from me! I own you, you fucking cunt!"

I winced thinking he was about to beat my ass, but he stood over me while I scooted to the nearest wall. I knew he had money and power and always wondered why he hadn't come after me, but I knew it was because he thought I was going to come running back to him. Jokes on him. I didn't. I just had to accept whatever came with it because getting my ass beat for sport wasn't it for me.

"When I came to Jagoda Bay all those years ago, I never thought this is where you'd be. Then I saw you one day, out with an ex acquaintance of mine, and thought my eyes were deceiving me. I could have ended you right then and there three years ago, but I'm a patient man. I watched and waited. I knew the opportunity would present itself."

I spit at his foot again. If he kicked me, I was going to pull his ass down here and fight for my fucking life. I wasn't seventeen no fucking more.

"So you followed me?"

He scoffed.

"Me, follow you? Nah. I'm far too busy of a man for that. I knew you weren't going anywhere, but I do have listen in every now and again. Today was just pure opportunity."

He kneeled down so that he was eye level with me, and I winced again.

"Still so fucking beautiful and pure. I missed you dearly. Your mother wasn't nearly as fresh as you. As a matter of fact, you have her to thank for stepping in your place and keeping me from tracking your ass down."

Thinking about my mother suffering at the hands of this man had me sick to my fucking stomach. She wasn't a bad mother, she just was dealt a bad hand. It caused me to have to grow up and raise her children while she struggled to provide.

"My man is going to kill you! He's going to fucking kill you! I swear to God he is!"

He licked his lips.

"I doubt that very seriously. I'm feeling good today though. So, I have a proposition for you. *Traela a mi! (Bring her to me.)*"

All the color from my face drained. This time instead of feeling sick, I actually barfed my insides out on the side of me. Mcgriddle got all over my pants leg.

"Is she okay? We need to clean her up and take her to a doctor!"

"She's okay, hija... Wait in the toy room for me."

The child he called out hesitantly turned and went in the opposite direction.

"You're...sick! You are fucking sick! How could you do some cruel shit like that? Why? When? For what? You're just raising both these kids as your own? Is she who I think she is? God no!" I had so many questions as my head spun. My eye was starting to close up on me so I knew it would be black, but that didn't even matter to me right now. I was so lost, confused, and afraid.

"That situation was personal and had nothing to do with you. Now back to my proposition. You can walk out of here and continue to be a shoulder for your man to lean on for the rest of his life. Or you stay here with me and our son and I release her and in turn, *that* will make your man Baguette the happiest soul in Jagoda Bay today. What will it be? After all, our son does thinks his madre is pretty."

When I say I left any and everything behind when I escaped this man, I meant that. Including my son. Our son. The same son I just came face to face with in the store. What I wasn't expecting was for him to have...*her. Could I really walk out of here and live my life, knowing what I know now?*

CHAPTER 15

Aphrodite "Ditey" "Pretty Pretty" "AP" Greer

Today was special because not only was it the housewarming that I didn't want, but my baby girl's birthday. I'd been sleeping in the new house for two weeks now, and I was in fucking love. Of course I damn near had to kick Tuscany out after she saw the house decorated the day after Goal and I's first date. He had the movers come as promised, but my mom, Tuscany and I still had to unpack everything and that took all damn day. I even called my cousins to help, and my auntie brought the damn punch. Before I knew it, fish was being fried in the garage, and we'd turned me unpacking into a damn unofficial get together.

Walking around the house and seeing everyone in the cream and lavender while enjoying my home had me feeling wholesome. I still had to pinch myself every day that I woke up in this place. It was truly a dream that I didn't think I would ever life out. Goal hadn't left my bed since that damn night, and although my sensitive pussy wasn't complaining, my sore jaws was. That man had a sex drive out of this world, and with me not getting laid for five years, I basically jumped on him anytime he was in my presence.

I learned quickly that Goal is a busy man. He started his days at five or six a.m. It didn't matter if were up being nasty till four. He hit my home gym, and while he did that, I had my sleepy ass in the kitchen making him a protein smoothie and omelet. I had to laugh at the thought because the old me would have fucking never. I don't give a damn what he bought. No way in hell would I get up out my sleep to fix a man breakfast. But I did. Every damn day.

After Goal showered, ate, and had his morning pussy, he left for the day and made it back to my house around nine. I busied myself with my boutique and dodged Tuscany's calls because her ass was here like she didn't have several businesses to tend too. She was so fucking happy I had a man that she asked questions all damn day. Baguette stayed while the movers loaded us up, but then he left and I hadn't really heard from him since. I already knew why he was distant and decided to give him his space. He'd just texted me though, saying he was on the way and asking me if Tuscany had arrived but her ass hadn't. Knowing her, she was still out getting gifts.

"You look so cute, boo! Aht Aht! Sit yo' ass down, Rhea! Rayna and Red jr, y'all know better!" Sora waltzed up to me with a drink in her hand that the mixologist was making. She was set up in the corner of the dining room, and the themed drinks she was making was a hit. I had two Goddess Potions already and was barely walking in my heels.

I brushed my hand down my dress as Sora yelled at her kids. She'd been telling them to sit down since they got here thirty minutes ago, and although I told her it was fine, she insisted that they acted like they had some home training—her voice. I chose to wear a cream silk camisole dress that fit snug and stopped just below my calf. On my feet were a pair of cream Jimmy Choo strappy heels, and I finished my look with a thick Gold chain choker and a beat face.

"Thank you, boo."

"I love when you wear your real hair. It's gotten so damn thick. I know when it's pressed out its long. Lord, you've always been God's favorite."

Today was a rare occasion in which I was wearing my real hair. I had my stylist clip my ends and do me a twist out. Goal couldn't keep his fingers out of my head. Thoughts of him beating it from the back this morning while gripping my curls had me shaking my head from the nasty thoughts I was having.

"Girl, please. Your hair is long too."

"Not as thick as yours though. Uggh!"

We both laughed, and then she ran off to fuck with her kids again.

The DJ played Juvenile's Back That Ass up, and my mama hyped Bobby's ass up to dance. Even he was looking good in his lavender jeans, lavender Chucks, and cream Polo top. He was probably going to sell the shit once the event was over, making my mama mad as hell. She'd bought his fit yesterday when she was at the mall picking up my gift.

Even though I didn't want this housewarming, Tuscany outdid herself. The décor featured a white and purple floral garland that wrapped around my staircase and across the catwalk, two chefs, food from their bars, a mixologist on the drinks, a DJ, and later on, we were releasing doves. I was hoping the garland lasted a while because it was so beautiful to me in my home.

"Where yo' fine ass man at?"

My auntie asked while sipping from a purple cup.

"He's with his family. Today is his birthday too, so I didn't expect him to cancel his plans. That's not my man either, auntie."

Goal and I hadn't put a title on anything, but he was who I woke up and went to bed to. I was cool with what we had now because although I wasn't letting up off him, my heart was still healing, and my trust was fucked up. A few times when his phone went off in the middle of the night, I had to check myself. Five damn years and I was still scorned, but God is still working on me.

"Chile, he bought you a house, a car, a truck, and I bet he hasn't left that cat since he handed you the deed. That's definitely yo' man. He better carry his ass through that door or I'ma cuss his ass out the next time I see him. I don't give a damn how fine he is.

Sora, stop hollering at my grandkids and send them upstairs with Litty and the rest of the big kids. They don't need to be left alone like that anyway. Some of them brought friends, and ain't no fucking going on under my roof. Bad enough, I smell pregnancy in the air! Somebody expecting and it bet not be a little ass girl." This wasn't my auntie's roof, but I was gone let her rock and her ass need to stop drinking talking about smelling pregnancy.

Ding dong.

"There his ass go right there. He knew better!"

187

I playfully rolled my eyes at my auntie, but I was secretly hoping she was right. The way my heart was beating in my chest, my body was hoping it was his ass too.

"Auntie, this is nobody but late ass Tuscany. Or my realtor."

Quasie had texted and said she was running behind because her mother wanted to come, so she had to stop and get her. The videographer she hired was already here, as well as her assistant Kassie, who was so sweet and pretty.

"Oh, my girl, the sister wife. Tell her bring her ass on in."

I waved my auntie off and switched to the door. I wasn't wearing a bra, but I was glad I opted for these pasties because my nipples were definitely pebbled in this dress. I opened the door and was confused because no one was outside. I went to close it back, and my phone dinged in my hands.

Tuscany: *Come outside*

Shrugging, I opened the door again and saw Tuscany standing in front of the door. Even though she had shades on her face, something about her didn't look right. When I noticed the blood on her clothes, and the vomit that was smeared down her pants leg, I reached at the shades that were on her face, and at the same time she drew back, but the shades went flying off anyway.

"Bitch, who the fuck put their hands on you?" I screamed so loud my voice cracked.

Tuscany started shaking as tears fell from her good eye. The other was red and puffy. I was so fucking mad, my eye was twitching.

"I'm so sorry. I'm so sorry, Aphrodite. Just know, it's not what you think. *Gilberto* made me choose."

Tuscany stepped aside, and when she did, all the wind was knocked out of me. I saw Tuscany running out of the corner of my eyes, but I was too stunned to speak. Standing at about forty-five inches in height, with two long ponytails sprouting from her head, in a purple dress was the exact same face as mine on a five year old.

"What are you doing out here, chile? Who is this baby- oh my lord." My mom came out of the house beside me, and at the same time tires streaked as well, as a door closed. I briefly tore my eyes away from the child to blink and noticed Baguette walking up with purple-wrapped gifts in his hands. Goal walked over to relieve him of a few with a lady and a younger version of him at his side, both the spitting image of Goal and dressed for the occasion.

Both Baguette and Goal were smiling until they noticed the look on my face. Baguette squinted his eyes, dropped the gifts and then ran full speed to the porch. He didn't even stop as he scooped the child up in his arms and turned her around to face him.

"Fuck! It is you! Athena baby! My fucking daughter!" Baguette was crying so hard his chest was heaving. The little girl looked confused but she didn't seem to be afraid. My mouth opened and then closed and then opened again. Baguette placed his forehead against the little girl's and then looked at me through his tears. His free arm went around my neck and he hugged me to his side.

"This our fucking daughter! Our fucking daughter is alive! Who the fuck brought her here? Where the fuck she been? How the fuck is this real? This her ain't it? She look just like you Ditey! What the fuck bruh?"

My mother war praying behind me as Goal and his family walked up, confused by it all.

"I...I...Tuscany brought her. She said...she said...*Gilberto...Gilberto...* made her choose."

Who the fuck is Gilberto and how is my child alive? Is this my child?

Baguette drew his head back and looked at Goal, and if looks could kill, he would have the same birthday and death day.

"Tuscany said what? Talking 'bout this nigga's daddy?"

Baguette handed me Athena and pulled his gun from the small of his back. At the same time, the young boy with Goal pointed a gun at Baguette. It felt so good having my baby in my arms, but I couldn't focus because the men in my life were about to blow each other's brains out. My mama snatched Athena out of my arms and ran in the house. She tried snatching me too, but my feet were planted.

"If you gone pull the strap, you gotta use it. 'Cuz my young nigga shol' using his," Goal calmly replied, still holding the gift's.

"Nigga, what the fuck yo' pops and my bitch got going on? They kidnapped my fucking daughter?"

What the fuck is going on?

To be continued...

Please join my group for a chance to win prices, get sneak peeks, and read FREE exclusive books!
www.Bit.ly/LisaAustinGroup

Also, I advise you to read Litty and Gage's story. It's short and only $5..the link takes you to paypal and the book will be in your email where you can download and enjoy the book via kindle They will both be in part 2.

www.bit.ly/Euphoricpreq

Part 2 IS COMING SOON AND WILL BE AVAILABLE ON AMAZON FOR KU

Lisa Austin Books

A Winter Crest Valentine's: Snowy & Sphere